Somma

A Novel

G.A. Chamberlin

Titles by

G.A.Chamberlin

The Handmaiden Legacy

Cultural Attache

Rare Earth Element

Outbound

Somma

Unintended Consequence

The Particle

The Kneeling Woman

At Auction

*

Kathleen The War Years

Somma
Printed in the United States
ISBN 978-0-9904027-4-9

Crown Eagle Publishing

Distributed by Ingram

Cover Design by Jennifer Chamberlin

Rare Earth Element

climate, culture, commerce...Too important to ignore, too well written to overlook. And too technically suspenseful not to wonder about...

* * *

The Handmaiden Legacy

The Handmaiden Legacy is a contemporary thriller full of corporate interests, beautiful seas and ancient legacies...
>---*G.A. Chamberlin is an International Thriller Writer!*

>"International Thriller Writers ...that will surprise "
>--Agent, Thriller Fest, New York City

* * *

Cultural Attache

"...Amanda Wells is lecturing on the historical integrity of medieval works at the University when she is informed that the original manuscript of a major work...has been stolen from the vault.

Somma...

...an International Thriller

In a flight from abductors whose plan to kidnap her daughter had been foiled, Amanda Wells can identify them...

Except for the loss of an important antiquity that must find its way to a celebrated Museum - across a world of ancient legacies and intrigue.

Worse. Amanda and her children are in a rental sedan - suitable for sunny rides down the beach promenade. Ahead of them is a climb of six thousand feet into the Alps...

And those whom she needed most... were facing horrific new realities. "You see, what we are describing..." explained Dr. Keanan "will bury Europe!"

Somma

A Novel

G.A. Chamberlin

One

London, England

The Minister put down his cigar and let the pages of the report rest on his lap. How to prepare for something such as this, exactly?
He would relinquish his position, he decided. Make for a Joint Coalition government.
This was too much for him. This was too much for the world! His heart, they told him, was weak.
He reached for his brandy, a touch of cinder dropped to the floor.
The report had been freshly issued by London scientists.

* *

Helen McConaught had been a career Executive Secretary for 35 years. She knew her way about these premises. She had entered the main office through the Carriage house where she normally parked her car, and checked her watch. She was hours early. Always had been.

She walked around the office suite, touched the window arrangements just so, allowing for the sunlight to cast its long beams across the chamber by mid-morning; and the reading lights she tipped to best advantage. The room had its quirks. It had hosted many officials over the years.

She moved to the desk and laid out the essentials, dossiers neat and square, and the Report at the top right hand corner of the desk. Her fingers lingered, the dark red coloring of the classified document clearly marked and stamped. She looked at the title. SUSAN.

A terrifying report, her boss told her, before leaving office. Something that only the new man can deal with.

The first page she touched ever so gently.

"The Toba event eruption occurred about 73,000 years ago. It is the last of the known super volcanic eruptions in recent history. It is the most studied event by scientists presently although the phenomenon of hot spots is only now revealing its urgency. Such catastrophic events are viewed to have taken place on all continents as tectonic plates pass over hot spots.

"This eruption took place in the region now recognized as Indonesia. The eruption was so vast that it deposited 15 centimeters of ash entirely over South Asia. A layer of volcanic ash fell upon the Indian Ocean, the Arabian and South China Sea. And it produced a darkening of the earth's atmosphere that resulted in what is known as the volcanic winter, followed by an ice age.

"Magma rises into the earth's crust from a hotspot but is unable to break through the crust. A "magma lake" spreads beneath the surface until the crust can no longer restrain the pressure.

"In recent studies, the human species bottleneck theory has been connected to this eruption. This bottleneck theory supported by scientists like Gibbons, Rampino & Ambrose in 2000 imply by their studies that the human population suffered a severe population decrease—only 3,000 to 10,000 individuals survived—followed eventually by rapid population increase, innovation, progress and migration.

"The climate change effects of the Toba eruption resulted in a global ecological disaster with extreme phenomena that implicated the complete picture of genetic human lineages, including present-day levels of human genetic variation, thus allowing the theory of a Toba-induced human population bottleneck.

"Whereas Neanderthal are said to have been extinguished in the colder climate of Europe due to its dependence upon large game that faltered, it is currently not known *where* human populations were living at the time of the eruption, or how some survived. The most plausible scenario is that all survivors were populations who migrated to Africa, and whose descendants would go on to populate the world as we know it today.

"In the UK, scientists claim that an area the size of North America would be devastated by one super volcanic eruption. Global climate would be pronounced deteriorating for a few years following the eruption: This would result in the devastation of world agriculture, severe disruption of food supplies, and mass starvation. These effects could be sufficiently severe to threaten the fabric of civilization."

"The warning is not new. Geologists in the United States detail in their findings of 2001 evidence for the existence of volcanic activity in Yellowstone National Park, which will eventually lead to a colossal eruption. If such an event were to occur, half the United States would be buried under 3 feet of ash. *Earth and Planetary Science Letters* did not find this a survivable extinction event.

"While our technology can shield us with its many advances in the case of fall-out from other threats like asteroids, nuclear attacks and global warming anomalies that leave humans vulnerable to disaster… there is little to do about such an eruption.

""The eruption pumps dust and chemicals into the atmosphere for years, screening the Sun and cooling the planet. Earth is plunged into a perpetual winter, causing widespread ecological collapse.

"The only hope for humans is to be prepared with intelligent and graduated plans to build up an infrastructure for long term sustainable survival. A

Sustainable Underground Survival Network. SUSAN.

"Those lucky enough to survive may be able to carry the seeds of civilized society into the future. Otherwise, it should be considered a global extinction event"

* *

They arrived en troupe.

Amanda Wells walked down the train platform in a black satin coat to match a tailored dress and satin trim hat touched by grouse. She was not one to be outclassed in appearance. Nor was the retinue that trailed her.

Adam, aged 7, she held by the hand, his necktie and coat buttoned up, if lopsided with one arm up. His darkly polished Clarks treaded firmly beneath grey flannel pants.

Behind them walked Ms. Prettyman leading the twins Trevor-Reginald and Sandra by the hand. They had to keep up, even if smoke belched from tracks under trains, and their eyes were wide with curiosity.

Amanda stopped, leaned down for Adam and whispered "Doing ok?"

He nodded dubiously, looked into her eyes and quickly became emboldened. Up came the other hand as she switched sides and marched on with him.

The others caught up.

Ms. Prettyman was American, formerly employed by the Airlines and experienced at accompanying children. The twins, aged 3, were happy to follow Adam anywhere.

Amanda was alert, and pressed her troupe briskly up the elevators and out the main entrance of the Great Railway Station.

The crowd on the street mingled with provocative overtones of riots and unrest. Some paused, reviewing the party. This was London.

A man advanced, placard in his hand which he hid, now having full recognition of his charge. He took a briefcase from Amanda and lifted the travel bag off Ms. Prettyman.

"Please, this way Ma'am" he said politely.

They piled into the black RR like a relieved party of space travelers, all seating and rearranging themselves with excitement.

Amanda hugged the twins and unbuttoned Adam's coat. She cast a thankful smile at Prettyman who was pulling out water bottles, peanuts and yogurt chocolate raisins.

"Good job everybody!" said Amanda finally, and they all giggled.

The car slid smoothly through slow traffic and turned into Downing Street.

Two policemen stood at the wrought iron fencing that sheltered the townhouse at Number 10. The great door opened and Trevor MacDonald stepped out.

A gathering of the Press began their imaging of the new family arriving. One held out a microphone over the children.

"Daddy!" screamed the twins, tumbling out together and racing forward into his outstretched arms.

Adam stepped out of the car, waved and waited for his mother to straighten up before moving forward.

They all clasped and hugged in a fairly unscripted tangle, still standing on the doorstep, something the police force would prefer them not to do in public given the risk of exposing vulnerable family members to stray cameras and surveying eyes.

Trevor managed to usher the reunion indoors. He offered a cordial welcome to Prettyman, but reserved for his wife a look, above the fray, of profound admiration and warmth.

Their eyes met. She smiled back at him, discretely.

"The soldiers! The soldiers!" implored Adam, pulling his father's arm towards the stairs.

Adam knew that upstairs, in a large drawing room and Library, there was an array of interesting things. At a table by the window a full display of miniature metal soldiers stood positioned for the battle of Waterloo, complete with trees, cannon and miniature horses.

"soyjers…" repeated Sandra negotiating the tall steps behind him. Trevor-Reginald followed.

"Your coats ma'am?" offered the House Gentleman.

"Yes. Thank you Dennison!" said Amanda

** *

Istanbul

The bomb that exploded worried the Turkish Police. Not because of its wreckage in an open market under shade trees, awnings and trellised vines - and certainly too close to a structure whose age exceeded one millennia; nor even that it killed six, but rather because of where it came from.

Unlike activist crime-scenes in the West, nothing claimed responsibility for its purpose of protest. Nothing was left recorded on a smart phone; no farewell text messages…

No. This was an incident with eyewitness accounts only: Four women dressed in black and decorative head-scarfs had gathered at the vendor kiosk of a friend, talking and sipping tea when they saw the assailant. He came by them, they said. He stood at the far end of the market courtyard and shouted. He scared everyone, they said. Then he blew himself up.

He spoke Arminian, they said. From Syria.

* *

Baltimore, Maryland.

"We're not sure *what* the manuscript is" said Dr. James, leaning forward. "It's a relic, probably authentic if we are to read the forensic analysis - and accurate in its portrayal of the world from which it came. But there is no way in hell to tell *who* the author was... whether he calls himself Judas or Justus the Great!"

"The Judas Manuscript *does* relate to the ministry of Jesus Christ..." pressed Shirley.

"Enough!" interrupted Tim. "We've reviewed this already. We can show the public the Exhibit in a scholarly way. Nothing more. I'll recommend to the Board of Trustees that we bid for the item. God knows what we're getting into..."

He turned to Shirley "We will exhibit it here for a season; host a Conference and invite scholarly analysis for publication. That'll be for your group to arrange?"

She nodded.

They sat back and paused.

The Museum Director touched his pad with his pencil and checked off an item. The end of the pencil pointed at Bob. "...After that we'll sent the Exhibit on a national tour. Those logistics will be for your team. Right?"

Dr. James sighed. "How many exhibits?"

"Three, max. Three large museums with adequate security - and willingness to cite us as the source institution. Then close it all down and return it to the host country. Disengage us cleanly from further exposure and liabilities to the relic - with all necessary inspections; repairs and curation. Do check in with Legal on the necessary paperwork, including all insurance; indemnification and Exit Certification documents before returning it to the owners, ok?"

Dr James nodded.

Tim looked directly at the far end of the Conference table. "Let's hope this Exhibit raises our profile sufficiently to solicit money from donations to our museum!"

He looked directly at Amanda Wells. "I have no idea where you begin your Fundraising campaign Amanda, but you'll have my full support for any planning. Just let us know if you need anything…"

Tim turned to the Intern on his left "Diane, allocate all the office resources necessary to support the Fundraising program, give top priority to Amanda. Yes? And a weekly update on running totals if you will, please."

She nodded.

"Meeting adjourned!" said the chair, smiling.

He got up, dug into his pocket for his cell phone and was talking to somebody with an apology for being tardy as he walked out the door.

"Busy man!" Shirley muttered.

They collected their papers. They had been at the conference table for over an hour and were slow to unwind.

"You *tried*…" said Diane, eying Shirley.

"I did" she answered. "As your Resident Advisor on theology of Middle Eastern Antiquities, I should tell you that it will be noticed that we omit theological discourse, or, for that matter any spiritual insight…"

"Absolutely right!" said Bob, standing up. "No religious proselytizing in the work we do here!" He grabbed his papers "*None* whatsoever girls!" he said, thrusting out his chin. He turned to go, but the arm-sling from his shoulder snagged on his books. He jerked it free and walked out.

Shirley turned to Amanda. "Pay no attention to *him…*" she said "His father tried to work with Strugnel on the Dead Sea Scrolls!"

"Oh?" asked Diane.

"Someone had to finally photograph the damn things after forty years of study!" said Shirley.

Amanda nodded.

Glory hoarding. In the academic world, professional jealousy was one thing. Glory hoarding was another. It kept things in the dark and ruined people's careers. She understood what Shirley meant.

Diane, and Shireley walked out with Amanda.

Professor Strugnel was with Harvard University when asked to examine the Dead Sea Scrolls. He studied them for decades before critics accused him of keeping the Dead Sea Scrolls hidden from the world. Harvard, being a Catholic Jesuit Institution, was accused of Catholic proselytizing. The Dead Sea Scrolls, it was alleged, belonged to peoples of the ancient world that predated Christianity: They held as much significance to the Jewish and Muslim traditions as any other. Harvard had hoarded the scholarship for its own purposes and for the Catholic Church.

The fall-out was immense. It rendered suspect all ancient texts, and it placed ancient relics on the target list of dealers betting on high-priced antiquities - many of their client's high-stakes bidders from every culture and creed. The results were ugly. The higher the price, the deadlier the game.

"…Anyway, are *you* alright?" asked Shirley when Diane left.

They walked around the central lobby balustrade and reached for the elevator button. It was full of people. They looked at each other and nodded towards the stairwell.

"Yep!"said Amanda.

Down they went on wide granite stairs flanked by a generous marble columned barrier to the grand lobby where Security officers were checking bags of tourists entering the Museum.

Dancing down the large museum steps looking like a pair of working museum professionals - Amanda, in a Kors suite and silk white blouse; Shirley a stylish Trench coat billowing away as the knees, they contemplated the crowd. Tourists threatened to overwhelm the building.

"Excuse me. Miss…Miss… Are you our tourist guides?..." yelled one man.

They turned left.

"It's just that you've got a lot on your plate" said Shirley. "Your trip to Italy, is it? Trevor to join you there…with the children? Can you manage everything in time?"

"Yep!"

"Just asking!"

"Yep!"

More steps. "Don't get wordy on me now!" laughed Shirley, breathless.

Amanda stopped.

"Shirley… I'm fine! *Really*. I'll get things going. Arrangements will be as much done as possible before I leave, and then…well, I can rendezvous with the family in Rome. Or even on the way back from Turkey. I'll think of something…"

"The sonofbitch!" muttered Shirley "*He* should be the one going. He didn't even offer. In fact, he refused to go! What the hell are we paying him for? That's *his* job. Head of Acquisitions. So. *You're* on your own with this delivery. Are you sure you can handle it?"

"Look. We'll make it. We always do on these Fundraising Gala events."

"Yes I know… But walking around Europe with a treasure it not safe these days…" insisted Shirley.

"Don't worry. It'll be quickly over!" said Amanda.

Without Amanda Wells the Museum would not have flourished with funds pouring in from all over the globe and receiving worldwide recognition for its exhibits and shows.

In fact, if ever there was an indispensable professional on the Board that saved their jobs and the city's tourism industry, it was Amanda Wells!

Yet Shirley remained apprehensive. To go the Middle East to collect an antiquity was no trifle. So much could go so wrong! The world of relics from the Holy Land was her area of expertise. She knew about the dangers of underground markets. And a woman…? It was big business. "You *sure* you're alright with this?"

"Yep!"

They laughed.

"Just let me know if there is *anything* I can do to help, OK? You, Trevor and the kids have time coming to you…"

They were outside, Shirley hailing a cab.

Amanda had her car parked below in the public parking Garage.

They parted.

* *

Less than an hour later Amanda's cell vibrated with a message. It was Tim.

"Expect calls from Trustees. They have leads for potential sponsors of the Exhibit…"

Amanda had to admire the man. Not for nothing was he the Director of one of the most venerated Museums on the East Coast, if broke.

The week passed quickly enough, and finally the day of departure arrive.

Outside it was hot and humid, Amanda's hair lost its sheen and developed a halo of fizzy, being naturally curly. Plus it was drizzling - not one of those summer storms that could split the sky then bathe the landscape quickly in silvery sunlight, but a pernicious dampness that drenched everything as a three-day Nor'easter. She popped open her umbrella, and got into the taxi.

Her cell buzzed. It was Diane.

"Hia! Just wanted to check in and see if there was anything you needed, right off the bat…"

"Well, a good coffee in an air-conditioned Spa somewhere!" laughed Amanda. "No. Yes. Thanks for checking: The budget needs extra funds for Security. We'll need to upgrade and refresh our security systems' contracts; camera surveillance, floor-sensors, electrical-perimeters, vaults and personnel. I'll meet with Mr. Byrnes personally, too." She paused. "Our security capability will doubtless be the first question I'll have to answer" she explained.

"Ok."

"Also…" She hesitated. Was she asking too much? "Set up appointments with Legal about docs for *Deed of Gift* and *Acquisition Agreements* etc. That's before I can start any vending or representation…"

 "Got it! When do you want to begin?"

"Not until we're certain we are getting the Asset" said Amanda.

"Right."

* *

The plane had been circling for almost an hour and the flight from Frankfurt had been cramped. Flight-crew came on the speaker.

"Ladies and Gentlemen, we do regret the delay in landing and we hope you will enjoy your stay in Istanbul. Please remain seated with your seatbelts on. Mesdames et Messieurs, nous sommes justament …."

Amanda looked out the window.

The plane belly-dropped with an accelerated roar and quite suddenly lurched forward for a descent for landing. Amanda's arms stiffened and her palms dug in as she pushed back from her seat. She hoped Air Traffic Controllers knew their skills.

Processing over 45 million passengers a year, Istanbul Atuturk International was one of the busiest airports in Europe. Located 15 miles west of the city center, Amanda had chosen well. To have gone to the next largest airport, Sabiha Gokcen International which was some 30 miles south of the city, her trip would have taken all day, especially at this time of year when it was over-subscribed as the favored landing site of low-cost carriers.

Still, she wanted to take in Sikeci Terminal for International rail service. She liked railroads. Had she had her way, she'd have taken the Orient Express! Launched in 1889 with a line between Bucharest and Paris, it was known for its comfort and intrigue as seen in the celebrated Agatha Christie's mystery novel *The Orient Express.*

As it was, the baggage Amanda Wells was to take back to the United States from Istanbul was considered too valuable to be exposed to anything but the shortest duration travel time and the tightest security. A special commercial flight to Rome was already booked. She had three days.

* *

Amanda was Fundraising for the Museum, this she had to inform Customs. After all, she would be leaving with one of their national treasures, and they had to know she was honest about her intentions, if asked…

They asked.

Dr. James was supposed to be with her. But he, as Shirley had pointed out, saw little reasons to go out of his way for the Museum, much less travel to Turkey for it!

Amanda was alone. Turkish officials found this most puzzling. Even if her Director had a plan to import an important discovery, and certainly, in this city, he had channels to support the effort. But Amanda was alone. They worried.

In American newspapers the news was brimming with anticipation. Only partial information had been leaked, and even then, it was all up for corroboration. The Director had been cautious. These rare collections placed on Exhibit didn't happen by accident. It took aggressive stewardship of a museum to acquire them, achieve the event, and unless you had a team of US Navy Seals accompanying the relic, anything could happen before it reached your premises!

Unquestionably, with the relic at the museum, Amanda knew that she could manage a splendid Fundraising campaign. However, it was one thing to leak information about something you aspired to acquire, and something else to boast about what you had sitting in the vault. That made all the difference in the world. People responded, they felt involved. And so they should be! This was their community effort, and for that reason, their Museum to patronize.

Most people, if Amanda's experiences offered any insight, liked to deal in paperwork, and from desks. Amanda liked to deal in realities. To her, this was the secret to sparking the imagination…

If one soul in the ancient world had dedicated his labor and effort to something of value so long ago, then surely the modern world should be moved…

In fact, as far as Amanda was concerned, it was inspiriting - one human to another, divided by history and centuries and cultures – if not a noble quest.

So it was the least she could do. If it meant travelling to Turkey alone… then so be it! This, she had decided.

Still, Shirley's words rang in her ears. *It's just that you've got a lot on your plate.*

Shirley specialized in the History of iconography, mainly religious icons of the middle periods. This was her academic expertise and she knew a great deal about the subject, including the scholars, the institutions, the circumstances of the commercial world in which such items circulated. She also knew about the danger. More than anything, that was what she was referring to when she expressed her concerns. Too late now, thought Amanda. She wanted to check out of the Airport and into the sunlight.

Nothing had happened for the Museum in a long time. The Temple scroll was the last great Exhibit that they had shown. Part of the Dead Sea Scrolls, it had become their specialty: The Temple Scroll was a brass-plated "shopping list" for supplies to run a Temple in times of antiquity. It was splendid! The museum had set the standard for all that could be discovered, discussed, shared and enjoyed. From specialists to institutions; from highly trained forensic technicians to fans volunteering their feedback and sharing.

And here she would do so once again.

Her task here was a formality: All the arrangements had been made. Administrative in nature, she would have no trouble from the local authorities.

These things, in the interests of human interest, always worked well.

But there was more that Shirley had said. *Trevor to join you there…with the children. Can you manage everything in time?.*

Well there was some pressure, actually. How to fit everything in, get it all done, without incident, and to carry on with a scheduled vacation…?

Yes. The waiting was long.

The kids, Trevor, Rome! Italy!

She wanted to rush away.

But both she and Trevor understood that as a pair of professionals there was no evading their responsibilities. Especially Trevor!

No. They had to do this!

Plus the children. Safe in London as they were - she so missed them! But again, that was the nature of their relationship: Trevor a senior Advisor working in Great Britain; and she in the Washington DC where they had a home in Chevy Chase. Her absence was scheduled for no longer than three months.

This then was their vacation time together. Well, almost-vacation. Trevor had some banking business in Italy, but apart from that there was family there… A world of memories, family, fun, sun and oh, those beautiful days by the Mediterranean sea; those vineyard-meals under trellised grapevines, and those warm evenings under a moon too full to shut out. So, yes, Shirley was right. There was no way she was going to miss their family vacation!

Keep a grip and walk through the paces methodically, she decided. Make no mistakes, stay clear of complications and keep things simple. That was the method of good management, she told herself.

So, it came as something of an irritation that Customs held her up. If she could just get past all these slow-moving people!

Slow down, she told herself.

* *

The transcontinental city had combined East and West over the centuries. Founded on the Sarayburnu promontory around 660 BC as Byzantium, the city was now known as Istanbul, seat of Alexander the Great at Constantinople in 330 AD, and capital of four empires: the Roman Empire; the Byzantine Empire; the Latin Empire and the Ottoman Empire.

Amanda walked out to the Hotel balcony, a roofed terrace of vaulted ceiling and granite columns that marked the parapet. It was once a palace by the sea. Below her the Bosphorus was teeming with ships as one of the world's business waterways positioned between the Sea of Marmara and the Black Sea. Here early Christianity had advanced during the Roman and Byzantine eras. The Ottomans conquered the city in 1453 and transformed it into an Islamic stronghold, seat of the caliphate. It was a remarkable sight, and Amanda took it all in.

Today, the region marked the center of modern trade in a vast agglomeration of some 13 million people - the second largest city in the world. She had read the brochures.

It was both new and old at the same time. Yet nothing seemed as it appeared: Everything held double meanings, from the sacred design of Islam to the iconoclastic ornamentation of Temples turned Cathedrals.

Istanbul had seen turmoil, she knew. Even the food, smells and sounds of the ancient city emitted evidence of a temporary standoff between peoples strongly divided by culture, yet united by expediency of its central location to all points of the Mediterranean sea.

Amanda's business appointment was not until 3.00 P.M. Hotel Management offered a tour. She wanted to take pictures for Trevor and the children, and she decided to go.

Wearing a white chemise over long pants, her hair pulled back in a severe chignon beneath a veil that covered all, she was driven through the city with four tourists from the hotel, and they were shown the delights of each district.

They found each venue as colorful and enigmatic as the last, if redolent with ancient tales, human effort and modern impulse. Amanda checked her watch.

Amanda returned to her room shortly after lunch. She showered and put on a fresh shirt and a Lauren suit, a silk scarf for her head was tucked into her satchel.

She consulted her Notes before leaving.

The manuscript she was about to be shown had caused a stir in the markets. Some claimed it entirely a fraud. Others, a real find.

It surfaced during the 1970s, near Beni Masar, Egypt. Known as the Codex Tchacos, after the antiquities dealer Frieda Nussberger-Tchacos, it dated from the 2nd century AD. It claimed to be titled the "Gospel of Judas" with an account of the story of Jesus' death from the perspective of his disciple, Judas Iscariot.

Amanda had prepared for her meeting with the Turkish Authorities. She decided she was not about to enter into a debate as to its epistemology, religious doctrine or content, just an acquisition for a museum. Far be it from her to get into arguments about the ancient relic. She was just the delivery boy, she told herself.

This, she made quite clear when she met with Mrs. Ollahman, Drs. Savron and Populas at the Center of Cultural Affairs at the Turkish Antiquities Administration that held an office at the University in Istanbul.

* *

Three men from the House of Lords were admitted, the heavy gates preceding large medieval iron-studded oak doors closed behind them. They entered the Court Chamber in the deepest parts of the palace where writ in stone they passed under the arch carvings of a seated watchman bearing the words *Eternal Vigilance is the Price of Liberty.*

At the center table, old and buffed to a shine in the dark glossy shadows of an overhead chandelier, three others were seated and already in conference. Here, they could speak, and nothing from this chamber was repeated or overheard on the outside of the medieval structure.

Not that they were unfamiliar with the very latest in technology, surveillance, or for that matter, intelligence for the Eyes of Ministers only, but theirs was a special responsibility - time honored and appointed only to those deserving, as it was stated, and those descendants of an early legacy.

The chair of one man was vacant.

Their topic was money. Or rather banking.

Since the Companies Act of 1862 wherein was introduced the concept of limited liability – the method by which investors could hold a trust able to float bonds, the matter of money bank notes had been a highly controversial one, if not contested on the floor of the House of Commons…

Thus if fell upon the House of Lords to adjudicate. Especially with regards to the true value of Sterling and the Bank of England's holdings. Moreover, it had been an ongoing issue for multiple generations: Commencing with the American railroads linking vast new territories for commerce, trade and development, the transcontinental railroads were shipped coal and steel to feed an industrial revolution. It proceeded to shape the modern world.

With bank-notes, securities could be sold to European investors. Especially those wanting to buy American bonds in the development of the Industrial Revolution.

Investments had been remarkable. In Europe, the road to Empire wealth was laid in track. In America, the Pennsylvania Union Pacific and Atchinson-Topeka and Santa Fee, along with Transcontinental Canadian railroads, ran on investor's money held by Notes. Even through

Depressions, investments kept coming backed by the railroads.

Sailing across oceans in ships, was cycling back and forth, even as trade flourished to other parts of the world across the British Empire, including the Anglo-Persian Oil Company. Many had made their fortunes.

Those seated at the table were familiar with the financial instruments whereby banks and bankers like Pierpont Morgan; Schiff at Kyhn Loeb and the New York Warburgs had prospered.

As had the Treasuries of sovereign governments.

However, things had turned. The Trade Agreements and Social upheavals that swept across Europe left many on the streets, others in turmoil and insecurity following WWI. Modernism itself had been strangely haunted the experiences of The Great War.

How could they fathom the consequences that came at the turn of the century when territorial boundaries were rooted in agrarian economies still able to sustain themselves?

The British Empire had grown, and ruled. But new pressures of growing populations had emerged; industrial centralization intensified; labor demands and technological advancements developed only to hurt smaller nations, and the seeds of destruction were sown…

The road to war happened quickly, unexpectedly. These men present knew very well the signs of lesser threats that could take down a giant. They knew the events well indeed. Especially one.

They staged a fake act of provocation, and resulted in an attack by the Kwantung Army, Japan's field army in China, with the aim to occupy the whole of the province.

The League of Nations, a body of the greater powers designed to aid unfairness and keep peace, did little to object to Japan's assault in its 1931 plot to seize Manchuria and its rich resources.

The 1930s hit many nations hard. Especially those who had come to depend on trade between nations – relying entirely on their own production of goods for export.

Those with strong Trade Agreements, like the Imperial and Colonial powers had international political and economic standing. But lesser nations were neither recognized, nor supported by the League of Nations.

Thus, with none vigilant to watch, and as Germany allied with Japan to arms, socialism took root in aggregate, amassing laborers and unemployed…

Moreover, curbed of their power and influence, the House of Lords came under scrutiny.

Whereas the Appellate Jurisdiction Act of 1876 to the House of Lords allowed Law Lords - Lords of Appeal in Ordinary to perform judicial functions as the highest court of appeal, their role was reformed: A legacy of their function now served the purpose of reviewing bills passed by the House of Commons.

The checks and balances of power had dissipated. Guardians of England's monetary and sovereign assets were gone – leaving only areas of dispute.

Except for the few. They met. They gathered, like forgotten warriors. Those who believed that *Eternal Vigilance is the Price of Liberty.*

This matter before them now, due to its legacy and circumstance, was before them by default. It had been left at their doorstep like an unwanted baby.

Whereas the Companies Act of 1862 changed the world with industrialization, here was a new problem.

This was different time. They had left behind the concept of bank notes; gold currency and dusty ledgers.

They had shifted to digital transactions - if not in railroads…in emerging global markets, international investments; integrated technologies and transcontinental financial computations of billions of trades per day. Entire corporations depended on sales, acquisitions, bonds and stocks. Sovereign states invested heavily in currencies; commodities, energy and resource allocations in a filigree network of connectivity and electronic interaction.

Yet economies were collapsing. Something had gone terribly wrong.

The consequences for Britain and her banks were profound. They must deflect the impact of a massive draw-down on English resources as the Central Bank offered assistance to sovereign states in distress…

Belgium. Greece. Cyprus. Spain. Ireland…

Assembled today they reviewed the growing list of defaulting economies. How should they protect Britain going over the cliff…?

They were a handful of men, inadequate really. Those that knew *Eternal Vigilance is the Price of Liberty*. How to aid society …in the storms ahead?

"Does he know yet?" said Mr. Eldridge, nodding to towards the vacant chair.

"No. He does not."

"He is a senior advisor, and if he was aware he would be honor-bound to disclose our Findings to his superiors…"

"…whose interests we are also honor-bound to defend!"

"True. But not in this fashion of old assumptions, my friend. We are today a popular plebiscite, and all must come forward for the scrutiny of the populace!"

"Many of whom do not transact their business at this level. Neither do they have understanding of the greater consequences to the nation…"

"Nor do they care…" said Mr. Eldridge.

"I understand your sentiments. But as *he* says, people do understand – given the chance. Still, we are under increasing pressure here. How do we draw a line in the sand?"

"That, we must do!"

"We declare a state of Emergency!"

"An Emergency? What kind of Emergency?"

"…anything that would bring the country together…"

"Or divide us, every one!"

"If we make it a financial emergency, then we will have panic in the markets…"

"Then make it an environmental emergency…"

"Gentlemen" said the principle speaker, "How can we keep this from one of our most trusted members?" again he nodded towards the vacant chair.

"We shield him! Keep him in the dark…Let him deal with the crisis at hand…In his position of leadership, it would change nothing!"
There was a silence.
"Is this truly necessary?"
"I'm afraid so!"
They thought about it.
"For England" said one.
"For England" they echoed.

* *

The Taxi driver was most helpful. He and his family had lived in Turkey since before the war, he said. Originally Syrian, his father was a cement mixer then a mason, and eventually started a cement factory for the construction of the city. Especially as Europeans moved into the region during the 20th century and a building explosion began for the many populations of today.
"You come from America Madam?" he asked.
"Yes, I do!" answered Amanda.
"Is here… very, very old place, here Madam! Long time ago the lands, once have villages, cities, all…all…all… from the beginning of time, it go all…all to the sea, it come up in great flood" he said, his hand flourishing his words.
"Yes. This town has a long history!" said Amanda.
He grinned at her in the rear view mirror.
They drove to Stamboul along the walled peninsula between the Golden Horn and the Sea of Marmara. The driver was enjoying being a tour guide.

"The word Pera, in Greek, it mean *across from*, that is the crossing between the Golden Horn and Bosphorus. We call it Beyoglu district, and it has its constituency like to err…how you say? vote in district election of the Turkish Governmnent!"

"We not have elections and democracy for a long long time, and we now have!" he added proudly.

"Islambol, that is like Istambul, it mean City of Islam, especially with great Ottoman Empire, and it make it picture on its money. But it also very old in ancient times!"

"I see" smiled Amanda.

He navigated traffic as it surged and stopped with unremitting urgency, humans in flight from place to place in continuous motion.

Amanda looked out across the sea of diamonds glimmering in the sun, knowing its ancient origins. Moreover, Shirley had refreshed her history with a primer. She had read the material on the plane. There had been Neolithic artifacts uncovered by archaeologists at the beginning of the 21st century, suggesting that the peninsula was settled as early as the 7th millennium BC. That was an important find because the region coalesced over time, into a Neoloithic Revolution that had spread from the Near East to Europe. It endured for a millennium before a sudden collapse caused by inundation from rising water levels, allegorically said to be Noah's Biblical flood. More probably derived from a volcanic eruption and ensuing tsunami effect that opened seas and crested any barrier.

Amanda was mesmerized. Sunlight flashed off golden domes and minarets as the Taxi proceeded through the city, its noisy battleground receding, in

Amanda's mind, like a musical call from the past where the world was ancient and man was feeling his way through time.

Long ago this horizon of walled concrete across the sea division was the region of the Thracian tribes, one, the famed Phrygians who began settling in the Sarayburnu in the 6ᵗʰ millennium BC.

The study of the Thracian tribes, Amanda knew, was known as Thracology. The study of their language was a combination of early Indo-European, a language family distinguishable in modern scholarship. They had inhabited the Central and Southeastern planes of Europe, bordered by the Scythians to the north; the Celts and the Illyrians to the west, and the Ancient Greeks to the South. Celebrated in history, the *Illiad* described them as allies of the Trojans in the Trojan War against the Greeks.

The discovery caused a sensation, Amanda knew. Known as a people of Red Heads, they were discovered shortly after WWII in the territory south of Bulgaria in archaeological tombs like Tomb of Sveshtari, Kazaniak, Tatul, Seuthopolois; and in Romania at Sarmizegetusa. Within the tombs were funerary artifacts of gold and silver of the 5ᵗʰ and 4ᵗʰ century BC unrivaled in human history. Famed treasure finds were made at Panagyurishte, Rogozen, Valchitran and Borovo.

According to Herodotus, the Phrygians came from those early settlements. Thus it was known that the Indo-European people living south of the Balkans created the state of Phrygia around the 8ᵗʰ century BC with its capital at Gordium.

Moreover, they spread eastward, progenitors of early Biblical peoples, asserting themselves upon the Urarty, Hurrians until invaded by the Cimmerians in 690 BC, passing eventually into the Persian Empire. Here then, were the ancient tribes of the Bible.

Along the "Asian side" of the Bosphorus peninsula at Istanbul, Amanda knew that old artifacts of the 4th millennium had been found in a place called Fikirtepe, the site of a Phoenician trading post known in the 1st millennium, possibly the town of Calcedon which appeared in ancient writings.

Most remarkably, here was the seat of the ancient Semitic civilization situated on the Fertile Crescent, centered on the coastline of modern Lebanon and Tartus Governorate in Syria, propelling a maritime trading culture that spanned the world.

On the European side of the Bosphorus was the acropolis of the Byzantium, center of recognized Greek settlers from Megara who fashioned it as the heart of the Roman Empire..

It was just too amazing. Amanda would write it all down when she returned to her hotel tonight, she decided. It was one thing to read about it, another to witness the large vistas and vast spreads of landscape that inspired early civilizations!

Gradually, the golden shapes of the past turned into bleached sunlight of hot white modern concrete structures – and the financial district in Maslak appeared.

The taxi took a turn and negotiated a wave of business-suited pedestrians; traffic and tourists amid a city of skyscrapers 200 meters high.

Maslak competed with the Levent business district for financial activities its high tech steel structures; power plants and glass enclosures distinguished it as ultra-modern world moving for a global set of concerns, Eastern and Western.

Amanda had to smile. University campus structures appeared, and here was any city in Europe or America competing for commercial, cultural and political presence in blue jeans; book-bags, white tees and lover's looks.

Here, Amanda had her first appointment.

* *

A discussion on the intrinsic and historical integrity of the manuscript would be necessary amongst scholars in this cool and ambient environment of intellectual exchange.

Amanda, being the only representative from the Museum, had to revert to her academic skills to accommodate them. Not that she was unqualified since she had logged her time at academic institutions - both as a scholar and instructor. But the predominant reason for her meeting was to be more than just another debate. It was to be a respectful courtesy visit to the source of the antiquity in question.

They trusted her reputation. They knew her. If anyone could tell the West what this manuscript was all about, it would be Amanda Wells.

Here was the forensic technology ground that informed ancient artifacts and their authenticity - let alone their provenance for insurance purposes.

Still, she felt a little daunted, not only because she would be the only woman on-deck in a field of highly acclaimed archaeologists from Europe and the Middle East, but topically, she would be in the midst of Biblical scholars; anthropologists; sociologists and linguists. They of course, would know of her limitations, and she, as a guest would remind them of her field being outside theirs for comparison or competition.

If she thought her field of medieval literature was hardly appropriate for a manuscript almost two millennium in age, she was wrong. She belonged in the room, they said.

"Ms Wells!" said the woman in a semi-burka and pretty veil, clasping manda's hands in greeting. Within minutes, all predispositions were swept aside. A scholar was a scholar, as far as they were concerned. And as such, there was a certain code of ethics that tied them to their passion.

Introduced, there was Mrs Ollahman, the Administrator; Drs Savron and Populas. two professors, one conservator, and two technical experts from a forensic laboratory that was *sans pareille* in the Middle East. Amanda was pleased to have Mrs. Ollahman join them.

It wasn't long before she was in a room wearing a white overall, dust gloves and protective light glasses. At a table irradiated for the examination was an ancient text.

It took her breath away.

Here was an oiled skin illumined leather-bound papyrus, written in the Coptic language, the Codex Tchacos.

"According to Timothy Jull" said Savron "the manuscript was radiocarbon-dated between the third and fourth century."

Amanda had heard of Jull at the University of Arizona's physics center.

"…That is roughly consistent with the analysis brought forward by the National Geographic, AD 280 plus or minus 60 years."

"Yes" said Amanda.

"We have a manuscript that is in about a thousand pieces, entire sections missing from age, poor storage and bad handling…"

"Umm" said Amanda, leaning over and almost purring from the wonder of it.

"According to Radolphe Kasser," he continued "the codex might well have once held 31 pages, with writing on both sides; here you see the ink, here, and here…"

"But by the time it came to us, or arrived on the market, it had only 13 pages. Some say that individual pages have been sold off already…"said Dr. Populas.

"I see" said Amanda "Has there been any textual analysis?

"Oh yes!" they all nodded.

Savron took the lead. "There are features of inflection from Greek loan words, words that have meaning and idiom to add to the text, and we believe the Coptic text may be a translation from an earlier Greek manuscript, dating to AD 130-180."

"Supporting this theory" said Ollahman "is a citation from the early Christian writer *Irenaeus of Lyons*, who argues strenuously against Gnosticism, and calls this assertion a "fictitious history…" She paused, the rest leaving her clearly a little hesitant such that Populas stepped forward and completed the theory.

Amanda noticed that none could utter the words of its potential sacredness.

"It is speculated that this is the Coptic 'Gospel of Judas' -now the Codex Tchachos: It is the account which claims to be the story of Jesus' death from the viewpoint of Judas Iscariot, his betrayer. It is labeled as *"Gospel of Judas Evangelion Ioudas"* They held their breath.

Amanda looked down, her own effect hidden from her onlookers, to examine the manuscript. She could find no words.

"A.J.Levine, as you know, said this manuscript contains no new historical information concerning Jesus or Judas..." said the Conservator.

"Yes. He says it explores the arguments, rather, of Gnosticism, particularly for the early Coptic-speaking areas!" Savron said.

Amanda looked up "...But you don't agree?"

They looked at each other, the look that scholars give when they have reached the boundaries of their specializations, and are reluctant to stray into another's field of expertise.

"For that, Dr. Wells, it would be better to consult with the religious specialists and theological theorists."

"Of course!" she said, knowing that she was being passed along.

Like looking into the face of a beloved, there was no hurry to avert their eyes. Together they stood, lingering over the manuscript before them, torn, aged and inked over from the hand of a beautiful ancient calligraphy...Even in the modern lighting, and sterile white lab conditions, it beckoned from an era redolent with urgency and passion.

The Judas Manuscript.

Here was something that, if true, was written by the hand of a human embroiled in a story that would frame history with words uttered from profound beliefs and avowals of the ancient Jewish world.

Or, at least, tried to…

They could look at it no longer, as if this sacred text could mute all who pondered upon it.

Finally, it was the conservator who tented over the parchment its soft chamoe covering, and switched off the examination-table light.

They spoke in the hallways, profoundly moved by the text within, yet able to pull themselves together as scholars and analysts.

Her next appointment, they knew, was at the Sultan Ahmed Mosque.

Having viewed the relic, they retreated to the small office where Amanda made a formal presentation assuring them that she had a full itinerary for the secure removal and transportation of the manuscript to America.

They all nodded, bravely.

Amanda stepped out into the sunlight. She chose to walk, and finally settled for a small outdoor café where she ordered a cappuccino and watched the city block unfurl around her.

Amanda knew that she could not remove the relic from Istanbul without the courtesy of consulting with the religious authorities at the Mosque, a gesture made out of professional respect for the Muslim tradition at Istanbul. Even as official authorization had been granted by the Government.

* *

Amanda approached the southern courtyard of the Blue Mosque and observed worshipers entering from all sides. It was as popular a house of prayer and worship today as it had been for centuries.

She paused in the courtyard and looked up. Surrounded by a vaulted arcade, the medieval structure rose to a central dome with six minarets and eight secondary domes surrounding the main. It stood as a magnificent monument of Islamic architecture.

Colorfully depicted with iconography of Islamic art Amanda knew that while Islam was generally considered an iconoclastic religion in which the representation of living things was prohibited from the beginning, the development of abstract ornamental design in which geometric and vegetal arabesque patterns of leaves; palmettes and sometimes animal-like motifs could resembled calligraphy for amazing adornment.

Amanda moved to the historical elementary school where the Mosque Information Center was located, adjacent to the outer wall on the side of Hagia Sophia. There, she found Persian decorative paintings on ceramics, stylized with animal or human figures in scenes from unidentified tales and romances.

"The Director will be with you shortly Ms. Wells." said an Administrator wearing a colorful headdress. "He offers his apologies for his tardiness, and

invites you to tour the premises at your leisure…"
Amanda was handed a guide brochure.
She stepped out into the sunny courtyard. Emerging from the main entrance of prayer, a Sultan in flowing white garment descended to his waiting Limousine which, judging from the three Mercedes cars and security personnel that followed, denoted an official of some importance.
Amanda walked inside. She quietly took off her shoes placed them in a corner and pulled out a silk scarf from her bag. She placed it over her head with a knot at the chin.
Immediately the temperature differential was felt. Whereas it had hot and was humid outside, the cold air in the Mosque was calming, like a wash of atmosphere.
She stood there. She had read the brochure, but nothing prepared her for this scenery.
Thousands of handmade ceramic tiles lined the walls at every pier of the vast open interior. Made at Iznik - the ancient town of Nicaea, the tiles glistened in more than fifty ways colorful and differently. Arranged in tiers, they represented simple tulip designs at the lower levels, then became markedly more ornate at the higher levels with displays of flowers, fruit and cypress.
Above her, high within the interior of the massive domes, over 200 stained-glass windows of intricate designs admitted light, illuminating with decorative ornamentation sacred verses from the Qur'an.
More domes, exedra and semi-domes were constructed with fenestration of colored-glass - gifts from the Venetian house of the early sultan.

At the center stood the mihrab, an alter of finely carved and sculptured marble; a stalactite niche and a double-inscriptive panel above it. To the right was a richly decorated miber, or pulpit, where the Imam stood to deliver his sermon.

Amanda stood in wonder. God lived here, she was sure of it, feeling like the many visitors of all faiths including the Pope who came here during his visit of diplomacy to Turkey.

A gentleman approached her and bowed respectfully. "The Director will see you now, Ms. Wells" he said.

She had been carefully watched. And she was now courteously escorted.

** **

The Director was an elderly man, comfortable in his surroundings of books, cushions, benches, and plain oak tables. He stood at the center of a room whose walls, stone and stark ceilings held a reverence about them. Only in the far corner purred the electronics of a highly sophisticated computer station.

"If I were a Christian" he said, his eyes smiling "I would be a very contented monk, as you can see from my place of study and contemplation…"

He put her immediately at ease.

Amanda smiled.

"Please!" he said, offering her a seat in a small lattice-worked divan.

She accepted coffee from an attendant, a circular brass table tray between them.

"I understand that you wish to take the Judas Manuscript to America for a public exhibit?"

"Yes, the Mendhelsson Gallery of Baltimore, Maryland."

"And then you wish to send it on a tour to various other museums across America?"

"It deserves no less, if it is authentic…" she said quietly.

"I agree! And I understand that you have satisfied the authorities with all the security precautions necessary…"

"Yes."

"Well, in that case" he said, leaning forward to offer her a small plate of delicate confections "who am I to object?"

Amanda nodded, knowing very well that the traditions of self-deprecation and humility were the sophisticated ways of Islamic courtesy.

And she had to ask.

"I ask for your understanding of the manuscript, and your approval of our moving the manuscript from your boundaries."

"I see" he said, sipping his coffee. "In that case, I am honored that you should ask!"

She thanked him. She saw something else in his querying eyes.

"Do you intend…" Ms. Wells, "to use this for profit, or for… understanding?"

"As you know, it is the way of charitable non-profit organizations in America to appeal for generous donors and gifts from the viewing public. Thus, we have to keep money in mind as we operate the business in the public domain. Operations and management, as you know, are paid for with good salaries for talented individuals, and the services of good vendors whose bills are all paid in a timely manner. This is our tax-reporting system. However, as long as we remain within the strictures of our assigned charter-mission, were are entitled to show material and items that have public appeal as a way to appeal for public financial support."

Amanda knew that he was aware of the laws and charters that governed museums. But his was a larger philosophical question.

"I understand." He put down his cup and stood up. "Come!" he said. "Let me show you our exhibits!"

They walked through the ancient Library containing scrolls and papyrus. He pointed to religious items that held meaning for the faithful of Islam.

"It would be ill-suited Ms. Wells, for the manuscript to be jeered at by unbelievers!" he cautioned.

He surprised her. Being an item generally known as Christian, he was concerned for its integrity and historical significance and meaning, regardless theology.

They had paused.

He put his hands behind his back, and looked down, strolling. "We live not in the same world where relics hold people captive, but… we are a world of skeptics, idolaters and factions - all living beside the Faithful!" He paused. "The sacred… seem to matter little, regardless the religion. Surely you understand my concern…?"

"I do understand" said Amanda. "Our exhibit will be simple and respectful in presentation" she assured him. We have no agenda, other than to show an item of antiquity for people to ponder and view.

"We may be of different religions, you and I, but we are all descendants of Abraham are we not?"

Amanda smiled. "I fail to see how any woman cannot be moved by a God who responds to the appeal of a handmaiden Hagar, alone with a son and separated from the only household she ever knew…"

"I see you are a woman of the Scriptures" he said "Thank you!"

 Amanda accepted the complement, knowing that in the ancient world, such an invocation separated the civilized from the uncivilized.

"Now, tell me what *you* know of the Judas Manuscript Ms. Wells?"

"Well, I know of the presentation of Joseph Barabe to the American Chemical Society Meeting in his analysis of the ink used on the manuscript…The analysis was used to authenticate the book.

Further, the manuscript is probably a text derived from an earlier Greek version. But beyond the translation published in 2006 by the National Geographic Society, I know very little, I'm afraid."

"You are most modest Ms. Wells. The content of the manuscript, as you know, is a hotly debated issue. The Gospel of Judas is a Gnostic gospel containing the conversations between the Apostle Judas Iscariot and Jesus Christ the Jew, descendent of King David - named as the first prince amongst princes, or son, in the Judaic tradition. After Jesus the Prophet was crucified for his teachings, he was believed to be the son of God and progenitor of your Christiana faith. Judas Iscariot was the apostle who purportedly betrayed him…?"

"Yes, it is believed to have been written by Gnostic followers of Jesus, and contains late 2nd century theology. Since Irenaeus, the Bishop of Lyons wrote a document railing against the gospel in 198 AD, it is believed that the gospel was already circulating with a following of believers…" she said. He nodded.

"The only copy we know of is the Coptic language text, which as you know, has been carbon dated to AD 280 or so…"

He spoke softly. "The conventional story is that Judas delivered Christ to the authorities for crucifixion in exchange for money. As the Bible writes, Judas' actions are viewed as that of a betrayer…"

He paused, looking up in thought, as if hesitating.

"But the Judas manuscript implies that Judas was only conforming to the wishes of Christ himself, suggesting that the events of this ministry, and death, were planned…much like other planning, such as the Innkeeper's room reservation for the Last Supper?"

Amanda nodded.

"It is argued" he proceeded "that since Gnosticism believes the human form to be in spiritual confinement, Judas serves to release the soul of Christ. This implies two beings: The one of the immortal soul which is 'from the eternal realms – with no ruler over it' (and I quote); and the other being is the majority of mankind, mortal and unable to reach salvation."

"But the teachings of Christ offer forgiveness by God and salvation…" offered Amanda.

"They do. And in that, they differ from Judaism and Islam. However, it is here suggested that Judas stood alone in his understanding of Jesus. The other disciples, by inference, were less informed about his true mission and meaning. It is almost as if Judas held some exalted position of favor with Christ."

"The account says that he is overcome by remorse and kills himself" said Amanda.

"Yes, according to the Biblical story. But in the few narrative elements of this manuscript, whereas it is generally agreed that Jesus *had* to die in order to atone for the sins of humanity, Judas suggests this to hold *lesser* purpose."

"Oh?"

"Yes. The prevailing scholarship explores the suggestion that the true God, as understood at the time, is gracious and thus does not demand any sacrifice. In the Gospel of Judas, the death of Jesus is simply a final release from the realm of the flesh."

"Is there room for any other interpretation?" asked Amanda.

"There is. Other scholars say that the proto-Nicenian church fathers had their approaches to understanding Christianity. Yet others say that non-Nicenian texts show that the early Church fathers tended to 'oversimplify' when contradicting doctrinal assertions…"

"Sounds a bit like politics today really…" chuckled Amanda.

"It does indeed!" he smiled. "But the Gospel of Judas has allowed scholars to develop deeper understandings of the movements. Gnostic or not, there is much subtlety and sophistication in these words."

Amanda walked with him.

"There is much to learn and understand here. It depends on how open is your mind, and how generous is your heart for learning the words of such a prophet. For example, the four canonical gospels show the life of Christ. Judas however, speaks only of the spiritual conversations between him and Christ. Was there a connection? Did they have a mission? Was the account for *them*, or for us…?" he said.

"The New Testament apocrypha has several dialogue narratives, like the Gospel of Mary Magdalene" said Amanda.

 "True. They were popular during the early decades of Christianity, were they not?"

"Yes."

"I see you know your history Ms. Wells!" he smiled. "Of course, as history later shows, it depends on whose interests are being served, and which Institution is doing the proselytizing - or even which scriptures as gospels are chosen for inclusion in the cannon! Remember, if you owned the hearts and minds of people, you owned their body; their labor and their resources!"

Amanda knew he was referring to the Holy Roman Empire who decided in the 2nd century AD which gospels should be used for the Christian Bible, and which gospels should be omitted.

He hesitated, walking more slowly. They had moved around the perimeter of the great mosque discussing the meaning of the manuscript.

"…Whereas Judas is viewed as the one who betrays Christ for money in the canonical gospels - the villain of sorts, in this Judas manuscript, he is seen as a divinely appointed instrument, as if a fate of remorse awaits those who find no accounting for their lives…Theological discussion will be lievely!"

"I see. The matter of contention being that of self-determination. Free Choice, if you will, and independence as God's intended?"

"You, Ms. Wells…should not be afraid to find learning in this manuscript. There is much yet to see from that era…I hope that you will explore your scholarship…"

"Thank you. But no! My job is not to question the contents, but to deliver it safely for others to ponder…"

They resumed their stroll.

She then added "The Judas manuscript is a different interpretation from that of the conventional religious narrative: Few words are legible, of course. But some are. Assuming they are authentic…I cannot pretend to know their meaning…"

He stopped, and spoke more quietly. "It is a controversial question. The main words in the Judas manuscript still legible were ascribed to secret words uttered by Jesus where he tells Judas that his mission is to reform Judaism: God the personification is found within us all, he says. Implying that self-determination and self- reliance are endorsed by God in the Judaic tradition. This, he tells to the Treasurer! We must wonder why, since he also recognizes the authority of Caesar for taxation?"

They walked. He raised his hands to his bowed head where his fingers touched, thinking.

"I believe you will find the same words spoken by Paul in your Bible in the Epistle to the Philippians where he reminds them of the mind of Christ Jesus who '*being in the form of God, thought it not robbery to be equal with God. But he made himself of no reputation, and took upon himself the form of a servant…And being in the fashion as man he humbled himself, and became obedient unto death, even the death of the Cross*'?"

"Surely that implies self-sufficiency and independent agency?" she said, drawn into the question of human choices.

"Exactly!"

"Forgiveness, then, is also a choice?"

"Forgiveness is a position that each religion must decide – and defend - for itself."

"Of course!"

"In modern terms, forgiveness often suggests the world of second-chances!"

"Like, the forgiveness-of-student-loans?"

He laughed. "I see that you are as greedy as the rest of us!"

They were at the end of their walk, she knew.

"I am teasing of course! You see, in the end, the nature of man must be judged by the rules of God in any scripture."

* *

Amanda left the Mosque feeling as if she had walked the clouds with a grand master of understanding. She had even been exhorted to examine the content with him! It had been a most memorable experience if not a privilege, she decided.

She looked at her watch.

Amanda had one more stop to make, and hailed a Taxi.

How could she put out of her mind words spoken under the great domes of the Mosque? Words about an event that had occurred so long ago? In one manner or another, those moments had shaped the modern world…

Amanda could not wait to return to her Hotel for the evening. For now, she was exhausted. Yet she felt pleased with the accomplishments of the day. She had achieved her objectives to meet with the scholars and religious leaders in the city.

All that remained were some Administrative obligations at the American Consulate, followed by a brief visit to meet with the Bank.

Then she could fly to…to …*Italy!*

Her heart skipped a beat. Oh, how wonderful to be meeting up with her family in Italy. The prospect thrilled her.

Tonight she would make notes; send out correspondence to Baltimore about her progress, and inform them of her itinerary. Then she'd shower, dress and dine in the Restaurant of the Hotel before retiring for the night.

Amanda checked the time. Her agenda was on target.

Next the American Consulate…That was to be done tomorrow.

Two hours later, she was well her way to completing the day, she realized.

Having seen the manuscript at the University this morning and found it to be authentic in her professional opinion; then a visit to the cultural constituency for permission to remove the treasure from Turkish soil, she was now scheduled to meet with the Bank Manager of a designated American branch bank in Istanbul.

At the bank, she was to meet with the Vault Manager and she would receive the full dossier of the vault accounts for certified repositories.

The bank was easily found, and she introduced herself. They were expecting her.

There were safeguard 'Stops' in which to deposit the treasure while in transit to America. Rome was the first Stop. London, the second Stop. This, they said, was for insurance purposes - bond deposit account numbers; security code assignations and passwords.

"Please keep your password simple" admonished the bank manager. "The burden of responsibility that attends the transportation of treasure often places a courier under duress, and passwords elude them when under stress…"

Amanda understood, and grinned. "Tess" she said, "my mother's name!"

"Well then Ms. Wells. Remember, once you activate the secure box in the vault of the bank, a timing begins. It will change the password in 30 days unless the treasure is reclaimed. So you have only 30 days to move it on to its next leg of the destination. Rome is your first bank deposit with this material. After that, you have arranged for London. Yes?"

"Yes. My husband and I plan to return to London after a short stay in Italy. Then I travel to the United States with it. As arranged."

"Right! So you must not forget the Passwords or account combinations to gain access to the vault. Remember, only three people know this password now: You, me and…your mother Tess!"

"Well, she died some years ago…"

"I see" he said. "But you understand the importance of revealing those passwords to no one! With them, they can access your vault box…You understand?"

She signed off on the documents and stepped into the sunshine. Already, she felt the weight of liability of travelling across Europe carrying a treasure.

The taxi finally brought her to her hotel.

The sky was a golden blue, now casting purple shadows from tropical palm trees; bougainvillea vines and flora. She took a deep breath. How beautiful!

So far, so good.

Two messages were waiting for her at the hotel lobby. One from her Embassy contact in Istanbul inviting her to luncheon the next day; the other from Trevor, which she received with a suppressed squeal of excitement. He would call tomorrow.

She walked across the lobby, elated and already recounting the highlights to talk about, including the flight over, the visit to the University and the relic itself, although she should guard her words carefully for security reasons. Still, she would tell him about her talk with the Imam Director at the Mosque. There was so much to say, and so much to ask him about. Her mind turned to the children in Italy, imagine.

"Amanda!" yelled a voice. It drew her to a halt. Unsure, she felt as if she recognized the voice.

"Amanda!"

Of course! How could she forget that French accent? Jacques de Torraine, French Antiquities Dealer.

"Jacques!"

"My dear Ms. Wells!" he said, arriving breathlessly from across the lobby. "How pleased I am to see you here….and to say hello again!"

"It's a pleasure to see you too!" she said, offering her hand in greeting.

He took her hand, then embraced her French style in a gesture of public hugging. The effect dislodged the gaze of all in the lobby looking on. Back to business – these being clearly friends reuniting.

"Please, sit? You have a moment for an old friend?"

"Of course!" she said, wondering if he were friend or foe after their encounter in London two years ago over a matter of questionable intentions.

But he swept all doubts away with a fresh "How are you? Trevor? The children? Tell me!"

They chatted.

"I was in Istanbul buying some inventory for my Antique Gallery in Paris when I heard rumors of an American scholar come to review the manuscript for a touring exhibit in America!" he said simply.

Well, at least he was being honest, thought Amanda.

"…And *I knew* it must be you, my dearest Amanda. That most knowledgeable expert of texts!"

She held up her hand "Not exactly Jacques…. This era is way earlier than anything I'm trained in. But yes, I'm here to plea for the Judas manuscript to come to our museum in Baltimore, Maryland."

"Of which you are on the board of Directors for fundraising, yes?"

She smiled. He would be informed, naturally.

"Well, in that case, my dear, you will want to know the background information on this manuscript that comes to your museum… Not only for provenance, but as a matter of the market and insurance value, yes?"

He had a point there. If a museum was about to expose itself with an exhibit, there had better be a clear survey of what they were getting, and what the background rumor was. At this point, she would be derelict in her duty not to pay attention, especially to one such as Jacques de Torraine - one of Europe's most eminent collectors of Antiquities.

"Dinner?" he grinned. "Tonight?"

She smiled. "Jacques I fear for my life when I am with you! Charming as you are, I may be swept off my feet…But yes, if there is anything I need to know about this manuscript, then you'd be the one to know, the one to tell me. So yes. Dinner will do fine!"

They laughed.

"I know of a place…" he began.

"No. Thank you Jacques. Here! I shall be coming down to have dinner in the Hotel Restaurant at 7 P.M., and I'd be happy to dine with you if you care to join me…?"

"*Absolument* my darling!" he said with great flourish "I look forward to it with pleasure. Tonight, 7 PM here then! At the Hotel Restaurant. That is perfect." He kissed her on oth cheeks again, and was gone.

7.00 PM then. Amanda braced herself for the prospect and pressed the elevator button to her room, messages from the front desk still in her hand.

From her room balcony, the Bosphorus looked calm, like a blue mirror reflecting the sky in quiet and sober warning of turbulence that could lay beneath the surface.

* *

She secured her valuables in the Safe, opened her laptop for Notes and finally took a shower before turning to her suitcase to dress for dinner.

None of her clothes were suitable!

She had packed business suits for Istanbul; casual gear for herself and the kids in Italy, and maybe an evening dress or two for the man she loved, Trevor! That was it. Her options for a dinner downstairs with Jacques were few.

If she had counted on a smart dinner to relax by herself this evening, she was mistaken. Now it was dinner with a Jacques de Torraine.

She tied back her hair and picked a blouse and a business suit. Then, reviewing an austere composite in the mirror, added a simple broach and tiny diamond earrings for formal wear. No more.

She made for the door, and hesitated. She looked at the phone, then made a decision. She called the Concierge requesting in-house Hotel Valet Escort service to her room from the Restaurant at 9.30 PM sharp. She gave her name and room number, and would leave her name card with the Maitre D' of the Restaurant for identification purposes. Yes, Master Key Access for her room door to be opened was permitted for the escort service valet only.

* *

"Do you know where the manuscript came from?" Amanda looked down at her shrimp aperitif and thought about the question. She did not know. Or rather, she did know, but only that which had been presented. She took a deep breath. It was time to find out.

He leaned forward, his face lit by the candlelight of their small and secluded table.

"No. I don't."

"It turned up in the 'grey market' in Geneva in May 1983" said Jacques, his silver fork waving a small circle in the air.

She understood immediately. It came from a sort of quasi-legal parallel market, trading as a commodity through unauthorized distribution channels, usually preserved for the illegal importation of goods for cost benefits like pharmaceutical drug manufacturers importing equivalent drugs for different prices.

Known as arbitrage, the process was encouraged to promote free markets and reduce tariffs to stimulate growth, she knew. But she asked, anyway.

"Without provenance? Was it even legal?"

"Not all of it. Partially legal" he said. "Well. Once you enter the grey economy…"

Or worse, thought Amanda. The dark market was an underground economy, like unissued securities not yet traded in official markets.

"Like the commodity futures on crude oil sold in 2008…" he was saying.

"I understand, Jacques…But I don't know of anyone going to jail over it?"

"No" said Jacques "but still, if not illegal exactly, then without accountable third party traders."

The shrimp was gone, all that remained was her salad and role. She was hungry and had not eaten all day, except for a coffee in the morning with a croissant for breakfast, and a cappuccino in the city square.

"Ok. It's not the black market. But as you know, Amanda, antiquities circulate in a number of ways. Anyway, such a gospel text was unknown until this..this…Coptic *Gospel of Judas* turns up!"

She looked up. He was sitting still, and if she wasn't dreaming, he looked as if there was wonder in his eyes.

"Imagine, Amanda…the *Gospel of Judas*! The man who spoke to Jesus Christ on a daily basis…?"

She decided she liked Jacques, after all.

He had a heart, even if his wallet led him to places less than scrupulous. She put down her fork and smiled. "Yes, it is a remarkable thing, isn't it?"

"Right!" he said, nudged from his reverie. "So! Anyway, it was mixed up with a group of Greek and Coptic manuscripts when this student at Yale, Stephen Emmel, was approached by the Southern Methodist University to take a look. He was *stunned*!"

Amanda could only imagine that effect, how it might impact someone with the realization that this stood to corroborate a moment in history.

"How exactly was this manuscript found?' she asked.

"Well that's the thing. Nobody knows for sure. Apparently, the Codex Tchacos - that was the name of the Antiquities dealer, was discovered in the late 1970s, and it had not been fully documented. It is believed that an Egyptian "treasure hunter" discovered the codex near El Minya, Egypt, near Beni Masar and sold it to a dealer called Hanna who resided in Cairo."

Amanda knew this part. She pierced into her salad loaded with feta cheese and olives and broke off a chunk of bread from her bread plate.

They munched.

"Shortly after" he continued "the Hanna dealer, well his stuff was stolen, including the manuscript. The thief was a Greek trader named Nokolas Koutoulakis, and everything was smuggled into Geneva. Hanna and another Swiss antiquity trader paid Koutoulakis to get it all back."

Amanda swallowed and then teased gently

"…Not you Jacques?"

He laughed. "No. *Unfortunately!*"

He took her jest as compliment to his fine expertise on such things. He raised a glass to her in complementary manner and continued. "…So they paid a large sum of money between $3 million and $10 million, just to recover the manuscript, and offer it to experts who saw it for what it was…"

"Wow!" she said.

"What happened next, for a couple decades, is well known. The manuscript was….err… offered to various buyers - including libraries and museums in Egypt. But they were nervous about the it's dubious provenance."

Amanda raised her eyes discretely. After all, she had first met Jacques with Trevor when they were Beirut, his undertakings in Egypt less than clear. Not an unknown turf for Jacques, of course.

The bread tray arrived.

Jacques smiled and proceeded with his account.

"Michel van Rijn published the course of this material and its journey in 2003. Finally, the 62-page leather-bound codex was purchased by the Maecenas Foundation in Basel...."

Amanda waited. There was more, she was certain. Even as the waiter presented her soup.

"Well of course, the previous owners then came forward to say that it had been found in Muhafazat al Minya during the 50s and 60s. They claimed that its significance was not recognized at that time."

"Umm..." she said.

"Finally, a Rodolphe Kasser, a scholar at a Coptic conference in Paris disclosed the details in 2004, and the next year the Foundation announced plans for its translation. But only after a forensic study at the University of Geneva. That's when Jull at the National Science Foundation analyzed the ink and then, well you know the rest...."

Amanda finished her mouthful, then sipped from her glass of water. Sooner or later, he would arrive at his quest.

"Dating though...it is less uncertain, yes?" he said.

"Well, as you know" said Amanda "The University of Arizona has conducted radiocarbon dating procedures and fixed it to somewhere between 220 and 340 when they did their study in 2005. But that puts is in the 3rd and 4th centuries - *earlier* than what had been thought from the original review of the papyrus script."

He was raptly attentive, then spoke. "But this Ohio bankruptcy lawyer claimed 'ee had parts of the manuscript, eh?... and since 'ee refuses to have the parts authenticated, we don't really know much..."

"Umm"

"Quite a story, eh?" said Jacques scooping up his soup.

"Yes, it is Jacques. It would be interesting to review the various responses, and to its contemporary finds..."

"I knew you would ask, Amanda! You are such a clever one. We know through a Dutch paper *Het Parool* that Professor Kasser revealed a few details about it in 2004. He say the language is Sahidic, like Coptic, you know, like those of Nag Hammadi Library. Then, the original codex had four parts to it"

He raised his hand as if to count off the sequences: "First, the *Letter of Peter to Philip,* - (already known to the Nag Hammadi Library of course)...

Second, the *First Apocalypse of James*, (also known to the same library).

Third, the front pages to something called *Allogenes.* Fourth the *Gospel of Judas*. Most of it still illegible." He grinned, the entrée arrived.

 "A paper was started somewhere, but then the National Geographic Society in Washington DC got hold of it, and away we go with American celebrity-ville..." he said in his swaying French accent.

"They filmed it, I believe, in 2006 or so?"

"Oh yes. It was aired on their own TV channel. Their Executive of Programs declared it the most significant ancient non-biblical find since the 1940s!"

Amanda knew of the arrogance of Media when drumming up sensationalism to boost profits. His disdain was not without merit. Still, the item was in the sunlight, at least.

They ate, and after a while, she said quietly "You know, of course, that James Robinson, a leading expert on ancient religious texts suggested that little was new here about Judas since it was derived from an older manuscript…Implying that the text will only show the situation of the Gnostic movement rather than alter the biblical narrative…"

Jacques nearly erupted from his chair "Biblical..Biblical…Biblical. Eh bien! One man says Judas was fooled into believing he was *helping* Jesus, another that Judas was a *demon*…"

Amanda put up her hand "you know as well as a I, Jacques, that when it comes to theology, the faith of each if differently interpreted. Are we the ones to known enough, let alone judge?"

"*Bien sur!* Amanda. I give you that. And semantics, like the business with err…err…*Whats'eesname?*"

"DeConick – who said the text shows Judas not as 'set apart *for* the holy generation,' but rather 'he is set apart *from* the holy generation.' In his view that reverses the direction…"

"*Exactement!*" said Jacques, wiping off his mouth with his table napkin.

He was remarkably well informed, decided Amanda.

She looked down at her plate. She had devoured a lamb dish of the most delectable quality she had ever tasted. She pointed to it. "The savory flavors…they were amazing!" But her mouth did feel rather like a spice-rack.

"*Absolutement!* Amanda. You are sitting at one of the best Hotels in Istantul - transection of East and West where they have the best spices in the world!" They laughed.

Amanda looked down at her watch. It was just past 9 PM.

"Jacques, I shall have to retire shortly if you don't mind… I've had a very long day!"

Of course he understood. And yes, she would have coffee, she said, the waiter hovering over her.

Her mouth was on fire. She turned to Jacques, and asked him to excuse her just a minute as she went to the powder room. He stood up.

When she returned, Jacques announced that he had ordered an *apres-café* Brandy to sip before "saying farewell."

She agreed, if just a sip.

"The manuscript that you carry is one of the most remarkable things that has ever happened to the world of antiquities" he said.

Amanda finished her coffee; popped a little mint chocolate in her mouth, and lifted the exotic glass of brandy. It went down smoothly and relaxed her immediately, the day's stress seeping away.

"As a collector," Jacques said "I would be so privileged to show it in our gallery in Paris. But only in photographs you understand, since the original must be kept always under lock and key…."

"Of course!" she said, sipping.

His voice was moving outward, like a drone that had left behind a Doppler signal. Her spine was loosening as the Brandy surged through her system, she felt a little tingle in her toes.

The coffee was refilled by the waiter. She drank it all, feeling suddenly thirsty.

"Jacques, if you will excuse me…"

Her vision was altered, peripheral focus narrowing slightly. She saw only what was before her.

What was he saying?

"Of course! You know I understand completely 'ow busy someone like you…I thought I could accompany you as your travelling companion and serve as your Courier service also…"

"No need. Jacques. But thank you! All my arrangements have been made" she managed.

Now her head was spinning.

She felt good. The evening had been a success; they had met socially over dinner. Conversations were pleasant - like old acquaintances sharing a professional interest in the field.

Jacques was smiling at her, and still talking.

Her head was more than spinning. It was cartwheeling. She nodded graciously, still stable. But she clutched the edge of the table.

What was he saying?

"I could image the original, and to show the world that I 'ave access to the famous manuscript…But only as an image, of course…"

Not much was different, his lips were moving and his hands gesticulating with words, but for just one instant she thought she registered something in his expression, just a fleeting glance, it seemed, when his eyes settled upon her Brandy glass, then quickly away.

What was he asking? Did he think she had the manuscript with her now?

 What was he saying?

"If you were able to share the passwords…"

 Amanda looked down at the plate before her and saw instead her name on a little white business card. She recognized the graphic design, a blue-lined perimeter that closed with a bow above her name. The hand of the person holding the card belonged to the Hotel Bellboy come to discharge his duties as Hotel Escort Service to her room. Her card was being presented as identification, as per her instructions beforehand.

She looked up.

 "9.30 PM Madam?"

She smiled.

The Maitre D' showed up beside him and he blocked out her view of Jacques.

"Is Mrs. Macdonald ready now for her escort service?"

She raised her chin slowly and nodded. She stood up, Jacque's voice in protest, was it?

She took the Bellboy's arm where the stripes of his hotel uniform met his hand, and she held on, teeth clenched and legs unsteady.

The Bellboy guided her steps to the elevator. Up they went and he marched her to her room number where he opened her door with authorized Master Key.

"Madam?" said the bellboy, courteously presenting her room as his duty required.

She smiled numbly and stepped through, the door firmly closing behind her.

 She stood there, her head spinning like a whirling derby.

The seconds passed, her legs folding beneath her. Deep consciousness left her with an impression of relief. She was *safe* ....

She then went out, cold.

* *

Two

Amanda came around. She went to the bathroom, it was 2 A.M. She felt drowsy, thirsty, her stomach queasy. She threw up. It took half an hour to empty her stomach.

An hour later she was standing in the shower, warm water drizzling over stains of make-up and her hair stuck to her face. It felt good.

She brushed her teeth, drank water and rested. She popped aspirin and seltzer from her bag, and wearing only her bath robe, lay down on the bed.

The thoughts of the evening with Jacques materialized. She sat up suddenly and eyed the Safe in her room. All was well…

It was the Brandy. What did he put in it? What was he hoping to achieve?

She felt tired. Whatever happened…Hell, it was no longer a worry.

She dozed off for a few more hours sleep. It came restfully.

* *

Amanda awoke to a cool and darkened room. She dozed lightly for another half hour and then got up to open the curtains to the veranda. The room filled with sunlight, the view spectacular.

She had recovered well, she decided, coffee in hand.

Whether Jacques had tampered with her drink or the rich brandy went to her head after a long day of anxiety with little food or drink, she could not tell. Jacques was, and always would be - an avaricious antiquities dealer. That he was prospecting for his business last night was neither against the law, not her problem. He was out of the picture, she knew. He had his bounds, and even he had his pride. Were it not for the fact that Trevor had known him for a long time, she would have reported him as an issue. But she did not.

She ate a quiet breakfast downstairs on the hotel veranda café, coffee and a croissant, then returned to her room for an hour of work on her laptop - work that been forfeited for a dinner with Jacques. She had much to say in her Report, and she would completed all the requirement details for insurance purposes later. Besides, it was classified information until she handed it in to her superiors at the Museum personally when she returned to Baltimore. For now, she could send a few simple email messages of assurance and logistics. They would want to know at the Museum, especially Shirley.

Amanda gathered her belongings together, and decided for a swim down at the swimming pool. The hour in the sun would relax her before her Luncheon appointment at the Embassy Consulate. And she was right. By the time the phone rang from the Concierge, she had showered and was dressed in a simple white silk summer smock with pockets and a drawstring tiebelt. White espadrilles sandals and a straw hat in hand, she went down to be driven to the Consulate.

The arrangements had been made in advance. Mr. Hadid was to pick her up.

Lunch at the Consulate was on the top floor of the building where white damask dining tables were served by waiters for the senior staff of the diplomatic colony. The Cultural Attache was one of them, and he entertained Amanda cordially for an hour over lunch before leading her to his office. Clearly, the official briefing was for the safe passage of the valuable cargo.

Also in the room was a Mr. Hadid who stepped forward to shake her hand again. He then retreated to the rear of the room.

"You will be picked up from your Hotel at 9 AM.

"You will have special security disposition as a courier; Safe-Passage papers to correspond. You will be taken to the University where the manuscript will be delivered to you in secure, sealed packaging.

"After that you go to the Bank for the signing of courier papers; insurance and that sort of thing…

"The Turkish have asked for indemnifications certificates, and they want your signature. OK?"

"How heavy… and what size will it be?" she asked.

"It will be in a shallow box, like a small Vuitton piece of luggage. It will have two simple latches. Simple enough to fit it into a backpack: *Yours!* It's a specialty backpack bag which you can heft on your back easily. Nothing too strenuous or conspicuous. But it will be on your person *at all times.* It will have a beacon and tracing device in it, so you won't be alone…"

He paused. "Any questions?"

Amanda shook her head.

"You will also be given a special cell phone to contact various agents along the way. We will have made arrangements for you through Customs. But the Flight might be changed. Be ready for small alterations. Consider them routine precautions…"

She must have looked worried.

"Don't worry, you will have seating to yourself! First Class compartment seat will be yours, double berth, and you can place the bag at your feet, or beside you. But it must be kept in sight at all times. If you have to withdraw somewhere for privacy, you must take it with you. Period….Got that Ms. Wells?

"Yes."

"Once you arrive in Rome Airport, you will be picked up by a regular limousine and the driver will be an agent. Together you will go to our bank deposit box to lock the backpack in the bank vault…."

"Phew! What a relief!" she sighed.

"Yes, at that point, I imagine you will be relieved to be unburdened. Until the time you pick it up again, you are free to relax…to enjoy your vacation! Just be yourself as a normal citizen of the United States visiting Italy."

"Right."

"The same procedure must be done when you exit the country: So, you pick up the backpack from the bank vault, sign off with the vault manager etc. etc…got it?"

She eyed him. He looked impatient and annoyed. He caught her drift.

"Look Ms. Wells, I can't pretend that I like this arrangement. In fact, I'm surprised a commercial flight was arranged for you. But State said *no fuss*, just a cultural delivery! But I need hardly remind you that this ain't a pair of silver cufflinks you're transporting. As a Biblical text there are religious overtones, and national tensions. There are dangers with this kind of cargo. Assailants, terrorists, angry competitors, cultural objectors, political enemies and black marketeering to worry about…. We have been informed of a group who are watching the manuscript…:"

Amanda straightened up. If there were any surprises, this was it. She had no idea she was a moving target.

No wonder Dr. James turned down the assignment!

".So, I've made a decision to accept the help of a source of intelligence on this issue, the Israeli Authority of Antiquities, Mr. Hadid's group."

He stepped forward and bowed politely.

"Mr. Hadid's group are attuned to details related to antiquities; religious artifacts and cultural icons of the Holy Land eras that require special security precautions."

He paused. "Any questions?"

She shook her head.

"Ms. Wells, you are to be commended. You are not only travelling with the blessing of the Islamists with this manuscript, but being offered special protection by the Israeli authorities. You can be assured of safe passage!"

Amanda wasn't sure if she should salute or not. But it helped hearing those words, and she stood up.

"Thank you. The Museum thanks you! I'm sure I'll be fine" she said. "Besides, who would want to rob the public of exposure to this manuscript?"

His mouth smiled, but his eyes turned to Hadid standing behind her.

"True! Nevertheless, what you will be carrying around on your back is almost two millennia in age, regardless. The world, if you wish, has been altered by it."

"I understand" she said. They shook hands.

"Good Luck!"

Hadid came forward. "I don't want to be in your way Ms. Wells…" he opened the door "but you understand we want this to be an uneventful transfer, and a happy solution for all parties."

"I understand" she said again, feeling a little over-protected, fatigued, if not instruction-weary. She thanked him.

They walked in silence. Amanda could tell Hadid was wanting to say more.

"The Temple was a mess" said Hadid in a low voice. "You know that of course!"

"Of course…" repeated Amanda. "No. Wait. I *don't* know that, and frankly, I'm totally surprised by this interpretation. What exactly *are* you saying…?"

"The meaning of the Judas manuscript. As an Israeli National, I can tell you it's bullshit…"

They reached the elevator. It was posted with a "Maintenance" sign on it. They should use the steps.

They walked back the length of the hall and down a flight of steps.

"I'm surprised the Muslims didn't tell you the same!" said Hadid.

Amanda was being pushed.

The American Consulate was a large building, and this intrusion was almost more than she could handle, let alone the pace of their steps. It was as if he were running her.

She stopped, a little breathless. "Look, I know you have your opinion. You are entitled to an opinion. But I'm not here to collect opinions on this thing. I'm just the messenger-boy. It's all I can do to absorb the enormity of this manuscript and what it implies down through the ages. So give me a break, will you?'

He had stopped. "Of course. How inconsiderate of me! I should have realized. It's just that I'm here for a different purpose. And yes, I do have an opinion. Everyone who reads scripture does. It's just that you of all people should be sympathetic to hear all sides of the story, and all interpretations of the meaning of this manuscript…"

"Ahh, now wait a minute, Mr. Hadid. I am no theologian! And besides, I am sure this manuscript will be the topic of debate amongst the learned and scholarly for *years* to come. I welcome your interest! Perhaps you will come to the States and visit the Museum Exhibit? Perhaps *our* specialists will offer some insight when it is put on display?"

"OK" he said. "I will. On one condition, I'll trade: A visit to America to see this thing, - only if you agree to a cup of coffee with me across the street to discuss it!"

She was taken aback.

Business was behind them, and, since all she had little else to do for the day but to prepare herself for her departure in the morning, she should allow him time. Hadid was, after all, her designated security travel companion.

She consulted her watch. "Alright! Just a brief cup of coffee at that. Does your café also serve Coke? I'm parched!"

"Sure! Right over there," he pointed "…left of the square!"

They crossed the street together. Two taxi's went by. Hadid missed nothing as he waved them by. They were not looking for passengers. They were surveying the woman at his side.

"Judas was a Jew, you know!" he said.

She looked at him. "So was Jesus Christ?"

"Right." he said, his official demeanor returned.

"Mr. Hadid. You seem to be… well informed about this manuscript?"

He looked at her, and smiled. "You are gracious to observe. And I thank you for asking…"

He had a serious face, his eyes sharp and sincere. She noticed he wore a small prayer hat, black, delicately trimmed with fine gold thread in the design of the star points. Clearly, this manuscript had the power to move many, as it had through the centuries.

"…It's not at all what you *think* it is…?"

"Oh?" she paused. "you think it a fake?...It's a holy relic. Found in Egypt! It has been authenticated by…"

"I know. I know. We have our share of holy relics at the Antiquities Authority of Israel. The Holy Land, remember?"

He looked at her. "Yes. It was found in Egypt. It has a provenance, rather, a history. I understand that. But Egypt is not the most stable country right now."

"Look, Mr. Hadid. I'm not a politician. But need I remind you that the Arabs were keepers in the early eras of all things sacred and learned…"

"As was the Holy Roman Empire protector of civilization during the Dark Ages. No problem!"

Amanda resisted the urge to make some quip about the longevity of the Judaic tradition. This was not the time. He was clearly of an opinion on this manuscript.

"No…" he continued "It is authentic, of that I'm sure. But the manuscript interpretation, *the meaning* about Judas… the story has been entirely misconstrued…"

He ordered.

 "And…?"

"…the message transmitted to Judas was made by Christ. The reason was simple. By the time of Christ, materialism *was* framing God's justice, and the Temple culture was dictating new commandments for behavior.…The Temple was a mess! He did not kill Jesus Christ, they did! And he threw away its legacy in disgust "

It took her aback. "Well…*that's* a surprise!"

He had to repeat himself at least twice.

* *

Hadid explained himself over the coffee, in earnest wanting to share his view, but he was cautious with his words nonetheless.

"In a reversal of the assumption that Judas was a betrayer, the Judas Manuscript reveals a basic doctrine of the Children of God. God loves his people as his children, and they must love him as their father – not as a coerced collective, but as *individuals.* Christ, being a Jew, assumed this directive voluntarily, asserting the agency of free will under One God…What was made of Judas by the Catholic Church fathers was entirely *bullshit!*"

"I'm not sure I follow your train of thought…" said Amanda, sucking on her straw from a coke.

"… Judas sells the Temple Title - not the kiss of death, for 30 pieces of silver, ending exploitation of the Temple Culture by a highly material world. Why? Because as keeper of the Treasure he had the Title to the Land upon which the Temple was built; it's mission directive compromised; its proceeds to feed the First sons of the Jewish tradition for services at the alter only. And who were they? The kingly descendants in the line of succession from David. Judas was Trustee to Christ's inheritance! If he threw away the Title, he threw away the Temple culture! Christ, first son, represented the tie to the Holy Spirit of the Temple!"

"But… why would Judas be a Trustee? By your argument, he must have had something to do with Christ to know all this stuff…his story, his mission, his intentions etc..Yet he betrayed Jesus?"

"Don't you get it?"

"Get what?" she said, her throat filling with soda bubbles.

"Judas was the brother of Christ!"

She burped, her hand flew apologetically to her mouth.

This was no laughing matter. Hadid was not amused. Furthermore, the conversation was clearly over. He got up.

"Can I call you a taxi to your hotel?"

Just as she was climbing in he said one more thing. "If he threw away the silver, he was throwing away the Temple culture because it was corrupt! He slammed the door on Judaic corruption! What the Catholics made of Judas was bullshit!"

A taxi arrived and she climbed in it. He gave the driver instruction to the hotel, and then shut the door and the taxi took off.

Amanda thought about his words. Her medieval literature told her that the Temple had various meanings throughout the ages.

Amongst other responsibilities, it had commercial authority vested by judicial and moral codes of conduct. Such was the tradition of the "Keep" "Treasury" and *"Temple" places of worship of* old…

Hadid had implied that Judas was not only Tresurer of the Temple culture and responsible for its mission, but his behavior and his understanding of Jesus held significance. He was the presumed next heir as the next son in line to *what…?*

What did all that mean?

******

The day spent at the Hotel was pleasant. She caught up her correspondence, worked on her Report, and ordered dinner to be sent to her room.

She was painting her toenails a bright orchid-red nail polish color.

"Hello My Darling…"said Trevor.

They were all the words she needed. They chatted away. His talking made her float between a dreamy world of reality mixed with romance. They spoke of the children, their delights at being on vacation. They were having a wonderful time, he said.

She lay flat on the bed listening and laughing; telling and sharing wonders of ornamental ceramics at the Mosque; then traffic in a city of white washed houses with tiled roofs laced with bougainvillea; and market square foods and barbeque smells in quarters steeped in oldness…

Nor was any detail too small to hear. Trevor was travelling with children who were discovering glass and chrome airports; strange little Italian cars and funny languages on their way to pizzas…

Such was the sensation of their relationship. Words and interests and humor creating a world that encompassed them. It was all too short. Yet Trevor understood every word, every nuance and heart-beat of her being…

Just a few more days apart, and they would all be together enjoying a vacation at Aunt Anna's in Naples!

She explained that she might be delayed a day in Rome. He understood. He assured her that the children were secured. Oh, and he did have some banking business to conduct himself…

"In my luggage is everything we need" she said, her toenail polish drying nicely "from a pretty white and sexy bathing suit to Turkish sandals for the kids…"

He laughed.

"*You*, however, will have to *work* for your turban!" she admonished, twinkling her toes.

"Umm" he said, before they could hang up.

It was all too delicious.

She did not mention Jacques.

The evening passed easily. She stayed in her room, watching the news intermittently, preferring to read to soft music mostly and achieving all the rest she could.

She walked out to the veranda. The city on the Bosphorus lay before her, its jeweled lights lacing around the night sea like a garland. This was a dream world.

And Trevor was waiting for her!

** **

Amanda accepted a petit breakfast in her room; showered, applied a little make-up and selected from her Jacob pouch Cartier diamond earrings. She began packing her bags for the day's delivery program. She would need to be practical with her clothing, and comfortable.

She chose simply. Her head popped through an easy Land's End cover up T-Shirt and she landed a pair of loose linen black Celine pants; tying off a pair of brown leather flat Valentine espadrilles when she received the call from Concierge.

She was ready.

She grabbed her luggage, put on a grey Scottish wool alpaca jacket, vacated the room and descended to the Lobby.

Amanda was still walking on air when Hadid said good morning.

The procedures of the day had been rehearsed. All was to go according to plan.

First stop was the University Registrar's office where she signed off on the package placed in a backpack, Hadid at her side.

"Once you put that on your back…" said Hadid, escorting her to the vehicle, "you will not want to be taking it off! Here, let's get it secured in the trunk of the car until you do. Got it?"

Next, the Bank where she signed papers of accession, including documents about security and insurance.

Finally, back into the vehicle to drive to the Airport. She was perfectly relaxed in the rear. She observed Hadid's small prayer hat, black, always placed at the back of head - delicately trimmed with a fine gold thread in a design of the star points. She caught him twice peeking into the rear view mirror.

"Mr. Hadid" she said "Is there something wrong?"

"No. Not at all, Ms. Wells" he said flatly. Then peeking just one more time, he grinned, saying "…It's just that I was wondering how such plain clothes could make a woman look so beautiful…"

Her chin went up. "Well thank you Mr. Hadid. I take that as a compliment!"

He grinned.

They passed streets of white-washed walls; paused at traffic lights and waited for pedestrians crossing wide boulevards flanked by grass and palm trees.

The sun held the city by the sea in a shimmering mirage - gold domes and white dust dodging tree shadows, and everywhere the sounds of worshipful minarets rang through the air.

Amanda was focused out the window, a breeze filtering her hair and absorbing her thoughts. If life were not an illusion, then here was the passage of time played upon peoples through the centuries... And here she sat, transporting a manuscript that was almost two thousand years old!

"It shows... you know!" said Hadid, interrupting her thoughts.

She looked at the driver, puzzled. "*What* shows?"

"That you are in love!"

She suppressed a response, and looked out at the window. "Yes, Mr. Hadid. With my husband Trevor..." Not that it was any of his business, she thought. But of course he already knew that from her dossier. He was only being chivalrous, testing her disposition perhaps. She smiled.

If these moments of wonder were any indication of a world without illusion, then life was still good, she decided.

At the airport, she was prepared.

First came the backpack, then the procedures of identification at the airport followed by the passport check in.

Next came the security scanning and finally into the lounge with her gear, belongings and precious cargo.

She gave him a look: So far so good.

Hadid entered the lounge area with her. He had a security pass, yes, but he was hardly striking in his casual shorts and Hawaiian shirt of all things.

"To see you off" he grinned.

Amanda looked up and saw his small prayer hat with the gold thread making a call...

She nodded at him. They chatted. Tourists in these parts came from everywhere, he said. Hadid was so subdued that Amanda almost forgot the person she had met yesterday at the American Consulate.

He was casual, even flip, and moved about the lobby. He strolled for a hot dog and soda. Then he got a newspaper. Over again to check flights. Then back for a coffee and another check at the flights… It was almost comical as he ducked into the gaming arcade briefly.

Amanda got the drift of his movements. He was observing other passengers, his eyes missing little.

Finally, her flight was called.

Amanda picked up her gear and stood in line to show her pass. Just before leaving, she turned and waved goodbye to Hadid now sitting beside a few passengers. He waved back, and Amanda Wells walked down the walkway to the plane. There, a stewardess welcomed all embarking passengers. She found her seat.

The doors sealed tightly, and before long the plane crawled to the center tarmac of the airport. It taxied.

Engines humming, the Captain introduced himself and the drill of emergency procedures was underway. The plane left the ground - a drink cart already prepared for making its way down the aisles.

* *

Amanda had walked away not a second too early.

Hadid had spotted the man and sat just behind him as he prepared to board the plane.

African, he was definitely the build, body type and face that Hadid expected, and even as he stood up to leave, Hadid recognized the feature on his ear that gave him away. Scars of a gun battle fought long ago, the dossier had said. A thug of many trades and thefts.

The African leaned down to pick up his bag, and that's when Hadid's foot nudged the bag a tad. Enough to make the man reach for it before looking up.

Hadid caught him as he sank back into his seat, a small bullet hole in his chest. Together they sat side by side, erectly, so that nothing amiss could be noticed when Amanda looked back to wave.

Later, much later, when the cabin lights allowed for cell phones, Amanda read her latest message from Hadid: "If your plane is slow, don't worry. Relax and enjoy! You are safe. Bon Voyage!"
She smiled.

* *

The approach to Rome was a long shoreline that marked the boot shape of Italy along the Adriatic Sea.

The plane landed smoothly. Amanda was anxious to proceed with the program, if only because it put her one day closer to joining Trevor the next day in Naples.

Tonight was reserved for Rome. She was to rendezvous with the Bank designated to hold the treasure…

The passengers disembarked from a sleep-like ytip that had transported them from the center of the Islamic world to the center of the Holy Roman world.

Fiumcino Airport was all business and bustle, a routine as predictable as Amsterdam or London: First the long walk out of the docking gates, then down the sequestered hallways and into the channels for baggage, and Customs inspections.

She noticed a message on her cell. It was Hadid with a text message: "If you see me in bella Roma…you dunna-know-me!" he joked "Have fun!"

Sometimes - and only sometimes - you could catch a glimpse of waiting parties. *Rarely.*

Since security measures had tightened, little was left to chance, let alone artistic tampering. Barriers herded people offloading planes like cattle.

Amanda sighed.

Inspectors were nowhere seen. Uniforms, if any, represented some authority or other. In fact, the place looked relatively police-free, if not sterile. But they were far from alone, she knew. Above them, the eyes of cameras watched everything. They were all under digital surveillance.

Amanda's steps had been carefully pre-charted. First to the Desk for designated passengers. Then the Desk for special delivery baggage, and finally the Desk and counters for customs…

She was wearing her backpack. She felt a little unaccompanied, and she tugged at the shoulder straps a little more tightly. What bothered Amanda was the lack of any sign of an escort. There should have been someone stepping forward according to the planning. Someone should have identified himself to her the moment she got off the plane… That's when she heard the commotion coming from the exterior of the passenger clearing lounge

- the area where waiting family and friends stood watching for loved ones to emerge. She peered out. Some had flowers in hand, others small children struggling to be free from clutches.

Amanda stepped up on her toes, and could barely see through the partition openings. Only one head seemed familiar. Was that the head of a prayer hat?

A surge of officials went running to the area. But it seemed to be under control.

Amanda walked through the various clearances, expected little eventfulness.

All but one. The last Customs officer, an African.

"Please open your bag" Ms. Wells.

It caught her by surprise.

No such request was anticipated. Come to think of it, the bag was never opened! It was given to her at the University and signed off at the bank. She never even got to examine the contents for herself…What would she be showing?

Again she was asked to unpack her bag "I am sorry Ms. Wells, but you will have to comply with our regulations. We can offer no guarantees of safety for anyone without our inspections!"

She nodded, her mouth going dry. *Why hadn't she been prepared for this?*

A second officer strolled out of his office and the backpack was placed on the counter, her hand still firmly on the strap.

The rest was a blur, and her pulse began to race as if she were engaged in a criminal act. She kept her head calm, and her responses even.

Could she pass it through the scanners? They wanted her to do so.

She said she thought the request unusual for disembarking passengers...

It was the wrong response.

She was obviously mistaken for someone else, she said. She was not...*Stop!*

Could she speak with the Supervisor?

He came out, and she had to explain her mission.

"American?" he asked.

"Yes, American" she said.

Jesus, they were behaving like complete strangers. Didn't they know she had special dispensation?

She presented her Special Courier Pass. She had a license to transport a precious cargo.

Another man joined them.

Now four men were arrayed before her. They examined her pass, looked at the bag.

She started to sweat. "All arrangements have been made in advance" she protested. "I was assured by the Consulate that there would be no problem... Above all else, I am not to be parted from it. I'm sorry, I cannot surrender the bag to anyone!"

They thought about her words, and finally the superintendent responded.

"In that case, Ms. Wells, you shall have a long wait!"

Two others stepped forward. They were armed.

They opened the bag. When they did, she got a surprise. These were no manuscripts in the containment box. Just files.

"You baggage is not what you say it is...Ms. Wells. Please excuse us for intercepting! The contents of your knapsack must be inspected by the local police in order to pass this area."

The commotion beyond the partitions was increasing. A loud shouting occurred, and a crowded public scuffling roared through the terminal.

The two armed guards stood down and turned to the matter beyond the partition.

It didn't take long after that, but her affairs were cleared away as being a distraction.

Amanda proceeded through the gate with her back pack on her shoulder. She looked normal, but she was steaming.

No one had shown up!

She was alone. What in the world was going on?

She stepped sideways into a Ladies Room and splashed water on her face, her backpack still on her shoulder. It was calming, the cold water, and she pulled herself together.

Security measures attending her cargo had been somehow compromised. *What did that mean?*

She walked out, and passed the crowd gathered now at the site of the commotion. Several paramedics were attending to people. One, a patient; another, the victim of a gunshot wound evidently she overhead them say. He was being lifted onto a gurney, a white sheet covering his head.

She passed on. Her mission would not allow her to take on the affairs of Airport scuffles. No. *Move on!*

Except that on the floor, near a vending machine, inadvertently kicked by a passing passenger lugging luggage, was an item that belonged to the corpse. Amanda recognized it at once. It was the small black prayer hat, trimmed with gold thread...

Amanda moved to the vending machine and, putting coins in the slot, inspected the items for purchase while deftly bending down to swoop it up and place it in her bag.

She wanted to say something, but she said nothing. She wanted to surge forward and speak up on behalf of the man on the gurney. Did they need his name? She knew him! *She knew him!*

Hadid!

If you see me in bella Rome, you don't know me…

* *

The driver that greeted her was on station, just like any other driver waiting with a limousine to take her to her Hotel.

Just as planned.

She was mortified.

"Ms. Wells?" he asked.

"Yes"

"Please step this way, if you would. We have transportation for you to your Hotel."

She followed. Her mind racing, the details, the people around her. It had all happened so …so…*unexpectedly.* What happened?

Hadid, dead on the gurney. Imagine! My God…As if he knew in advance, she was to *ignore him*…How strange was that? What was going on?

It was raining in Rome. Then that business at the Customs Desk… What was it she was carrying on her back now anyway? Who was playing her? Why?

She accepted the limousine, as planned. The driver opened the door, they had arrived.

It was a downpour of rain. The driver handed her a letter.

"From Mr. Hadid" he said, then closed the door shut.

She said nothing. What could this possibly be? *Something had gone wrong.*

Her baggage was carried to the desk and left at the concierge. She felt alone. Somehow abandoned.

"Your room Madam, is Number 202. The Bellboy will take your luggage if you would follow, please?" She did, the letter still in her hand. She felt numb.

She sat on her bed, the rain still running off her gear. She called the Concierge and asked for dialing privileges. Then she took off her shoulder-straps and unzipped the backpack. She stood there, stunned.

She did not have the manuscript.

 Twice she called the house. Mr. Trevor was not there. "No! Niente. Nianche I bambini…"said the housekeeper.

She called the office, her cousin Anna. No one was answering.

She felt alone.

* *

Dear Ms. Wells,

Forgive me, but if you are receiving this letter, it is because I have failed to shield you. Truth is, you were in danger, and whatever you have undergone, it was for your protection and for the protection of your cargo!

The Manuscript is Safe! You will see it again, I promise…

The backpack you carried was switched by me: Do you remember the car trunk in which I placed the backpack after you received it at the University? The backpack you were given at the Airport was identical, but not the same one you had collected…

Again, I apologize. But we had reason to believe you were a target. This way, with nothing to show at Customs, you are safe.

The price may have been high, I know… But these are the risks of things that matter. Even our lives are fleeting in the greater passage of time.

Your mission is worthy. The cargo you carry has endured the test of time. And however it is brought back to favor, or whose religion it pleases, God makes no error in the deployment of his accounting.

You may wish to abandon the project. But I ask you to proceed: Please go on with the arranged plan as if all is in order. That is all I ask. Pretend that nothing is amiss…

Go to the bank. Deposit the backpack you have. You may find this ritual unnecessary, but it is a precaution.

The cargo is safe.

By now, your Museum in Baltimore will have been informed that the offer to show the Artifact has been withdrawn by the Turkish authority for reasons of finances and insurance.

Please carry on with your everyday affairs!

With kind regards,
Saul Hadid.

She cried. Furious with Hadid for getting himself killed. Furious with herself for under estimating the matter of transporting a relic of value. *What was she thinking? A toy for a museum…?*

Furious with the futility of it all...

She would call Trevor. The Embassy. The National Guard.

Hadid had died.

The whole affair was a mess.

Amanda wept.

*** ***

With all obligations completed, the backpack deposited into the bank vault as per her instructions from Istanbul - plus the wishes of Hadid, Amanda stepped outside, never having uttered a word about anything being amiss.

"Thank you Ms. Wells," said the bank manager. "We look forward to your return…"

And that was that.

Strange as it was, she felt relieved. A duty discharged in full, as it were, if without the satisfaction of a mission accomplished.

Her thoughts went round and round. Certainly the hotel was comfortable and good for a rest. But she felt frustrated beyond measure with the whole situation. Who to tell? What was safe? Where to turn?

She would contact the American Consulate for sure. There would be more instructions, certainly. But perhaps not immediately. She would give it a few days, let the situation sink in, and then call the Consulate.

What else was she to do? She thought about it. Was she to toss the backpack somewhere? *Not* make the deposit?

She walked, the fresh air felt good, the sunshine warm on her face.

She stopped and ordered a café. Doubts still plagued her, if somewhat with less intensity. But the shock of the last days came close to overwhelming her.

Was she supposed to call the Museum, and say what, exactly? *Hi guys, I lost the manuscript?*

To Trevor, that is, if she got a chance to speak to him first, she could only say that she had something she'd like to discuss. Meaning, a level of discretion and security was required.

Some security she was! Shit!

One thing to be on the board of a Museum and volunteer for the transportation of an exhibit, quite another to have a man killed because of it. What was the price of it all..?

 Only gradually did the incident dissipate into the sights and sounds that surrounded her. For now, anyway.

She could put her feelings on hold, if she needed to.

She called Anna and announced she was in Rome. Cousins they were, if distant, and by marriage only. Anna was on the phone with her usual cheery singsong voice and welcomed Amanda to Italy.

If Amanda's senses were lackluster, her manners were not. Still, it was the case that she was calling family and arriving on their soil. All that remained, seemingly, was the joy of reuniting with family Anna insisted, as if sensing something remiss.

Anna admonished Amanda to take the First Class Europe Rail pass to come down to Naples via Pozzuoli. Then take the ferry across to their island.

Amanda booked a rail pass on the *Leonardo da Vinci Express* train. Once onboard she could relax, and think of nothing but reaching Naples…Or so she thought. The fact was, conversations with Hadid were still in her head. Not that she knew him, but he found value to what she was doing.

No, she decided. He would not consider it a waste. He was a professional, of course. And the execution of his tasks was what he did in the commission of duty. For him, the safeguarding of the culture was important. Even taking it to a museum in America was meaningful for him. Even knowing that avarice and commercial exploitation was the inevitable risk.

Please carry on…

What did Hadid say about the ancient text? What had he said, that day over coffee? *"The Temple was in a mess…"*

 Of course, his view would be Judaic. She hadn't had a chance to review the content and didn't have any particular opinion. But the questions were intriguing.

"The Temple was in a mess…?"

That implied a real physical building, with a function, an authority, if not a communal meaning of ownership and community value, right? So, what did that mean 'The Temple was in a mess…'?"

What did Christ say about the Temple?

In the mortal realm, the Scriptures said he threw out the "money-changers" from the Temple, asserting it as a House of Prayer, a place holy and not to be corrupted for private gain.

In the spiritual realm, he said he could tear it down and rebuild it three days…

 In saying that he could rebuilt it in three days, that was the point of law for which he was finally indicted. Yet he was speaking metaphorically using contemporary terms, obviously.

Was Hadid onto something?

By the time of the mission of Christ, clearly, materialism was corrupting the meaning of God's justice.

Perhaps by introducing the concept of "forgiveness" Jesus was *unbinding* all Temple corruption. *The Temple was in a mess…?"*

Moreover, Judas was a Treasurer. An accountant of financial obligations and commitments. That included land ownership, laws, and licenses to trade, human slavery, communal resources, and infrastructure of taxes, tithes and a hierarchy of society.

Of course, to challenge the authority of the Temple was to threaten the order of the day: The *Reforms* of Jesus were tantamount to nationalization!

Amanda thought about it.

And there was something the Imam said…

He said the legible words found on the Judas manuscript were seemingly those of Jesus telling Judas about his mission to *Reform* Judaism: God the "personification is found within us all," he had said, implying that God endorsed self-determination.

The Temple authorities had centralized their interpretations …of God's justice!

Just as the Catholic tradition had done in the first century when then sealed the cannon of the Holy Bible. Other gospels were excluded. And Judas was demonstrably *demonized….*

It was getting tiresome all this argument, decided Amanda. No wonder no two theologians could agree on anything!

Amanda had taken the Rome-Naples Direttissima, a rain line integrated with the traditional main North-South trunk line of the rail network. Newly constructed, it hugged the coast. Planned as early as 1870, it had taken over a century to be constructed.

Moving at extreme high speeds, the railroad pounded beneath her. She was alone at a window seat, the cabins almost empty. As the countryside unfurled, Amanda felt as if she was leaving behind the events of the past few days, and the three hour journey did wonders to help her refocus.

The high-speed train was like a space-age dream car. She appreciated the clean and sleek design of the Italians. As creative artists and visionary thinkers, their architectural skills and aesthetic was legendary. But she knew it had arrived after a controversial history.

Like much of Europe, the railroads defined the industrial revolution. Money to construct them came from bonds bought by early modern investors.

Amanda knew she was crossing territories once held as Papal States, bastions of the ancient Latin peninsula where people lived under the sovereign rule of the Holy Roman Popes for centuries.

The original railroad was never intended as a link from Rome to Naples, rather to connect the smaller localities along the way. It made passable the old Pontine Marshes, historically swampy and malarial, and it was the lifeline of distribution and flow of commerce for the Roman Catholic Church.

Harboring vestiges of that medieval culture however, impeded progress.

It was a difficult topography, especially in the Sacco River area. At the tributary of the Liri was a confluence of two streams, the Monti Simbruini in the Apennines of Abruzzo flowing southward; and the Ciociaria flowing from the mountain ranges of the Ernici and the Lepini to the southwest.

Europe was progressing in the late 19th century, and the new Railroad was authorized by legislation to connect passage from Rome to Naples - two mega city-ports and centers of national significance. The project promised progress; opportunities and hope for civil expansion and infrastructure development. But progress meant different things to different people. And political resolve was resistant to doctrinal change.

The design of the railroad appeared on paper in 1902. Five years later, construction begin when the State Railway Authority took over. The project had been ambitious, requiring the building of long inter-mountain tunnels, including the Monte Orso and the Vivola tunnels, both of which were about 7.5 km long.

The project had political opponents. Approved by engineers such as the famed Alfred Cottrau, a man of the 19th century known for his genius and experience, it was opposed and virtually halted by the politician Francesco Saverio Nitti, chosen in 1904 by the Radical Party to serve in the Italian Parliament. Nitti became Prime Minister of Italy in 1919. This region was his home.

Nitti's ideologies became the bedrock of battles over two world wars. He opposed the free market ideology of British economist Thomas Robert Malthus. Instead, Nitti called for socialism, especially in his manifesto and written work *"The Catholic-Socialism."*

At the end of WWI, Nitti opposed the Treaty of Versailles. It was signed to end the war and bring peace to Europe, even as European deposed monarchs and replaced them with socialist Dictators.

Nitti abhorred Benito Mussolini, and he tried to emigrate during WWII, but Nitti returned to lead the Socialist Party of Italy after the war ended, levelling private wealth for all Italians, and opposing NATO. The railroad stalled.

Amanda looked out the window. How sad that so much sorrow and unproductive waste had occurred.

But this was the new Italy. Vibrant, beautiful, sexy, people-friendly and a free and competitive state - long now removed from a past. This new rail line represented all that was budding in a new and independent commercial Italy.

The view said it all. The amble clouds and richly blue sky brushing across this Mediterranean Peninsula melted away apprehensions.

She looked forward to embracing Anna, to see Naples. Most of all, she couldn't wait to see the children, to hold them in her arms and listen to their chatter! And Trevor. Becoming once again — and *feeling* like Mrs. MacDonald was something she longed for…

*** ***

The Bay of Naples came into sight as shorebirds cartwheeled everywhere. It was circular, romantic, ephemeral and cluttered - all at the same time! Amanda's heart jumped.

Here her children were at play! And Trevor busy; Anna fussing, and everywhere the place teeming with excitement. She could hardly wait to disembark and embrace it all.

The Bay itself was perhaps some 15 kilometers wide, a gulf situated along the southwestern coast of Italy before the Mediterranean Sea.

Naples, ninth most populous urban area of Europe, four million living in the Naples metropolitan area, and recognized as the oldest continuously-inhabited city in the world.

Then there was Pozzuoli. Main city of the Phlegrean Peninsula, deriving its name from the Latin Puteoli, *stink* that came from its Solfatara crater as part of the Campi Flegrei volcanic area, emitting steam and sulfurous fumes.

Amanda consulted the brochure.

Here was the heart of the great emporium for the Alexandrian grain ships; hub for the Campania trades in blown glass, mosaics, wrought iron and marble. Here, the Roman naval base at nearby Misenum held the largest naval fleet in the ancient world.

Amanda spotted the island of Capri, Ischia and Procida located in the Gulf of Naples. There, tourist centers of Pompeii and Herculaneum perched at the foot of the Mount Vesuvius, a volcano that laid barren the Roman colony in its massive eruption in the first century AD.

The Peninsula separated the Gulf of Naples from the Gulf of Salerno, which then took to the Amalfi coast. It was too wonderful to see, thought Amanda, and she started to collect her things to disembark.

She switched on her cell phone and saw the message.

* *

"Amanda. What happened?"

It was Tim Samuelson, Director of the Museum.

"Bob James just informed me that he heard something went wrong. He can't find out a thing. I'm supposed to be meeting with the Department of State tomorrow!"

"It's a long story Tim, and I can't go into it right now. Just stay cool, and give me a chance to get back with an explanation…"

"Right. Right…" he calmed down. "You're alright?"

"Well, it got a little hairy for a while, but yes I'm fine. Thank you for asking."

"Enjoy your vacation then!"

After he hung up, Amanda appreciated that there were bosses and directors, and then there bosses and directors. Tim Samuelson was amongst the rarest who cared about people as much as he did about their performance. More than anything, he hated scandal. He was an enabler, a man who gave you the tools; the opportunity and the money to get done what you needed, and then left you alone to proceed.

However, he did expect results.

So, thought Amanda. The word was out, and hopefully, a resolution would be in sight once she got in touch with the Consulate.

The one to worry about was Bob James. He was an alarmist. No telling how he would respond. Especially if the media put a microphone in front of him.

* *

Trevor was in Geneva, Switzerland.

The lights in the small conference room were dim due to the digital presentation being given by an associate member IAEA, its blue crest displaying the words International Atomic Energy Agency.

Trevor sat back and listened attentively. Beside him were a small group of men come to discuss off-the-table matters of growing concern. The discussion was led by Tim Jennings, a silver haired former Congressman from Ohio, and retired Admiral. The red lighting of the command center showing the maps lit up him up like a great Santa Clause.

The Agency had been established in 1953 by President Eisenhower. The IAEA was to regulate and promote the peaceful use of atomic power. He had, after all, witnessed the deployment of two nuclear bombs in WWII in anger to stop an enemy. In his famous speech at the UN General Assembly in 1954 *Atoms for Peace,* Eisenhower called out for new uses of the technology, petitioning for the peaceful applications of nuclear energy in times of prosperity to generate power as electricity schools; municipalities and research institutions within the U.S. and throughout the world.

But that era belonged to the previous generation. This was a new threat.

"The initiative, as you well know Gentlemen, was serviceable during the Cold War as a strategy for containment - the policy to prevent the spread of communism..."said the speaker of the meeting.

"Yeah! And some good it did us!" chuckled Bennington, Director from the UN Security Council, a vocal Democrat.

"Well... to an extent, it worked" said Jennings. "As you know we brought the nuclear age forward into the sunlight, we built up our arsenal; created NSA and signed Non-Proliferation of Nuclear Weapons Treaties."

"True" said Bennington. "But the main purpose was to have NATO transition from conventional warfare to nuclear warfare."

"Yes" said Jennings. He switched off the viewer lights, and the houselights went up. At the table they faced each other for a normal meeting. "We're here to discuss NATO, Gentlemen. There is a problem" he nodded to Tom.

"We're exposed in the Pacific and Middle East" said Tom, Director from Vienna, headquarters of the IAEA. And it's been brought to our attention that we have leaks at NATO..."

"*Jesus!*" said Bennington, tossing his pencil.

"Trevor," said Jennings "you're going to have to get to the bottom of this at NATO, without so much as a whisper, right?"

Trevor nodded. It was known he was there with his family for a vacation. Even for some banking business, considering his background. But here was an opportunity to pry further into the intelligence behind the activism within NATO.

"We'd like to find out who is stirring the pot over there. And more importantly, why." said Jennings. "In fact, there's a reactivation program to resurrect those damned nuclear torpedo sea mines laid down in 1970. So we're looking at activism as well as cyber leaks" added Jennings.

"What mines?" asked Sorvenson.

"We don't know for sure. But they could be sitting on the sea floor in the Bay of Naples" said Jennings.

Trevor looked down, the soft overhead lighting sheltering his face, and some in the room sensed a hesitation on his part.

"Trev…if there's something else, please tell us!"

"There is something else, actually." He looked at them deliberatively, his voice even.

"Seismic disturbances on the sea-bed are worrisome. As you know, the torpedoes were laid by a Soviet November class Attack Submarine. So we know at what depth they could be. But we can't be sure as to their integrity in those seawaters. Nor do we know what are the response tolerance thresholds might be to external stress… "

"Jesus! Or even if they're there at all…" interjected Petersen, a Swedish man seated at the end of the table, now retired from his post at the IAEA, but active in his field of expertise.

"There is that question. We do need a confirmation from the Soviets. They may have removed them, some of them, or all… But I am concerned with the unpredictable event of sea bottom conditions" said Trevor

"Please go on!"

"If a natural disaster occurs in the region, not only will the populations suffer, but this could cause some kind of sea floor condition that is beyond us all, Gentlemen. The worst case scenario is that they are somehow detonated by external conditions. Such a multiplicity of detonations would cause a catastrophe the likes of which we've never seen. This, on top of a natural disaster may cause global havoc…"

"What are you saying Trevor?" asked Jennings "that this is a situation of Maximum Risk Status?"

"I am. It would be better if they were not there at all."

"Damned right" muttered Bennington.

"Deploying them is one thing. Containing them is another" said Petersen.

"Can we talk to them?"

"We can" said Trevor. "But we'd better know what we're dealing with. They may be unwilling or unable to alter anything at all. We may need to just get in there and help them through an extraction operation - without calling attention to it…"

"I see."

Peterson had Trevor's report open before him. "Once we embark on this road, we have to proceed with caution. If it came out in the open, such ideas would cause even more political instability. Worse. Some lunatic faction may try to steal the damned things. Imagine that!"

"Gentlemen. We clearly have work to do. The decision is to find a soft way to get them removed and minimize the risk of either disaster or exposure to un-friendlies. That's even as we try to curtail the nations seeking to expand their own nuclear programs. Anyway, see what you can do, and we meet next month in Vienna.

Questions? …So, Meeting adjourned."

Jennings talked to Trevor later. "Find out who in NATO is leaking information too, will you? This is not the kind of intelligence I should hear about outside our network."

** **

Amanda disembarked the train at Pozzuoli and decided to walk down to the Port rather than take a taxi. Her luggage was simple enough to haul. Without a backpack, she was down to her Banana Republic tote and a suitcase on wheels, laptop included.

She had an hour to kill before the Ferry arrived.

She strolled down to the Port of Pozzuoli and realized she was starved. She picked one of the prettiest cafés and ordered some food. She took in the sights and the smells of the sea.

This land district, said the brochure, was the original acropolis of the ancient Roman and Creek cities of Dicaerchia and Puteoili.

Many, including the Apostle Paul, had made the pilgrimage to this ancient site of the classical period. Archaeologists had unearthed a world of antiquity here. But only recently was it reopened to the public for tours. The 1980s earthquake demolished the region and rendered it unsafe for tourists.

Amanda scribbled on a post card for Shirely, then sent off a few quick messages on her laptop while finishing her coffee.

She strolled the dockside stalls and filled a basket with a bottle of wine, cheese, salamis and chocolates - tokens that would see her across the Ferry-ride, and delights for her hosts on the other side! The vendors grinned. *Si signora, very pretty Americana!*

She loved the atmosphere of the tiny port.

She relaxed, the sea calm. It gave her a chance to contemplate the moment, and she smiled. Yes, she was ready for family! This was exactly what she needed, to face the happy crowd waiting for her.

It put the incidents of the past few days behind her in a secure and manageable place.

For now.

* *

The news was not good. Regional conflict was not contained. Armored personnel carriers had deployed to Beirut Lebanon to prevent fighting between supporters and opponents of the spreading conflagration.

From a political standpoint, matters of international concern were far from quiet.

The Turkish government had shot down a Syrian plane violating Turkey's air space.

Israeli warplanes struck Syrian military posts in the Golan Heights after a roadside bombing wounded four, rendering the Syrian border a war zone for new insurgents.

As far as Israel was concerned, Iran was supplying the Assad regime of Syria with arms and bombs.

Such an alliance, they claimed, constituted the growth of a Pro-Iranian block stretching from western Afghanistan all the way to the Mediterranean Sea. Whereas official border defense was legitimate, recent espionage-type allegations of cross-border incursions left the West wondering what was going on.

It worried Trevor.

Turkey was a member of NATO. Headquartered in Brussels, the North Atlantic Treaty had been set up in 1949 for the collective defense of member states. All 28 member states, and newer ones joining in the Eastern block, as well as another 22 states participating in NATO Partnership for Peace program, were dedicated to defending peaceful conduct amongst nations. Article 5 of the Treaty was specific. The members agreed that an armed attack against any one of them in Europe -or North America would be considered an attack against them all.

If NATO was to take seriously its responsibilities, then such matters were not trivial. Especially since the budget to support and participate in NATO was often as much as 2% of a nation's GDP.

More importantly, NATO had a formidable arsenal.

The complications of achieving consensus amongst nations was challenging enough; but the remorse of making mistaken judgments based on wrong information was worse.

Moreover, financial instability strained borders. Trade and opportunity - the twin pillars of peace and prosperity that allowed for exchange between neighbors was seriously threatened and disrupted.

The unemployed; the disenchanted and those losing hope sowed malcontentment, Trevor knew. Especially among the young who might find no prospects in such a world.

Therefore containing smaller disputes was necessary in order to prevent greater conflagrations. This conflict was spreading from the streets of Beirut to the streets of Turkey. Any small spark might ignite the incendiary.

It worried Trevor more than a little as he approached the town of Lago Patria in a Jeep. The region of Campania was the site of NATO's new Allied Joint Force Command at Naples, Italy.

Built at a cost of more than 164M Euro, the new installation was designed to command the full spectrum of steady-state and contingency operations from here.

The Gate was guarded. "Trevor MacDonald to see General Hertz please!" said the driver.

Trevor presented his ID.

"Yes Sir! Your first visit Sir?"

"Yes."

"Welcome to Lago Patria Sir!" the security guard said as the gate opened up. They drove in.

Trevor entered the lobby of a remarkable building. Construction was still ongoing.

"Trevor!" called out the tall and greying General Hertz "*Good to see you*!" They shook hands "How's the family?"

"Very well indeed, thank you!"

They walked. Trevor looked around. "Wow!"

"The building is technologically advanced and bold in design. The Joint Operations Center had a multi-integrated conference complex built on a vision of futuristic functionality."

"Reflecting pools? Industrial facades, unique and modernistic style…elegant, I see!" smiled Trevor. They took the elevator to the upper decks.

"You bet! It's energy efficient; self- contained and a security stronghold in case the need should arise." Admiral Dunlap rose from his desk to greet Trevor, a member of the British Admiralty himself.

"Hope you like the place Trevor. Not at all like London, but new and a clean sweep…" he laughed.

"Plus sunshine that favors Italy more often than London!" added Trevor, shaking hands.

"Let's get some coffee!" they said. "How is that beautiful wife of yours? …What is she doing these days?"

Trevor told them and they were impressed. Dunlap remarked that he should like to visit the Museum Exhibit in Baltimore when it was unveiled.

"Let me show you around!" said Dunlap.

Trevor was shown the blueprints and floorplan as they toured the top floors.

The facility was enormous. Clubs, ceremonial courtyards, relaxing spaces, cafés, International Mess, Shops, barbers and exercise facilities with an Olympic size pool – all with a view of Lago Patria and the Tyrrhenian Sea. It was more exceptional than he expected.

Yet it also had open functions. The main Community Center was to be used for numerous Alliance and national ceremonial events with its theaters and public spaces.

It was at the café across the open space that they all settled at. "We're still getting accustomed to the facility ourselves!" chuckled Hertz. "That's all of us at the same time! We have an operational staff of 2,000 NATO and three separate commands, so there's a lot going on at once."

"Better than Bagnoli, for sure!" said Dunlap. "Here, we've a new facility that will provide JFC Naples with a much-needed modern, flexible and secure facility. We've all the services and facilities required by a Headquarters assigned challenging and important missions within the future NATO military command structure, as you know…"

"Yes."

"Hell, we're on 85,000 square meters of floor space. 600 kilometers of cabling; 2000 computer systems… 400 messing at all hours, and a 300 seat Auditorium!" said Hertz, clearly enjoying himself.

They laughed.

Trevor explained his visit was timely for his vacation in Italy – but just a couple of questions that he had, really.

"Whatever you need Trevor…"

Trevor wanted to know whether he could meet with the Russians about their weapons in Europe, firstly. And if so, where could he make contact locally?

"Sure! Right here. We'll arrange it…" said Dunlap.

"Things are not going too well with the Russians right now as you know " said Hertz. "But as they saying goes - 'once and ally, *always* an ally!'"

Trevor understood.

The Russian contribution to WWII was not easily forgotten, not even by later generations in the military. Certainly the world had changed. The cold war was over and Europe had reconstructed itself to become a healthy contributor to the global economies. But it was here at Caserta that the Allies prepared to defeat the enemy while the Russians held the Eastern Front for them with boots in the trenches.

"That's what I was hoping to hear. Are they much represented here?"

"Yes. They do have a presence. And we can make enquiries further. Do you have anything in particular we can help with?"

No. Not on that issue just now, thanks. But I am also wondering though about the latest information on Syria and the war spreading...

Trevor MacDonald was a British high-ranking Minister. He was entitled to know, and entitled to ask. They knew, and they looked at each other.

"You'd better come inside. We have things to show you…" they said, draining their coffee.

By the time he was walked back into the building, Trevor was completely briefed on the evolution of the conflict, and even some latest developments.

Inside secure premises with a digital display before them, Trevor was looking at the terrain of the war.

"We don't want to be dragged into this, tail-first" said Dunlap. "We can't understand what the Turkish are doing…much less the leaks coming out of their government"

"Here's what's coming out of Washington" added Hertz.

"Humanitarian overtures…with the compliance of an Assad still in place - have a long term agenda!"

"That's not quite Washington actually…" corrected Trevor. " But the Brookings Institution!"

"Well that's a relief. At least someone it looking at this situation besides us!"

"They are indeed."

"Well good. Because what's puzzling the hell out of us is why would Turkey be wanting to stimulate the conflict with Syria. Aren't enough people suffering over there?"

Trevor said nothing. He knew why. But it was not his position to update them. It had a lot to do outside interests in political negotiations.

"Well Gentlemen, as you know, I am no career politician. But the last thing we want are 'accidents' misread by an already unstable region. So we will require extreme temperance by our armed forces stationed over there. Even if we sustain damage! Let's be patient and careful with our men and our bullets, please! No confrontations. No media events…"

Dunlap eyed him carefully, as if he were a mealy-mouthed politician of the complacent type with a hidden agenda of his own. But Trevor was someone they trusted. This was a man who was no stranger to conflict.

"We understand…" Dunlap said finally.

Trevor waited, then continued in his soft-spoken manner "Was it not your own statesman, Averell Harriman, who conducted his mission for Roosevelt first with Supply to end the war; then with diplomacy for Reconstruction?" asked Trevor.

"Quite right!" said Hertz.

Dunlap made his decision. "We'll add you to the loop Trevor. Everything I get will be copied to you. Please stay close as an Advisor. I need to know what we're dealing with on a daily basis. Will you give me the benefit of your insight whenever you can?...I'd appreciate it."

Hertz walked him out.

"You're damned lucky he didn't throw you out by your ass" he said.

Trevor looked at him. "I have a tough ass!"

Trevor left with a dossier. In the dossier were the codes to their portals and current affairs. Including all the people in that division.

Tonight, he would study it carefully, and keep the material in his safe, that is, if he had to. Most of it was already keyed into the security protocols of his computer programs.

Hertz promised to keep in touch with him, and offered him all the help he needed if anything was to arise.

"Oh, just one more thing…" said Trevor. "Can I have a list of Civilians with access to the areas, and with what codes?"

Hertz stood there. "*All…?*"

Trevor knew it would be a long list with so many at the base.

"You got it! Give me a few days…"

"Certainly!"

* *

The IT technician entered the building was wearing the uniform of a Contractor. He was authorized as personnel who worked on the premises, a civilian, as his badge said.

Formerly trained in the military for computer hardware wiring technology, he was an expert on cyber-security.

He was a Guyana-born African who was early educated by his father, a doctor, to speak and read in English. He himself assisted at the hospital, then as member of the Red Cross, became trained as emergency transportation paramedic. Before long, he was signed up for duty in Afghanistan on an American military base.

Two years in helicopters; combat zones and extraction units offering aid for the wounded earned him their respect. And he was offered a position stateside.

He attended College in Boston as a foreign student, specializing in medicine and technology, including Information Technology.

He enlisted for whatever assignments he could get in the Middle East, then accepted work in Italy for a contractor.

His sister joined him.

They all knew him at NATO. In fact, the years of duty produced a few grey hairs at his temple, and he was considered trustworthy to receive the highest security clearances for IT support.

Once inside the dark IT center, he saw a dozen or so technicians working on programming support, screens, hardware, paper files and on one bench, open wiring. Technicians were often on the phone answering office assistants for help solving intransigent programming -usually related to security clearances. They were all projects-in-progress to support the staff of NATO.

"Hello Mike" yelled out someone.

He waved back, and moved on.

He took to the desk behind a screen, and worked an hour. It was late in the day, and as most of the technicians vacated the lab, he stayed behind.

Within an hour, he was completed with his work, and he left the building.

The Codes to the Admiral's office were transmitting on a cable that, for all intents and purposes, was using a stand-alone system for cyber-security purposes. Except for its power source which came from the local power plant. That's where had had added a transmission line.

On his laptop at home, he saw everything the Admiral saw.

* *

Trevor was to join his family. Amanda and he had spent over a year in London, and this vacation was long overdue.

True, she had taken a few academic trips back to the United States, and certainly, her position on the board of a few museums required her attention. It was part of their world together in Washington DC, even if now centered back in London.

She had wanted to server all ties to previous commitments. But he had insisted she carry on, she was American-born after all. And she seemed to be contributing to some very worthy causes. Still, she had never been gone long from his side, making only short visits back to Washington DC from London.

However, 'going home,' as he called it, suited her. Especially when she could add a little time for shopping in New York City!

This vacation was especially needed for the family, he knew. It had been a long year.

Even as the news was not good in his office of Minister, he had chosen to take the family to Italy – a place where he also had to conduct some banking business…

Further, Amanda was on a delicate mission, one whose peril and risk, he feared, she had underestimated considering the appraisals given to treasure insurances or exploitation these days. Especially now. Most people of lesser resolve would have avoided the responsibility. Transporting a valuable item of antiquity from Turkey to the United States, even with a stop in Italy, was particularly dangerous.

He checked his watch.

Amanda would doubtless have arrived by now.

He made one quick call to his office in London. He completed some notations and pressed on to Naples.

At times like this, one needed to think strategically. Necessary to facing a crisis, it was now essential to keep a clear head and even disposition.

Especially if the problem seemed insurmountable.

* *

Italy

The three year old stared at him. She blinked twice, girly curly hair frizzed, steady-gazed as a cat, watching.

Adam could read nothing in her look, his mind computing responses that could inflict instant revenge.

Sandra waited. She was half his age.

It had been perfectly executed, the longest noodle dangling from a silver fork, wavering thinly from her plate to his drink where it slithered gratefully like a snake to coil at the bottom of his raspberry juice.

He perched forward to peer into his glass.

He was about to speak when the juice came to life with vibration, along with everything else on the white dinner table cloth.

"Mummy! Mummy!" whimpered Sandra, eyes wide, lifting her arms.

Adam looked about to assess the other diners, all of them experiencing the tremor.

He leaped off his seat, which fell backwards, and he gripped the table. Then reversed himself with his arms out behind him to steady the table, facing the world in defense of his mother and sister, ground shaking beneath him.

** **

Amanda Wells had taken the children to Pozzuoli for the afternoon.

In a small piazza covered by trellised grape, she had chosen a cheerful Ristorante with small square tables and comfortable chairs. Her husband Trevor was in Naples on business, and the family had come along for the ride.

Or so it would seem. But actually, Amanda had stopped in Rome for a Conference which she attended only as an interested party from the academic world, not as a presenter, and only at the behest of her former employer and colleagues serving in Rome at the World Health Organization. Prettyman had accompanied the family to Rome. But with the party so large and the scheduling so rigorous, a few simplifications had to be made. The twins were tiring of it all.

Trevor-Reginald would be taken back home to Scotland and spend the weeks with his grandmother for the harvest festivities of the Glen, a prospect for which he very much implored. Granny, he wanted.

 Sandra would stay.

Furthermore, this was an opportunity for Trevor-Reginald to have his portrait painted. Sandra had sat beautifully for the portrait artist, and was done in a week, her steady blue eyes softly captured. Not even had the heather and blooms wilted in her hand. Adam's took two weeks. But Trevor-Reginald was a fidget. It became a fight. So they had postponed his portrait for a season.

So for Amanda here in Italy with Adam and Sandra, it was spaghetti; pizza and gelato at the Piazza Santa Anna in beautiful Sorrento before a visit to the Luna park, as she told her friend in New York. A plan that was met with great excitement. Daddy was to join them later…

Instead the earth shook.

The following day Amanda got a reply to her email.

"Re. A Jolt

" You sure got a jolt. - Wow! No Pompeii, I hope!

"I Googled tremors, and discovered something in a new study about universal signatures prior to a quake. (Bercovici's work at Yale): He says that although all volcanoes perform in different modes, their tremors all have the same pre-eruption signature, staying in a narrow band of frequencies …You're in a low pitch, I should think… So enjoy your ice-cream, and don't panic!

"Hugs to the children. "Best, Barbara."

That's a comfort sighed Amanda, texting "I don't know how the locals cope"

The answer came back quickly.

"Yep!"

* *

Stephen Tetlow was British. But he liked Baldwin and Dunkerton charts. He loved their 1999 work. And he loved America.

So he petitioned the University of London for a year's work in New England. They gave him the University of Maryland School of Earth and Atmospheric Sciences where frankly, all the fun was.

There were social connections; colleagues and a calendar of events that was never-ending. This was Washington DC for you, he told his Mum. – From ocean surfing to mountain skiing, you had it all…

Plus, here was the National Science Foundation just minutes away — using the subway - from the steps of the US Capital where all things funding was possible…

Anyway life was good.

It had been four years going on seven since he returned, his Irish- American wife commuting from Boston to DC on a regular basis. That is, for now. She was pregnant. And surely things would change, because she knew how important his work was, she said, calling his Baldwin and Dunkerton charts D&B just to annoy him. As in Dunn and Brad Street.

Still, he loved her. Only, the pressure was on.

This week was tough. Papers to grade. Reports to file for a General Faculty meeting. Proposals for funding. A week at the beach following, and damn it all, the sun was active as hell. Or so the emails were suggesting from NASA.

So he wanted to know with what frequency these anomalies were occurring.

What he had to do first was construct regressed three-dimensional perturbation structures representing the typical flow. Secondly, anomaly patterns for zero lag at the pressure questioned. Beginning with the highest pressure and working down, he could determine the typical flow pattern of the AO descent.

And that's where he paused. AO. Now there was a sacred word.

What did it mean? He gave it respect, this new finding, because it implied so much that he could never look at it full in the face.

Artic Oscillation. That's what it meant. Only recently had it been determined that there existed an actual downward stratosphere force that affected Surface Climate in the AO.

When the scholarly work of D&B was published, it blew people away. Steve himself was dumfounded when he read it. The authors themselves called their own work, as one newspaper put it, "eye-popping." According to their abstract they claimed that AO surface climate variations were the direct result of stratospheric polar vortex. These large-scale vorticity anomalies in the lower stratosphere were actually producing symmetrical zonal wind perturbations being pushed down to the earth from above. Meaning that the higher troposphere was more active than anyone thought, producing transient pulses in the mid-stratosphere.

Further, this *mechanism* they had the gall to boast, was now explaining surface climate; volcanic eruptions, solar cycle, ozone depletion and greenhouse gases. Even if proving it was a bitch!

He knew they were right of course.

He just knew it.

* *

A canary was what he needed.

Trevor was seated on a large stone slab, perhaps an ossuary or bench ledge. And he was underground.

The stone was cold, yellow with sulphurous seepage, but dry and chalky.

He looked about him. These walls were once lined by plaster, inhabited by a busy world of people eating in this space. Or sleeping. Or dreaming about things ancient and medieval. In one corner was a cistern well. Above him air ducts to the upper chambers, separated by bars. Such were his accommodations right now. A glorious historic underground basement in bank, locked up behind dinged wrought iron bars.

The canary would tell him if his could light his last cigarette. Was it safe down here? No toxic fumes? The canary of coal miners.

Actually, he had a lighter, and had used it periodically during the night. But today was different. He was in a cavernous basement of a man-made grotto. Period. No earthly other way to say it.

The Palace, or Palazzo, as they called it, was old. Medieval. With all the recognizable features of habitation.

He lit his last cigar and puffed.

There were beams of light that penetrated the space from somewhere above, possibly coming in through the overhead grillwork that served as windows.

How in the hell he got in here was beyond belief. He puffed.

What earthly reason could be gained from having him incarcerated? He had no wealth on his person. He had no strange and nefarious mission. He was just visiting the bank manager of the Banco di Tripoli.

He took another puff.

Yet, he was unafraid. His house was in order. All was well, even if he did perish down here the fate of a debtor in a debtor's prison. For that is what the structure had once been, in the darkness of the late medieval world, the brochure said.

He looked more closely. And he actually found elegance in the dimensions that surrounded him. The ceilings where high, the corners tall and straight, if damaged and crumbling. Even the overhead had stucco that swirled, it seemed, at the hand of the plasterer. Perhaps painted. But there was a curvature in the ceiling, as if the arch in cellars held importance for their owners. Perhaps it served as a wine cellar.

The Banco di Tripoli had restored the building.

Once owned by a family that funded Popes, armies, and missions of charitable causes, it was wealth derived from the seafaring trades of the medieval markets. That was the kind of wealth that brought statesmen to your table. And wine, even, from this cellar, he mused.

Another puff. This would be his last draw perhaps. And he watched it burn into a small cinder. The air was circulating enough to take his smoke upward, in a slow gentle spiral, so that it merged with the freight light and headed upward through the grate. Definitely. He was more than a prisoner. He was a hostage. And for that reason, he knew that time was on his side.

How it all happened, he could hardly recalculate. The appointment had been set up by his secretary to meet with the Manager of the Banco di Tripoli, Signore Ramibotti.

A car brought him from Pozzuoli where the family was staying and drove him through the streets of the city. Not much conversation, he noticed, but the driver was efficient, respectful and on time.

The door opened for him, and up to the main entrance of the historic building he went. A receptionist directed him through the bank lobby and into a paneled room of deep mahogany populated by white Louis IX chairs and a large desk. There sat Signore Ramibotti, Banker.

"Gracie, Sophia!" he said to the girl who ushered him. And as Trevor turned back to the door momentarily, he noticed a smile on her face reserved only for the intimate. Behind her though, patrons were leaving the bank. Closing time.

"I am so glad to receive you Mr. MacDonald" said the banker, seating himself and offering a place for Trevor.

Coffee arrived on a silver service, with an afternoon biscotti for Signore MacDonald, and a cigar for Signore Ramibotti, Banker.

"As you know, we are a small bank. But conservative, with a long history of deal-making…Please?" he asked, offering a cigar. Two bankers talking should be smoking cigars, he laughed.

And it was a good half hour of chatting before Trevor was invited to commence his business.

" As you know, we value your affiliation with the Bank of Sterling. I am come to be of assistance in assessing how our cash flows are helping you through this governmental transition of Euro-Aid from the Central Banks. We are committed to supporting their decisions, you know, and must keep our books in order …in these most difficult times, and ask how we might help with the recording elements of the accounting."

The smile spread across the banker's face like cracks. It was a look of relief. "But of Course Mr. MacDonnel. We are glad for your personal interest in our bank.."

The words that followed were effusive, such that Trevor had every inclination to believe that in the absence of reports, there were no records, period. In fact, what he was hearing, he felt certain, was thank God the English are such polite dolts.

That, he sort of expected. And even when Signore Ramibotti, Banker of Banco di Tripoli had to excuse himself, he knew he was sitting alone in an office being watched. The bank was now empty and firmly locked up.

In the economic turmoil that roiled Europe, anything was possible in this part of the world, a civilized world that was crumbling with social policies that brought the government to its knees; the unions to the table, and the criminals to their yachts.

Mr. Signore Ramibotti, Banker, had walked away!

Trevor finally helped himself to another cigar. That's when he heard the click at the door. The vast and church-like door harbored an automatic mechanism that bolted with a nasty click. It gave him pause, but not alarm.

What Trevor full knew was that the accounts had been on a run, and their assets already frozen by electronic measures in London… All the key codes had been changed. This then, was a true and genuine visit of concern to discover how he might help the bank.

The cigar was good. He had waited long enough. He got up. How unoriginal he thought.

A door behind him was open. Clearly a rear passage to exit the building. So, if exiting the building was an ignoble way to show the door to a creditor, albeit an English bank aiding in the financial rescue of institutions all over Europe, then so be it.

Signore Ramibotti, Banker, had lived all his life in conventions that worked. The question for him now was, what to do when things failed to work? How to deal with a long standing tradition of independent banking when creditors came calling and patrons drew down all their cash from your accounts?

Or, as Amanda would say, when the phones stopped ringing and business was over.

Trevor approached the rear side door, prepared to exit the building. Before him was a stairwell leading down.

It was a one way Exit.

And that's where he had been all night. And all the next day. He could get up as far as the passage to the top of the steps. But no re-entry.

Neither his cell, nor his laptop worked. Only once, when a fire truck followed by frantic polizia did his cell reception light up. He hit the last caller's identification, and waited. But it faded too soon.

No. Clearly, Trevor MacDonald was held captive in the empty vault rooms of the Banco di Tripoli.

Of that he was certain.

* *

Three

October 24, 79 AD

The ground had been shaking for days.

Tremors in these parts was normal.

But two men suddenly looked up. A dense cloud shot up to extraordinary height, shaped like a tree trunk before spreading out like branches.

From where they stood, across the Bay of Naples at Misenum about 22 miles away, the Admiral understood immediately. He turned to his young nephew and told him to get help.

The top of the mountain had erupted and the Plinian column, sustained by forces of gas and lightning plasmas started raining white pumice of clasti fragments up to 3 centimeters in size.

The Admiral asked his nephew to join him as he rushed to order his Captains to make ready for rescue operations. He said that a messenger had come from their friends asking the Admiral to rescue them by sea: They would wait at the foot of the mountain for his assistance. The Admiral deployed his fleet, reserving for himself a lighter vessel to make better headway.

But his nephew declined to go with him. He could help elsewhere, he was 17 and faster on his own. But the youth was afraid.

The erupting volcanic column was shooting fire 30 kilometers into the sky. For twenty hours it remained pyretic, spewing superheated steam caused by groundwater heated by magma.

It was terrifying.

When the shooting gases could no longer support solid contents, the collapsed column had dispersed 9ft of ash over the mountain.

Repeatedly, it released a pyroclastic surge, the column reorganizing itself and collapsing again, perhaps six times or more for two days.

The boy would later write "*I cannot give you a more exact description of its appearance than by comparing to a <u>pine</u> tree; for it shot up to a great height in the form of a tall trunk, which spread out at the top as though into branches. ... Occasionally it was brighter, occasionally darker and spotted, as it was either more or less filled with earth and cinders.*"

Rescue operations were occurring on the mountain, he deduced. He had tried to remain calm, to do normal things. Surely such a thing would not affect him and his family across the bay? He studied, bathed, slept, he said. But a tremor awoke him, and his mother ushered the entire household into the courtyard.

The pyroclastic flows spilling from the rim of the caldera now rolled down the mountain in slow rivers. It was magma moving at temperatures reaching 284 degrees F.

It melted tiles, granite and steel and rocks.

More eruption. The column had organized again and lifted itself aloft to spew grey pumice, with clastics up 10 cm in size for another 18 hours straight. The sound boomed across the skies.

By now terror had struck the hearts of people far beyond the mountain, including the youth's village across the bay as Misium, and the entire community evacuated.

The temperatures of the magma river increased. Magnetic iron mineral content *within* rocks was blocked from polar orientation, the earth's magnetic fields obliterated by heat, and the sea of rock was pouring into Herculaneum.

Pompeii was preserved for another fate.

By early morning the column had collapsed again, offering a grey cloud that obscured Point Misenum and the island of Capraia (Capri) across the bay.

Whereas the creeping flow of magma was cooling rapidly at the surface and the temperature differed along the ground as it flowed towards Pompeii, a change was now occuring.

In a second surge the difference in temperature between top and bottom of the flow combined, such that by the time the flow reached Pompeii, the city was as hot as the surrounding air which had reached 680 degrees Farenheight.

Across the bay, people ran to call to each other, and they moved back from the coast. Along the road, the young man's mother requested him to "*abandon her and save his own life, as she was too corpulent and aged to go further*". But he "*seized by her hand and led her away as best he could*", he wrote.

Ash carried across the bay. It rained everywhere. The youth found it necessary to shake off the ash periodically to avoid being buried. Later that same day the ash stopped falling, and the sun shone weakly through the cloud, encouraging the youth and his mother to return to their home and wait for news of his uncle, the Admiral.

 By dawn, another tremor hit the area, and the village was evacuated yet again. Still later another tremor occurred, and "*the sea seemed to roll back upon itself, and to be driven from its banks ...*"

By evening of the second day the eruption was over, leaving only haze in the atmosphere through which the sun could barely been seen.

Finally, one last surge erupted, but it was very diluted. Still, another meter deposits fell over the region.

The Admiral, it was decided had perished in his rescuing efforts. He was Pliny the Elder, and his newphew was Pliny the Younger. Few had lived to see the eruption of Mt Vesuvius in 79 AD. The record of Pliny the Younger would survive two millennium.

Yet, from afar off, there was one other who did survive and would witness the event. Someone located off shore, in a boat.

 A man named Saul.

He would later be known as St. Paul the Apostle.

* *

"Is Trevor there?" came the voice across the miles. The cell phone was cradled in a sturdy polyglass pedestal with notepaper beside it, an addition to their temporary furnishings for the summer made by Trevor and Amanda when they took residence of the house in Pozzuoli: It was to be their own private land-line communication system. And it was purposefully plugged in at the foyer entrance for all of them to reach. Even Adam… for when calls came in from his grandmother in Scotland.

"No. He is not available at this time. May we take a message?" responded Amanda politely.

Given the lapse of distance communications there was a marked pause at the end of the line.

"No need. Just tell him to call in for Susan please…"

"Certainly!" said Amanda, pulling for a pencil. And before she could speak again, the caller hung up.

Amanda looked down at the lighted digital display. The digits, whatever they might have been, evaporated as if wiped by an electronic eraser. There was no registered forwarding number, nor even a return number. She wrote down the message on a notepad, added the time and date, and left the message on the marble sideboard. Obviously, Trevor knew where and how to call back for Susan.

Trevor occasionally left his briefcase on the sideboard too, and his documents, in official folders, frequently found their way on the surface. Amanda tended to his paperwork, setting them safely aside on the table. A table that perched at the foot of the grand foyer stairway.

But the chief item on the Louis VXII wall table was a baroque vase of some antiquity with an colorful display of flowers, arranged daily by the Signora Vitoria. Amanda noted the tiny yellow roses of today as she climbed up the grand winding staircase with her hand on the brass balustrade.

They had rented a villa in Pozzuoli for six weeks of summer. It was attended by an elderly couple with the assistance of their efficient niece and her two sons.

On the second floor, Amanda threw open the windows and walked out onto the Veranda. The terrazzo surrounded the house and this allowed for running and playing by the children. In had shade spots, overhung by trellises bearing bright translucent green grapes. There they could sit, or play cards. And it was well railed, not high off grade level since the house itself was partially sunken into the sloping mountainside. Out back, an enormous walled garden offered a field, if not a vineyard in which the children could safely play.

And play they did.

There was a chicken coup which was routinely inspected for eggs. Not that the chickens were kept in their space particularly, they wandered all over the place, scratching and dancing for their daily feed of corn, which the children enjoyed dispensing.

Then there was the doggie-hound who followed them everywhere. They offered a small jump rope bar for him to jump over, which he roundly refused to do. So they skipped rope with it themselves.

There was a sandpit for building castles.

The local village clown came in one night and produced a puppet show. Susetta made a swimsuit for Sandra, for "la spiaggia" and her son whittled sticks with Adam "per il baltello di nave"

For Amanda Wells, it was a godsend.

The children had the run of the house, and Amanda became friends with the owners, finding old Signora Vitoria Rossa on the veranda, playing canasta with the children. This gave Amanda time to find cooler and quiet hours for computer work and private phone conversations. It suited her ideally, if unscheduled.

Food appeared mysteriously in the kitchen. The basics, Italian style, sometimes prepared and cooked, like lasagna. Or sometimes cold and insalada. Mornings presented croissants and pressed coffee on the sideboard, with occasional assortments of fresh sliced fruit and cream for the children. With this Amanda could argue little.

So she extended her arms and took a deep breath, blossom tingeing the air. The view of the Gulf of Pozzuoli was spectacular. There, beyond the green palm fronds that topped the roof lines, a sea surrounded by emerald mountains glistened in the morning sun with a blue ice glaze. If she leaned over she could see clear to the postcard town of Sorrento. The small islands, loosely necklaced around the four miles of the Gulf of Pozzuoli was the Camp Flegrei.

It was as if time had stopped.

* *

London

Outside University College in London it was drizzling. Silvery, with a summer sheen that bathed the city quickly with the heady promise of sunlight. "And this is a picture of the most recent movements in these two houses" the Italian said. He was one of three seated around a modern light oak table not far from the window.

"My God" said the Dr. Keanan, a tall lean balding man with a long angular nose.

"Yes. It's getting very bad" continued Mario.

The pictures he showed them depicted old city houses crumbling to the ground. One showed interior details. A home once vibrant now damaged by severe flooding and white mold. The second image showed a kitchen table, a bathroom shower curtain still hanging on its rail. But the coloring was deceptive. It wasn't water stains or age they were looking at. And it wasn't mold. It was deadly sulphurous deposit seeping up from the ground and invading every surface with a putrid covering of ash colored acid.

"Are they at least acknowledging there *is a problem?*" asked the third man.

"Yes. And no!" answered Mario. "For to admit to one is to admit to the whole…"

"Umm" the two said.

"But I have a few feelers still out. There are some reasonable men in the Government who are thinking. Particularly in the department of Civil Defense and the Italian Ministry of the Interior.

But generally speaking, they have a mess of social baggage; infrastructure and bureaucracy to navigate before they can say *anything*!"

The two looked up.

"I can pretend I'm taking site measurements on some *other* matters…even construction. Or postcard camera-shoots for tourism! We can sink drilling rods that way. They don't care what. It's happy land there. But I am not allowed to pronounce what *this* is…"

"I hate to mismanage information and play with the truth on foreign turf. Especially if we are making scientific findings" said Dr. Keanan.

The second man raised his finger off his cheek in agreement.

"And it's not as if they couldn't figure out what we do. After all, we are volcanologists!"

"No matter" said Mario "As long as you don't utter any *deadly* words…as you say. In fact, they are extremely interested. Just mute about it. So they don't mind. But they don't want to hear about alarm and mayhem"

"Very Nero-*esque*" muttered Kenean.

Mario shrugged. "it is how we keep…how you say…the song in our heart? Always hope!"

"So.." the third man said, hunching over the table with his thoughts "we'll just take the summer off… and make like tourists playing at geology specimen-collecting?"

"That means no funding for us -- or the research" said Keanan. "Can we afford it? Plus, we do need to make one hell of a data base, if we can…"

"In the name of science" said Mario "we must do all we can!"

"Right then. It's agreed. Summer at your house in Italy, Mario. I can do that!" they grinned.
"Bene!" he finished.

*** ***

Naples, Italy

Angelo had a fairly respectable office at the National Institute of Geophysics and Volcanology. It had a window, and with his desk, an enclosed cubicle or glass wall that partitioned him off from the main control center where a bank of screens entertained a host of scientists and technicians.

More than anything, he relished having some privacy for an occasional phone call. Actually, so did half his office who petitioned him periodically to have his room for 15 minutes to do just that, make private and personal phone calls. Being a personable man, he always agreed, and like a photographer, became the office favorite all round. Today, he had them clustered at his desk, two at the window, one sitting on the edge, and two in chairs across from him. It made for a hot room.

But so was the occasion hot. What to do about the increase in frequency?

They all knew that based on the mathematical model developed long ago by Bercovici and his colleague Mark Jellinek at UBC, tremors in nearly all volcanoes stay in a narrow band of frequencies from about 0.5 to 2 HZ.

But just before and during an eruption, the frequency climbs to a higher pitch, and the range spreads out to between 0.5 and 7 HZ.

They by turn alternated between talking, smoking, drinking and grumping. Was Ernesto, as the Department Under Director going to call the Civil

Defense and the Italian Ministry of the Interior or not?

One phone call. And it could terminate his career. One phone call, based on research findings made half way around the planet, and he could lose everything. Including his friends slouching all over his desk.

Even below them, at the control center, nobody looked up. They might as well have been all crowded in there with him. Secrets were hard to keep.

But someone below did look up. He had torn a sheet off a printer and held it up. They knew what it was, the night data from the night shift. He nodded his head. Bring it up! Nothing had changed! A tremor had shifted along the spectrum from below 2 HZ to 3.5.

What to do. What to do. What to do…they all said. Must be the plug, they said. Some of the most spectacular eruptions, had claimed Bercovici, was the oscillating plug of magma that was wagging against the walls of a cushion of gas bubbles as it rose… generating tremors at a consistent range of frequencies observed around the world. Or was it Mark Jellinek his partner who said that at the University of British Columbia, asked one.

In the end, it was not their decision, of course. In the end it was the Italian authorities. But since these guys had the technology, the education and the connections with other volcanologists, then the decision would be based on their recommendation. High price to pay for the Italians! Especially in an economic recession that was stressing the government beyond endurance.

So. Again. To call or not to call.

After all, what was at stake, exactly? At some point, someone in the room would have to say it.

What, precisely?

That they held the trust of the residents of the region? That dwellers who had been warned repeatedly not to expand, build or grow in the environs of Mount Vesuvius? These people relying on their decisions?

It was costly to manage. Costly to call.

3,000,000 million Napolitano's would have to be evacuated! And the needle that marked the tremor never subsided.

Angelo decided to postpone everything.

A few discrete calls he would make later. From his home, perhaps, if the wife and children would stay away a bit.

Because what he did not like was the source of the frequencies. This he could not express, not even to his colleagues. He would keep that part to himself, for now.

Part of his job was that he could receive reports from multiple sources and organize the information he was receiving. So far, he kept firewalls between his data sources. They all operated under the assumption that he would know what to do. It was his job as Under Director.

Sure, the funding was to monitor Vesuvius. But what he did *not* share was that the frequencies were all not local. They were coming from a wider sphere. A sphere he dare not even articulate.

He would call Mario about it in London, perhaps. But here, he dare not say it.

He shut his eyes.

* *

The food at the Chart House was good. Not exotic exactly, but good. Steve had a crab cake sandwich and Mel the blue cheese burger. It was salty, and he added hot sauce.

They were starved, Steve having fled the city to get to Annapolis an hour before the start of the Wednesday night racing. The Restaurant on the Waterfront was not far from the dock where the boat was being prepped.

Not that Mel had much of a boat. An older Albacore, basically, sailing about the bay amid a fleet of predominantly sleek-assed J boats, as he called them. But it suited his lifestyle in jeans and Tees. Working in boatyards during the summer, and Fawcett's in Winter. Annapolis was his home, Starbucks his center. And fortunately, he owned every square inch of his home in Eastport. No debts. No indebtedness. No foreclosures. And not much cash to spare.

He and Steve were friends. Steve crewed for him Wednesday nights, and they always had dinner.

"So. What's up?"

"Nothing" said Steve, finishing up his crab cake.

Mel dug into his pocket, pulled out a handful of debris like marlin spike, a penknife and a snatch of Dacron rope. Finally out came the pack of Camels and a lighter. He was going to be out on his boat and smoking was permitted by God, he always said.

"Ok…So, what's up?" he asked again, he blue eyes roving around like a stupid.

Steve peered at him.

"Aw comm'on man. I know that look…tell it, will ya?"

"What?"

"That 'you-won't-believe-me-look'. I seen it enough to know it on your face?"

"Ok" said Steve polishing off his French fries. "We know direct and indirect stratospheric influences require initial changes in the stratospheric circulation, and that there is a pattern. OK?"

Mel was staring at him.

"and, and… we've found how stratospheric circulation is strongly influenced by the troposphere. But, it's the mechanistic interpretation of such downward influences that worries me. .."

"Huh?" Mel said, in his slow way like he was utterly mystified.

"…only err… if it depends upon what processes are responsible for producing the initial stratospheric circulation anomalies…"

"And…?"

"It ain't what you think!" pronounced Steve. "Well. Wait. So here's the salt. Intraseasonal findings show planetary-scale tropospheric Rossby waves propagating upward into the stratosphere and they initiate changes in the stratospheric polar vortex, right?"

"So what?"

"In such cases, a subsequent downward stratospheric is a dynamical *feedback* . Based on the polar vortex, it's a downward stratospheric *forcing* rather than a feedback. Should be… right?"

"Huh?"

"It's breaking down, Mel. It's neither! In fact, it's *only* consistency is that with the magnetic fields…*also* breaking down"

"*What?* What are you saying?"

"Nothing" munched Steve, his French fry gone.

"Nothing *what?*"

"I'm saying that my data shows that this is not just affecting the atmosphere but the *geomagnetic fields of the earth*. We're discharging electro-magnetic impulses by rotating external electric fields with serious telluric currents."

Mel shifted, he was getting up, his so-what attitude grating on Steve. "The earth is a gigantic capacitor ain't it?" he said.

"No! Yes. Of course! I mean…only *they* aren't; I sent you charts. They're off the chart. They are rising in frequency like a bad fever… In fact," he leaned in, "they're in a state of subterranean flux!"

"*Really?*" grunted Steve, absently.

The Race Committee Boat was out.

From the water, the pre-start horn called like an angry goose. Mel's cell chirped. It was Mark - 'Leaving the dock in ten.'

They headed down together.

"So what are you saying?" exhaled Mel on his last puff of a cigarette.

"Major eruptions. Earthquakes. Volcanic activity."

"Oh yeah? …So are you gonna sail my boat tonight or not?"

"Okaayy!" swallowed Steve. *Christ, but the man could be dumb sometimes!*

Later that night Mel sent a text message to an old friend. Could they have lunch?

Mel wasn't just a physicist. He was a well connected physicist.

* *

"Do you like sex?" she asked in her pretty voice of New York Jewishness.

Steve was reading Kalnay's '96 article published by NCEP–NCAR, National Centers for Environmental Prediction and National Center for Atmospheric Research.

He looked up at her.

"Would you say that on a scale of one to ten, men your age like sex *more than* or *less than* men ten years older?" she asked, sitting on a chaise-long with a belly that resembled a watermelon.

She looked hot. Sand was everywhere, and the windy waves were kicking up a humidity that was almost unbearable. It was time to get her inside, he decided. Plus she was getting bored, clearly.

The baby was due in less than six weeks, and she was feeling uncomfortable. Perhaps less because of her condition, than because of the girls strutting their bodies along the beach. Trolling for guys, he said, taking her hand.

"*More* than. I mean *less* than? I dunno!" he grinned "I'm happy!"

"You may be good natured but don't know squat from squat. So let's go!" she said with some finality, adjourning the event at the beach.

She was working on her dissertation on the Social Sciences. Fertility Studies. As if there wasn't enough said on the topic. But no. It was an area of increasing fretfulness amongst research grants since the public demanded it, or so the universities said. Something to do with environmental factors and cultural stress - for which funds were always in abundance.

Anyway, Steve was glad for the break. He'd read enough to feel certain that his fears were no longer uncertain.

He was certain. Certain as could be. His data showed that what was once the case, was no longer the case! For consistency with recent findings, the patterns were no longer compatible with observed decadal trends in the AO.

He trudged through the sand, chair, cooler, beach umbrella, straw hat and backpack all dangling from his body. And he, thinking. The weather was changing damn it. Should he tell someone?

Who would believe him anyways? There was so much claptrap noise about the environmental global warming by liberal democrats wanting both equality and shares of the global wealth that the facts…didn't even *count* anymore. Besides, he wasn't talking about the weather, exactly. Well, not that it was that different in scientific terms…

No. He trudged on, his head down. He was talking about the weather beneath the crust of the earth! So what should he say…It was such an emerging science?

Could he tell them that titanic forces triggering earthquakes and volcanoes suggested that underground lightning was a major threat? Hell, the phenomenon of subterranean lightning traveling through huge deposits of quartz along earthquake fault lines was too new to articulate!

He was out of breath, paused, and chugged some water. Then trudged on, the car was a half mile away, across the far parking lot at the ocean resort. He never even heard his wife calling him.

And there was more that he was finding in his data. Plus anomalies from volcanologists: Volcanic lightning, though inconclusive was highly probable, they said, *because of its conductivity of the magnetic and electrical charges.* Ha! As if such things could be easily measured, he thought.

Old stories abounded, sure. But even recent eruptions, such as those in Indonesia, Iceland and the Mount Chaiten eruption in Chile during May 2008 witnessed gigantic lightning bolts. Ball lightning plasmas! This *was too cool* not to imagine! And electricity, it could be said, powers life. It powers the earth and the solar system.
Mel was right. The earth was a gigantic capacitor. Because of the low geomagnetic field, low frequency telluric currents have been recorded for centuries.
Truth is, the planet was a conductor and resonates thousands of amperes of raw energy.
But what interested him most was the science that suggested the evidence of the magnetic fields' beneath the crusts. Was such a thing possible to prove? Would it be him?
No, he decided. This was a whole different cocktail. Would he win a prize if he could prove…?
Now take *that* for explaining a change in the weather, he laughed. Still, he did not like the data on Solar Flares sent to him from NASA.

He stopped for breath, and actually turned to look at his wife. But he saw nothing.

His thoughts were thousands of miles away. Literally.

The sun, he was certain, in the last three months was related to the subterranean current interacting with increased geomagnetic inside the earth's liquid core generating a weird magnetic field.

Hell, the Solar flares were speeding up the subterranean current and setting off resonating oscillations in the troposphere and ionosphere, he knew it.

Except…with the troposphere and stratosphere conducting electrical discharges through water vapor, liquid magma was conducting the electricity of the telluric current.

OK. So the charges underground were attracted to opposite electrified charges in the ionosphere. But recently, the pressure was clearly releasing magnitudes of spontaneous discharges detonating underground – all of it being directed and intensified along fault lines by huge deposits of quartz. That meant that…

Jesus.

"Steve!" she screamed.

He hadn't looked where he was going. Later than day he was released from the hospital with bruises, scratches and a few stitches. Not enough to be in danger, but it scared them both.

She held him in her arms that night. "Tell you what. What do you say if you come up to New York and we stay at my parent's place to wait out the last month?"

She was worried about him.

Steve had seemed distracted this month. He wasn't even taking his medications properly. And the commute didn't end for the summer break because she was so close to completing her work up north. So they continued with their commuting. He wasn't just walking in front of cars because he hadn't looked up, he was bumping into things. And forgetting where he put things. And his blood sugar was off the wall.

Yes, this way she could keep an eye on him and keep him out of harm's way and get him stabilized again. Besides, it was calmer up north. Their apartment complex at College Park Maryland was hot, small and crammed with foreign "students" with no intention of learning English.

"Look" she murmured, lying beside him on the bed. "My parents aren't even there half the time. So they won't be intrusive. But the place is large, private, cooler and you can bring your research up…Just for a month eh? What do you say?"

Steve was asleep, exhausted.

* *

With high cheek bones and a demeanor to command respect, she was African America. Actually, more African than American, since her naturalization papers were freshly inked in Washington DC by an illegitimate paper mill for those of foreign origin.

But she had paid her money, and she did get a position as a teacher under mandate of law under Equal Employment Opportunity quotas.

Her father, a doctor licensed in India, was serving his country under the mediocre conditions of his various governments. And he had educated her in Somalia, at least she had that. More importantly, he had tutored her in English.

Like her brother, she was a Muslim. Her mother had died of AIDS.

She aimed to find retribution, one way or the other.

Fatima, or, *Naatisha* as she was now chose to be called was an African American fashionista, qualified for a teaching license of Alternative Schooling for distressed students. It got her into the educational system.

She had applied to the International School of NATO through the American EEO system of educational jobs listings. The International School of Naples followed the standard American college preparatory curriculum with additional specialized classes for the Italian State Exams. Sixty percent of the student body was from the NATO community, and this arrangement suited them well.

Further, there were programs for extra-curricular activities including sports, art, music, modern dance, newspaper, yearbook and drama.

Amanda MacDonald accepted their kind invitation to enroll the children in the summer school program during the period that Trevor was engaged in Italy on a mission of international concern and defense.

The children loved it. Amanda received accounts about school activities from Adam daily.

Sandra on the other hand, was often silent, her deep blue eyes brooding reproachfully. This was an unnecessary exercise, she seemed to be saying. Amanda knew that for Sandra, Naples would be fine without schooling. But since pre-K activities were available, Sandra went where Adam went..

Ms Prettyman enjoyed the respite from her charges during the hours of day time school. This teacher, Ms Naatisha Suti, however, was not someone she particularly engaged with. And Prettyman was frequently asked to wait outside as the children were taken from her by Suti.

This morning, when Ms Prettyman walked in the door with the two children, Naatisha Suti knew she had her victim.

The boy, Adam, was actually quite a good reader. And the young one would be going into the afternoon pre- kindergarten classes.

All she had to do was pick the right moment.

* *

Rome, Italy

The Conference on Cultural Treasures of the Mediterranean was a spectacular event.

For three days, the best of the Roman Empire would be featured in talks, forums, papers and exhibitions. For museum lovers, curators, collectors and scholars it was the thrill of the year. Attending the opening ceremony in the grand foyer of one of Rome's finest hotels was a gathering of patrons, donors, politicians and sponsors of the event, all mingling and having cocktails.

Here was the nursery for doctoral dissertations as new collections, public interest and antiquities valuations inflated. No longer satisfied with superficial exposure to works of art, frescos, sculptures and paintings, Italians developed a thirst for knowledge in writings, music, dressmaking and even hairstyling – all of it discussed in minute detail. Neither tolerance with authorities limiting access to treasure and its contribution to civilization, nor insufficiency of security satisfied the growing and voracious appetite about the ancient and medieval world: This was a period that defined the middle ages with its language roots and cultural foundations in Roman, Turkish, Greek and the Phonetician Empires. The Mediterranean culture had come to life!

Amanda was particularly delighted. Many of her colleagues - long faithful in their scholarship in the classics were now enjoying notoriety. Their books were selling; their names cited, their programs funded and their museums filling with viewers.

Further, there was a larger impact.

Not only did local tourism enlarge, but the entire tourist industry grew.

The academic community saw a resurgence of enrollment for scholarship from young people. Aspiring students wanting to open up fields of enquiry like archaeology, sociology, anthropology and even forensic history were drawn to the period like a magnet. Amongst them, topics of Pompeii and Herculeum.

Amanda enjoyed socializing with her professional cohorts and attended as many forums and lectures as possible. Many of them, now department heads and deans, were presenters.

Other attendees came to the Conference from tertiary and related industries, like private collectors and antiquities market dealerships. Of those she knew many, including Jacques de Torraine, an old acquaintance.

So with a schedule of frequent calls to the house; a leather jacket on her shoulders and a few Vespa tours through the streets of a City Amanda particularly loved, three days in Rome passed only too quickly.

Her evenings were also populated by acquaintances from her WHO career days. One or two joined them at the piazza ristorante where the entourage gathered for an evening meal.

On her last night out, Amanda had a private dinner with Santori, once deputy to her infamous boss, Fumosi, at the World Health Organization. Santori was now in charge of the Media events at the Conference.

"Yes. We have an incredible new mix here in the area. Gone are the simpler, regimented days of "El Capitano" said Santori "but it is vibrant with interest, and from all walks of life. Especially now, and with NATO's ranks that are swelling…"

Amanda noted as small catch in his voice even in his Italian inflections.

She took a sip of her Chianti, the beverage of tradition here on red chequered table cloths serving spaghetti. "I gather you have some regrets?"

"No! Not at all! Life is…much…much better than those miserable, impoverished days of autocratic rule and social custom…You have no idea how pig-headed the Italians can be!" he laughed.

"Money?" teased Amanda.

"Oh. Ma certo!" he grinned, also raising his glass.

"So…err…why the look of desolation?"

"What look?"

"Around the eyes, the underlying reason that you have me here, speaking to you separately. What is it Santorio?" she asked.

"Ahhh…Now I see why they trusted you above all others at the United Nations!"

Amanda smiled at him. "Kind of you to say so. But just doing my job!"

They sat quietly, days of crisis from the past filling their thoughts.

Finally Santori spoke. "I don't have to tell you how fortunate Trevor is to have you as his wife!"

"I remind him!" she grinned.

The waiter came, and they had coffee.

"It's like this: We are flooding with treasure in the area, it's for good money now to bring the authentic items here…But…"

"The costs….?"

"Oh *absolutamente!*" he chimed, rubbing his two fingers to denote lire "You have no idea!"

He leaned forward and hunched his shoulders, his two hands together itemizing the dilemma. "The insurance, the policing, the cataloguing, the upgrades to the building security, the tourism supports, the authorizations, the..the…eh!" he gave up, frustrated.

"But there is something else is there not Santorio?"

He looked at her steadily. "Yes" he said. "I want you as a paid consultant for an importante situazione…eh?"

"Umm"

"Eh bene. We have information of undercurrents from la polizia that we are likely to be robbed, and lose a lot to possible thefts and black-market selling…"

"Geese!"

"So. We were wondering if you could help us to find a *soluzione?*"

"Exactly, Santorio, what did you have in mind?"

"Well, how would you plan for a security place to hide our treasures?"

"Umm"

"If…that is…if something needs to be done to protect our assets. Against thieves and looters - Or if there was a breach or breakdown in our security systems…Where would we put them? How to hide them? When to protect them?"

Amanda was not entirely surprised by his request. She had been officially approached before by correspondence from one of the Director's of the Italian Authorities. She was yet to give them an answer.

Santori, evidently, was the footman come to prod her along.

"Well, as you may know Santorio, I've already been asked officially to lend my services to your endeavors here. And I have not entirely made my decision. But surely you realize that I am here with Trevor as an accompanying family, with children…and a small household, you understand…"

"Si! *Benissimo* for us to have you here with your familia!"

"So… I am hesitant to engage in professional commitments of any sorts, especially since it would require significant time and effort to be of service to you…"

"I understand!"

"But I will give it every thought, I promise Santori. And thank you for asking me. I am flattered."

"*Va bene!* We wait then, for your answer. And if it is NO, then I shall die from a broken heart!"

Amanda laughed "Thank you Santorio! I do appreciate your making me feel so welcome again…"

Before leaving the Penzione where she stayed, she said goodbye to the Concierge and promised to return. To show Rome to her children, she said.

** *

They were having tea not far from the green velvet billiards table that held the soldiers, if he recalled.

The Battle of Waterloo was changing slowly as more history was being revealed. Adding little vignettes handed down as lore. Diaries found in attics, mementoes that had passed through the generations, heirs wanting detail… That was what generated this work in progress: The battlefield tale still in the telling.

Why Waterloo was of such interest to the British Prime Ministers at 10 Downing Street was never really the question. Since most of the room, including the library, was shelved with a collection of valuables, it was not just an event but a statement. Maps. Strategies. Tactical and war compendiums, everything that added to the sheer weight and value of human effort and sacrifice that went into that war was present. As if the reminder of it all were part of the British resolve. The British culture as it called its shots as a leading world power, here in a room for Ministers.

And none had changed it. None since Churchill set it up. It was a family room almost. Even to Trevor now having tea with a few key scientists and scholars.

In that room, they could talk casually. Confidentially. Nothing in that room was repeated for any record.

What was it they told him that day?

He remembered the shock of hearing it for the first time. In fact, following that conversation, preparations were underway on three continents to deal with what they told him.

Dr. Keanan, it was… that was his name - who had taken the lead, with Mario Stramiere and the other two from London.

They wanted to make sure that Trevor understood. And that he would absorb the impact of what they were saying. After all, here was the man who must make decisions about a catastrophe so incredible… that averting it was impossible. Controlling it was out of the question, and preparing for it *might* offer the world some hope of surviving, as they put it.

"An Extinction Event" they called it. The kind that darkened the surface of the planet with such force and cold that an ice age would result.

Sitting beneath the surface of the planet was a super-volcano preparing to erupt. A hot spot approaching critical level.

As they explained it, the ground around the area was stretching, swelling, doming. Fumaroles – vents emitting columns of steam rich in CO_2 – were going to open up in the broken Tarmac. Four-and-a-half miles below the surface a bolt of magma had escaped the main reservoir and was rising upwards, changing and solidifying.

It had reached groundwater, was taking its time being converted into sponge-like stone.

Here Mario produced a small scale chart of what would happen as the water boiled, feeding critical amounts of gas into the sponge, and building up enough pressure to erupt.

"We're getting very little cooperation from the Italian Government" he said.

Trevor knew he was referring to Vesuvius, which was bad enough with all the projections and mortality rates expected. But still the melodrama was unfounded, he thought.

"Umm" he agreed. "But evacuating some three million people is an enormous expense for a government. Especially if it turns out to be a false alarm...?"

"*False alarm?*" they all echoed. As if the price of science and saving lives should even have a place on an economic scale.

"Vesuvius is not the problem!" said Kenean, standing up, hands in his pocket like the professor that he was.

"How do you mean?"

"What we are talking about is an unknown... Look at it this way, something that would make the Icelandic Eyjafjallajökull volcano look like a party candle. In terms of pressure, it would be 200 larger!"

"And Vesuvius is not, *not* ... a worry?" said Trevor, wondering what they were saying.

"No" said Mario, simply.

Mario spun around and walked to the window, watching the English weather.

It was Dr. Keanon who spoke "You see, what we are describing will... Will bury Europe!"

"What do you mean?"

They paused, giving him time.

Trevor put down his tea cup. His hand was shaking, he noted. This was too incredible to absorb. Surely!

He needed to collect his thoughts, he had read the report about Toba. But this was today.

"Excuse me" he said, adjusting his position "Where...Uh, *where* did you say this was, exactly?"

"In the Gulf of Pozzuoli. The caldera, marked by the mountains that rim it, is four miles wide at the opening. Beneath it is a super volcano preparing to erupt. Camp Flegrei."

A fog in his mind seemed to obfuscate…

Dr. Keanan drew closer and pulled up his chair. He used his hands. "As this four mile-wide caldera collapses and releases the larger maga reservoir into the atmosphere, it would wipe out all of Italy and bury Europe in 300 ft of ash…"

Mario took over the dialogue "Life as we know it would be over!"

"How do you mean?"

"An ice age would ensue" proceeded Rogers "We would lose all livestock, crops and three-quarters of our plant species, plunging us into a new dark age of rioting, starvation and perpetual winter"

Trevor asked how verifiable their information was. Research, they said, was deducted from the Toba super volcanic eruption that occurred 73,000 years ago. It was, by conservative if not under estimates, an M8 category eruption; its caldera complex was measured as being 100 X 30 km in size.

"We may be in a short period of uplift…" Mario was saying. "We could even have a decade, if we're lucky. Or we could have two weeks!"

"You are…certain?"

"Believe me. We've tried every invention to turn these computations on their head. But they don't go away. Spots in Italy are already rotting away from the gathering sulphur vapor alone. Some places report undrinkable well water…The tremor vibrations are pretty consistent…Hz Frequencies imply that the plug of the rising magma is already oscillating. And we do measure swelling and heating. It all adds up. ”

“How can you be *certain?*”

“Certain enough to be told by every volcanologist that the authorities need to make preparations…”

“That's the best kept secret I've heard…How come it's so sudden?”

“Fear” said Mario, unblinking.

“Umm” said Trevor. He was already thinking about the impact on Britain, his mind reaching for defensive measures.

“Can you send me full reports as to what we should expect, what vital elements are at risk, and what possible recommendations you can make for the aftermath and for the security of the nation”

Dr Rogers, Keanan's associate spoke next. He came closer.

“Security” he said firmly “is *not* on the table. Survival is!”

Trevor looked at him.

None of them spoke. It mattered little, each of them digesting the information.

“Survival then” said Trevor quietly, adjusting to the reality. “What elements of large scale survival should we plan for?”

Much of what followed was lost. Drowned by the scenarios that only imagination could provide. Who should know? How to prioritize? When to notify? Prepare? How, exactly? To whom and what resources were considered critical…The questions were endless.

They thanked him, he remembered, and they commented on his calmness. Truth be known, it didn't really sink in… Thoughts ran to his family, estate. And it shook him up sufficiently to find some excuse to drive to Scotland - absence for some constituency business, he said. Once there, he toured his estate, his thoughts in turmoil for three weeks.

By the time he returned to London, however, he had a full retinue of emergency preparedness specialists drawing up plans.

England, he decided, would survive. He had Adam, the twins. And above all, he had Amanda Wells as his wife. They would survive. That he would ensure.

The British Isles had stood the test of time for geologic epochs. The question was, how to prepare for this one? What were the critical elements needed for longevity, survival and endurance if a coldness were to follow…? Let alone the realignment of continental economies!

Trevor MacDonald was more than a Minister of the British Government.

He shook himself free of those underlying worries. For now, he was still stuck in the basement of a bank!

Bloody Hell…

Of course there would be an explanation! There had to be. Eventually. But his patience was reaching its end.

His own Scottish ancestral legacy included the ownership of a large Scottish Bank on whose board of Governors he served. Not often, mind, but as a sitting Governor nonetheless. His Sterling Bank, as it was called, had loaned a lot of money to other banks in Europe which were in distress.

What he didn't count on, exactly, was being incarcerated in the crypt of an Italian Bank who locked him up because he came calling. Certainly, they owed his bank a great deal of money. But what he had really come for was to alert them to new monetary policy! Bank Reserves. Bank Liquidity. This was new thinking that would require crisis management, redirection and restructuring for impending disaster.

Christ!

He would send someone later in the month to deal with the bank issues. That's… if they still had time for preparations…

What riled him most was that this delay was keeping him from other pressing duties as a Minister in his own Government…

In any event, he would call for a scientific forum of specialists to better brief them. If decisions had to be made, this was *far* beyond him: He would have to consult with many within the government, the leadership, the leading ventures and interests. The monarchy. And how *not* to induce panic? In fact, he wondered if the government could even cope with such a prospect.

It was overwhelming.

Surely, there was a flaw in their thinking. Test it, he must…that is, if he ever could get out of this hole!

* *

The statuesque form of a medieval Knight laid out on a stone slab in the crypt suddenly sat up and walked about, evidently trying to get red blooded circulation pumping through his veins.

Trevor had fallen asleep in the anti-vault of the bank structure that was at least three hundred years old. The temperature had dropped overnight, and he was shivering.

He was mad as hell.

He heard the sounds descending the stairs from the floor above him. A squeaking iron door was opening.

And before receiving the full invective of an angry Scotsman, the wailing of an abject Italian trickled down the steps in wretched apology and disbelief.

…How …How could they have done such a thing, the man pleaded? It was too miserable to contemplate…The bank manager would be fired! No. Thrown from the cliff …for lions for to feed…*Graze Dio!*

Il Signore MacDonald…He was alive and well! *Scuza! Signore Trevor…Oh, Oh, prega accettare il mio regretto a^gli condizione che se hanno qui arrivato... Oh! Dio Mio! Disgraziato! Che..Che..Vergonia! Oh Scuza* Signor Trevor…*per favore, Prega …Mi Scuza?*

A small rescue team followed the man down the stairs.

Trevor folded the blanket firmly around his shoulders.

He should sue the bastards.

Instead, he leaned back against the alter- height tomb that he had slept on, his eyes blue and cold as he glowered at his distraught rescuer.

"I'd like to know how your treat your clients with less money than I have!" he said finally.

The Italian looked up cautiously, appreciating the generosity in Trevor's words, and offered his hand for a handshake, perhaps wanting to weep.

Trevor gave him a pat on the back to avert further distress, and together they ascended the stairs.

Amanda was the first to greet him in the lobby, having called the police, the Embassy, the Joint Armed Forces and the Marines, she announced. Then Adam, who tugged at her, got his turn. "And Adam!" she added "He was the most concerned!"

Trevor looked at his son gravely, the two of them exchanging silent thoughts like Pinkertons who understood things nobody else could. Finally Adam took his father by the hand and led him from the building. Trevor handed off the grey issue blanket provided by the Rescue team.

"But actually" Amanda was saying as they drove home "… it was the bank management in their Main Offices of Milan that I had to take to task the most! I had no way of knowing of course, but I raised hell. You had disappeared… following a visit to the Bank Manager here at the Branch office of Naples…"

Trevor said nothing.

That evening at home, a subdued reunion brought them all together. But Trevor, Amanda noticed, was distracted. If not altogether withdrawn from his family.

Neither did things improve the next day.

An official visit was made by the Authorities. It was a personal visit by the Superintendent of Police for Investigations, attended by a younger Police Lieutenant. Outside was parked a full departmental escort of officers, waiting.

It was an official apology.

But it served more as a catharsis, if not a briefing.

The Superintendent spoke with them unofficially, explaining the full back story of the Bank. Mostly, his comments were directed at Trevor, his wife Amanda welcome to listen, he said..

"We have shut down the Bank Branch" he explained. "They were under investigation!"

All senior bank management had one-by-one disappeared over the last eighteen months, leaving new and unknown people to tend to the affairs of the bank, he said.   Everything appeared to be normal. The transition, trainings, routine and bank management…

'Actually it was hoax" he said.

"No. A *heist*.. - as they say in New York" interceded he young Police Lieutenant, grinning.

The Superintendent of Police put out his cigarette in a crystal ashtray provided by Amanda. At least he nodded.

"You see, the Bank Building – being a place of historic interest – housed some of the area's most famous paintings, statues and treasure. For civic pride and public display, you understand. Like a Museum that played the host to many popular events in the piazza, like concerts, touring Exhibits and Charity functions over the years…

He lit another cigarette, his thoughts on lighting up.

"Actually, it had some fame, you see. Its collections were not only celebrated and discussed in the local newspapers, but tourists from all over would come specifically here for to vies showings. Some our most prized items in Italy…Right here in *that* historic building!" he said, pointing definitively. He took a long draw and puffed, his storytelling distracted.

"Indeed, some of the great… *grand masters* of Art were on display on the Walls within the bank…" his hands flavoring the fame and memory of those moments. But his smile was fading. He looked down "A place considered to be safe from thieves wanting to steal money!" he laughed.

"But the bank was found robbed and denuded of all its precious and ancient icons, paintings, vault valuables, exhibits, art and statues…" He leaned over and extinguished his cigarette.

The gasp in the room was audible.

Trevor looked at him. Amanda raised her hand to her mouth. And the Lieutenant hid his face behind his fingers at the words.

"The estimated value of the stolen collection even exceeded that which was on display in the local Museum!" he concluded with a shrug, shaking the responsibility that lay on his shoulders. The *heist*.

He looked down then added, as if for the hundredth time in his head "That's because it was *assumed* that the bank not only had security, but could pay for the insurance to cover the collections!" He got up and walked to the window, seeing the assembly of policemen outside, as if attending a wake. He waved with a silly smile on his face.

"Much of it was on loan. Imagine! Paintings bought by the last Queen of Prussia after King Frederick had died…"

Amanda knew what treasure had been collected by the Queen of Prussia following the death of her husband. She had travelled to France in an disquiet quest to compete for collections with Catherine of Russia furnishing the *Hermitage*.

She could only imagine the religious iconography that dated from the first century through the Middle Ages.

Amanda looked at Trevor. If she could read his thoughts it would most certainly be along the lines of bank- related invective.

Amanda was appalled. Such a theft was almost incalculable.

Still, in an effort to pour oil over a troubled sea Amanda offered refreshments all around.

The Superintendent took a cool glass of lemonade, and drank thirstily, as did his Lieutenant.

The Superintendent returned to his seat. The memory of that day still *seared on his soul*, he said. The public disgrace could cost him his dearly, he confided.

The Security of that bank, it was known, was one of the highest technology systems in the city, he explained.

But clearly, the staff had been infiltrated for months, if not years, his voice trailed.

No, he concluded, staring down his empty glass. This had been planned for a long time!

He eyed Trevor. So when il Signore MacDonald showed up from the Bank of Sterling, and his fingerprints failed to register on their visual camera identification system…they thought…perhaps…*with greatest of apologies, Signore*! That he was suspect…And he was held underground.

He apologized. It was a precautionary move. And it was a plausible explanation, you understand?

Amanda kept her eye on the Lieutenant, a doleful youth who absorbed the enormity of the crisis on his face. The Superintendent raised his eyes to him on several occasions.

Amanda smiled at the young Lieutenant to relieve him of the burden of guilt, something his boss was lavishly laying on with melodrama. *This was only a crisis on the job*, she wanted to say to the Lieutenant. *Don't die!*

"I am sure you will recover the stolen collection" said Trevor, finally.

The Superintendent would go home to his wife tonight and enjoy a good meal, thought Amanda. This young man however, was taking it personally. A process of sorts, the Superintendent sloughing his responsibility and guilt onto the other. And just briefly, outside in the sunlight as they said goodbye, she saw the young Lieutenant look back at her with relief.

After supper Trevor went to his study and worked at his desk. With the children in bed, Amanda joined him in the study with some sewing. Just to be close.

Later that night she picked up the telephone that rang in the Lobby It was Santori.

He had emailed her.

"So, you see what I tell you? You heard from Il Superintendent of Polizia? What I tell you? …We are needing to consider what we do against thieves and looters if there was a breach or breakdown in our security systems…?"

Amanda paused. "Yes. I understand. Most distressing... Knowing that such a thing should have happened…and what a loss! Santorio. It must have been devastating…"

"You see Amanda. We are rich in history of Italia, but poor in how you say…new industry and technology for the protection of our most valuable heritage and assets…Please, you help us now find solutions?"

"Well…"

"Please! I do ask you from the bottom of my heart. And I shall give you Letters of Offizia for to do the task con *compenza* …With the government so unstable..We may have riots and difficulties. We need to rescue our valuables…"

"Ok. Santorio. I get it. Let me talk to Trevor about. I'd like to consult with his schedule. Let me find out if it all works out for the family arrangements. Again, as you know, I have the children with me…" She put down the receiver, knowing full well what Trevor would say. He would expect her to rise to the occasion of her professional duty. She paused. This was *Italy*!

Sandra came in, grinning. Chocolate on her face, she had confounded someone, her eyes said.

Amanda sighed.

Like mother like daughter, said Trevor.

* *

Anna was early. She could be heard throughout the house.

She was the self-designated Italian hostess. Sitting in her convertible Ferrari, wearing a pale orange silk scarf and white sunglasses that framed "the beautiful face of a fifty year old woman" she said in her accent. And she was laughing, her red hair peeking out at the shoulders.

"Eh, Amanda…*Andiamo!*" she said playfully, hitting the horn again from the driveway.

The children had left. Prettyman had taken them to school, and Trevor was on business downtown conferring with NATO officials.

Anna was the wife of a General, retired. And determined to inform Amanda about all things Napolitano.

When Amanda stepped outside, she wished that both Trevor and even young Adam could see what an Italian icon Anna was.

But appearances were deceiving. Anna was a scholar, deliberately permissive to induce critical thinking from passive students.

And she loved poking fun at serious matters

"So. Today, we tour *Il Catedrale di Napoli*…symbol of everything that is important in Europe, and everything that we have kept secret from the world…"

She pushed open the small door of the yellow sportscar.

 "Jump in! I show you!" she gesticulated, inviting Amanda to be seated beside her.

Amanda accommodated her in an open car on an open road with only a seat belt for deliverance.

"And this evening…" she proceeded, roaring up in noise through a Piazza of pedestrians "we have a party a la spiaggia where my brother have a boat for a tour of the grottos and graves of men!"

"Sounds charming…" began Amanda, wondering how much of this was thrill and how much was warning.

"E per carita`…bring… *ehhh*… I bambini for a little…frivolita` in the aqueous ways of Italy…Vabene?"

"Alright!" agreed Amanda, immediately worrying about her acquiescence.

"So!" she said, revving up.

Anna flew through turns and jolts, tires screeching and gears roaring in protest.

They came to a sudden halt, ears dulled in silence.

Anna peered into the rear view mirror to fix her hair.

Amanda looked up.

Marble portals towered above them.

"Built at the end of the 13th century, left over from a sixth century church incorporated into the Gothic architecture of the Cathedral of Naples" said Anna, pulling off her scarf.

"My God" said Amanda in amazement.

"Charles I of Angio decree!" said Anna frivolously getting out the car and slamming the tiny door. "Redone after the earthquake of 1788, then again one century later, exactly, 1987" she added. "But the marble portals never moved…"

At the entrance, Anna pointed above the door. "Charles I of Angio, Carles Martel, King of Hungary on his right, and his wife Clemenza of Hapsburg on the left".

Amanda wondered if these were the Angevin kings of the Crusades for whom the Knights Templar had raided Jerusalem.

Anna marched her through 100 meters of the interior. A towering space containing three naves divided by sixteen heavy pillars to incorporate 100 solid granite load-bearing columns.

"Ceilings are wood" pointed Anna. "Frescos of The Annunciation, The Presentation of the Temple, The Visitation of Mary with Nativity and The Epiphany"

The vivid images seemed to be circling the heavens above them.

"Those high on the walls of the Central Nave and the Transept are paintings of saints. These at the base of the pillars are busts of the first 16 bishops of the city of Naples"

Amanda followed Anna around the side chapels, her hat and sunglasses still in her hand.

She saw ornately carved containers…

"Funerary items" supplied Anna.

Amanda was surrounded by sculptures, frescoes and canvases that spanned a period of figurative art from 1200 to 1700.

"In this nave, the Fourth chapel, is the Brancaccio chapel. Beyond that, you enter the oldest part of the Cathedral, the Santa Restituta Basilica, resting on the oldest remains of a paleo-Christian structure. Here are the roots of Naples, if not Christianity itself!"

"Amazing" said Amanda. "It's hard to believe that all our cultural tradition had real life stories once…"

"All of Christianity does!" said Anna. "And most of it happened from right here"

"Geeze" said Amanda, almost in bewilderment.

"But wait till you hear the story of Charles!"

"Charles?"

"Ah ma si! He is buried here!" floated Anna. "I'll find him somewhere, and serve him to you in

"And this" said Anna, pausing in one nave "is the Bust of Saint Januarius!"
Amanda peered at the silver figure. It seemed out of place somehow. Even a touch intimidating.
"It was done by French craftsman. It is said to have preserved the Saint's skull as well as a vial of blood that will liquefy miraculously every year to protect Naples from a volcanic eruption from Vesuvius"
Amanda looked at Anna
 "This Miracle of San Gennaro is supposed to be one of the most remarkable manifestations of faith in all of Christendom!"
She walked on.
"In the Chapel of the Treasure of St. Januarius are frescoes by Domenichino and Giovanni Lanfranco. Massimo Stanzione and Jusepe Ribera are seen in the works of the altarpieces. To the right of the high alter is the work by Francesco Solimena. The bronze railing is by Cosimo Fanzago…"
Amanda followed, almost in a daze.
"There are many 14th century French masters who had their hand in the makings of the reliquary. .."
Amanda was amazed at the art work, the detail and the precision of the men working long ago with limited resources. This was a medieval, almost pagan world of the occult being unveiled through their works. From one dimensional primitive iconography to the vibrancy of images painted with human intensity, Amanda felt she was standing on holy ground. Here many had kneeled and prayed for deliverance through the centuries. . It almost took her breath away.

"This, as you know, is the original Orthodox Catholic Church. By that I mean it is the most dominant Christian denomination. This is the original site of the first original Apostolic Church established by Jesus Christ and his Apostles almost 2000 years ago. Today it is a religion, with an estimated 300 million followers"

"Wow" said Amanda again.

They lingered. Observing.

"A synod of bishops have the duty of preserving and teaching the Apostolic and Patristic traditions related to church practices.."

"Still?"

"Oh yes. They take their responsibilities very seriously!" admonished Anna. "They trace their lineage back to the Apostles Succession – through Byzantine Roman Empire to the earliest church *here* established by St. Paul the Apostle"

Amanda looked at her.

"So, you see. Not much has changed since this place was first venerated. It is based on the philosophy of learning in the original ancient traditions of growth-without-change, having shared its thinkers amongst Greek, Slavic and Middle Eastern Islamic traditions"

 Anna took a few paces. "And it still shapes the cultures of the world today…" she said.

"Like a monastery?" asked Amanda.

"Almost. They do have learned monks here, on rotation. They believe that the goal of the

Orthodox Christians is to walk as close to God as possible. A process called *theosis,* or "deification": A spiritual pilgrimage where each man strives to become as Christ like as possible"

"What a movement!" said Amanda looking up at the iconography.

Anna went to sit down.

"The Biblical text used by the Orthodox includes the Greek Septuaginet and the New Testament. And as you know, the seven Deutorocanonical Books – which the Protestants reject!"

Anna fanned herself, if tired her eyes burning with passion.

"So there is this term *Anagignoskomena,* meaning readable texts in Greek. Ten books that remain *outside* the 39 books of the Old Testament canon although they are included in the ancient Hebrew canon. Occasionally used by the devout purists…"

She got up.

Amanda followed.

"Over here.." continued Anna, nodding to acknowledge a priest appearing from the shadows in full vestment "are other artworks, including an Assumption by Pietro Perugino, canvasses by Luca Giordano and in the palaeo-Christian baptistery, mosaics from the 4th century…"

"My God" said Amanda. "That's *old*…"

"The main chapel is a restoration of the 18th century, with a Baroque relief by Pietro Bracci. …Over here, in the crypt, the work of Lombard Tommaso Malvito. And here, is the original 15th century portal, including sculptures by Tino da Camaino. …"

"Amazing!" was all Amanda found herself saying.

The priest came over with a little more fortitude and looked at them both in the face. Then he retreated.

Anna ignored him.

Amanda was staring at Saint Januarius. But Anna pulled her away with a disgusted *"Ugh!"*

"There are many kings buried here" continued Anna, walking on "Mainly, the one to know is Charles I…and by that I mean Charles of Anjou, King of Sicily by conquest from 1266. He did receive a papal grant but was expelled from the island after the Sicilian Vespers of 1282. His capital was Naples" she sang out to the vaulted echoes of the cathedral and crossed the great stone floor.

"He was the youngest son of Louis VIII of France and Blanche of Castile, younger brother of Louis IX of France, and Alfonso of Toulouse. And, an ambitious son of a bitch…" ended Anna.

Amanda laughed.

She understood of course. At the turn of the first millennium, this was the highly coveted region of a Mediterranean world flourishing with wealth, sea trade, early Christianity, Arabian rule and European conquest. Charles had fed his ambitions, setting in motion a stage for the second millennium. It was a legacy for a medieval Europe battling disease; distress and devotion for growing ambition of Empires and Holy Dominion.

"Like all young and promising Princes, Charles sailed with the Crusaders from Aigues Mortes in 1248. He fought at Damietta and Mansourah."

"A prince?" said Amanda.

Anna shook her head "Alas no! Even in fighting for the Faith, his brother Louis (who would rule

France) discovered him gambling on the Holy voyage, and ordered him returned in disgrace with his brother Alphonse in 1250."

"Ha!" laughed Amanda.

"During his crusade, a rebellion broke out in his Provence. Charles moved with alacrity to quell and seize control. Arles, Avignon, and Barral of Baux surrendered to him. Marseille held out. He demanded then his full panoply of comital rights and acknowledgement of his suzerainty by Marseille in a bloody threat…"

Anna twirled under the circle of busts and bronze statuary. "It was the start to a long career of seizing-and-taking. But where it held the greatest impact was upon the Holy Roman Catholic Church itself, now taking shape at the turn of the millennium."

Amanda nodded.

"So, already" said Anna "the pot was stirring…"

They paused in the light of a Cathedral fenestration.

The priest appeared.

They turned away, ignoring him.

He led two scholars up the main aisle carrying an icon. It was illuminated by a candle on a long stick, it's oil reeking with a dark trail of smoke. Amanda saw him look over his shoulder at them.

"At the death of his mother," continued Anna blithely "Charles went to Paris to assume Joint Regency of the kingdom - with his brother Alphonse: He was approached by Pope Innocent IV seeking to detach the Kingdom of Sicily from the Holy Roman Empire which was ruled by Conrad IV of Germany…"

"I thought it was offered to Charles' brother in law, Richard, Earl of Cromwell…" said Amanda.

"It was…" squinted Anna playfully. "But declined! Besides, France thought the idea bad. King Louis his older brother blocked it."

"Umm"

"So Charles took up the cause of Margaret II of Flanders against her son, John I, Count of German Hainaut in the War of the Succession of Flanders and Hainault. She made Charles the sovereign of the County of Hainault…Imagine!"

Amanda looked at her.

"This infuriated Louis of France who blocked it and returned the territory of Hainaut to John I of Germany!"

"And…?"

"Charles went back to Provence frustrated. Suddenly, the region became restive again. Manipulating money; conquest and political maneuvers, Charles accumulated high posts and new dominions de rigeur…"

"The Germans?" asked Amanda, loosing track.

"The titular Sicilian throne -owned by the Germanic Conradin Hohenstaufen *and* the Papacy - was his real battle plan. Now this was the power center of the world!"

"Oh"

"Pope Urban IV seized the Kingdom off his partner Conradin Hohenstaufen and offered the crown to Charles again!"

"Nice to have friends in the right places" laughed Amanda.

"The terms exacted were remarkable. Heavily in favor of the Pope; the Kingdom must never be re-united with the Empire, and the King was never to hold Imperial or Papal office, or interfere with ecclesiastical matters in the Kingdom!"

"Charles agreed…" finished Amanda

"Oh yes. He entered Rome on 23 May 1265 as King of Sicily. Now popular in Rome, he was next made a Senator! Like a Greek tribunal of ancient classical history!"

They strolled on.

"Some would say there are a few like him in Washington DC!" giggled Amanda.

They laughed.

They had moved to the West end of the Cathedral, and Amanda was begin to fatigue.

Anna was on a roll again.

Behind her, something else was going on. Or so it seemed. The priest was coming out periodically and staring at her. Once he just stood in the shadows.

Amanda finally sat down.

"He borrowed money from his Uncle Henry of Castille" Anna said "When the debt was never paid, a battle ensued in which Henry was captured by Charles. He imprisoned his uncle for 22 years. Imagine!"

Amanda looked up at the Priest.

He turned away.

She and Anna moved on.

And the priest followed them, his shoulders wide and sloping forward, his arms hanging broadly in a mildly belligerent way.

"Anna…" whispered Amanda, trying to slow her down.

Anna stopped suddenly and said "But Charles wasn't happy being just a Senator. He wanted Northern Italy. This alarmed the Pope…"

"Anna" said Amanda softly. "Can we take a break?"

"Charles wanted to be an Emperor!" Anna proceeded carelessly.

"Anna, slow down, please!"

The Priest edged forward, standing almost behind her.

Anna stepped away but continued.

Amanda had the uneasy feeling of concern creep over her. As if Anna was being provocative.

"Charles wanted the Latin Empire, and whereas the Kingdom of Sicily had controlled the ports and passages of wealth, gold and trade along the eastern Adriatic seaboard, he wanted to seize from the existing Nobility their entire Latin Empire…"

Amanda watched the Priest.

His eyes were following Anna, as if every word uttered was incendiary.

Amanda was getting worried.

"Perhaps he rescued the Roman Empire from a Greek and Turkish *feud*?" queried Amanda with a twinkle.

"Perhaps" acknowledged Anna.

The Priest suddenly spoke. "Pope Gregory X was consecrated on 27 March 1272. Charles launched a crusade and proclaimed he must arrange for the election of an Emperor!"

The priest placed both hands on his hips, and waited. As if he was about to spring a trap.

"Anna…" began Amanda. "It's time to go! I'm wearing down, please?"

Anna, hot and glowering, fairly stamped her foot in challenge, her eyes turning to steel and her voice angry. "Then Charles makes his kids marry Latin princes - with all Rights of Reversion of their kingdoms to *himself* should they be infertile!"

Amanda was about to make a joke about sexual proclivity when she realized this was no time to be flippant.

Amanda needed to steer Anna away. She led Anna by the elbow. She would have said something but Anna had angry tears in her eyes, and they stormed out to the rear of the church with their heads down.

"Anna. What was all that about?" asked Amanda.

 "He was the last man seen with the daughter of my friend" she rasped. "The girl was brought here for her Confirmation class by her mother."

"Was there an investigation?"

"Yes. But she was never found! It happened almost two years ago. She was 12."

Turning rapidly to face the guided tour assembling on the steps of the Cathedral she said loudly "And Charles proposed to the heiress of Hungary - and acquired the ancient state of Burgundy!"

"What a guy!" muttered Amanda. "Anna…" She looked down at her watch. She had to find a way to slow down this tension. "Can we sit for a bit?" she asked.

Anna would not be deterred, her eyes following the Priest as he circled behind them. She sat.

"Nor was she the first to disappear in the last twenty years here!" said Anna beneath her breath. She and the Priest were clearly in a dual.

Amanda sat down at a pew near by. "How can you be sure?" she whispered.

"Oh, I'm sure! But I can't prove…"

"Come on. Let's go!"

They both got up to leave. They began to walk up the aisle.

That's when it happened.

Anna barely averted the impact of a dangerously heavy iconostasis. The priest carrying it appeared from nowhere and without warning.

"Ah *scuzi!*" he said breathing roughly, and brushed off with it. The stand was being relocated within the church.

 Had the stand fallen onto Anna and hit her, it might have seriously hurt her.

Amanda was distraught, even if the priest seemed little more than indisposed.

Anna looked up, her mind centuries away and hardly listening "Neither were the Byzantines easily subdued, nor the Northern Europeans. This was world domination!" she said loudly "by a catholic priesthood!"

"Shhhhh…Ok…Anna, I'll read all about it, later!" said Amanda, leading her firmly by the elbow.

The priest was advancing towards them. The expression on his face gave Amanda cause to rush out.

"Anna. I want to go! Point out the tomb of King Charles and we are *done,* OK?" said Amanda.

"Sicily was left to the Aragonese" said Anna, absently, now standing in the narthex of the cathedral.

Amanda was no longer listening. She wanted out. Period.

"Charles' cousin Charles of Valois was to renounce the kingdom of Aragon for twenty thousand pounds of silver – he…evidently had a supply of coin minting. So that left Sicily as a Germanic territory…and the Valois region had never effectively been occupied."

"I have an Aunt and Uncle called deValois" spluttered Amanda "Anna are you *done?*"

Anna turned.

The Incense chalice came swinging from its pole to leave them standing in a cloud of white smoke.

Amanda felt claustrophobic and a sudden urge to re-orient herself.

She felt as if she was impulsively ducking a dangerous claymore. She needed air.

"*Come on!*" Amanda said to Anna. "I've heard enough. And I want to get out of here…!"

"I'm going to kill the sonofabitch!" blurted Anna shaking her fist at the sacred icon.

* *

"Tutti a tavola!" came the singsong invitation to eat.

The children came running from all corners of the vast garden that overlooked the sea of Anna's house.

Dora, Anna's daughter had a family of small children - friends for Sandra and Adam.

It was the cottage that Amanda loved most. The cottage sat on a ledge of rock just above the beach. There it had perched for almost a century, said Ernesto, Anna's husband. The place had been the home of his parents who remodeled it as a turn-of the-century nouveaux house, but the estate had been in the family for generations.

Whereas the main house was on top of the hill, now serving as a conservatory for its historic gardens; museum and visitors center, below it were the ancient waterside anchorages, now amenities of modern beach enjoyment for Anna and her husband. The children loved it.

Descending down to the sea, a pathway zigzagged down the cliff along stone platforms and flights of wooden steps, flanked by railing, tree plantings and view stations until finally reaching the original cedar- sided beach house, or bathhouse, complete with arched loggia and mosquito screened doors. It attached to a small side lodge of house comforts that bespoke if many happy gatherings.

Further down, in descending to the sandy beach was a small tack shack for horse riding excursions along the bay coastline, perhaps once for beasts of burden for ships at anchor.

At sea level almost was a cliff-carved marble basin and fountainhead debouching natural spring water, beside it a stone slab platform to process any sea catch of the day.

The sand was warm and firm to step on, having seen the tides of ages come and go. The beach was a bay, mountain promontories embracing it as if for secrecy from the world. With summer winds it had sheltered its players for centuries, perhaps swimming, sunning or collecting marvelous sea shells that washed in.

Along the cliff-face, only a single tree had taken root - finding seasonal sources of soil that offered little less than a year's worth of growth. Yet the saplings kept trying, bringing in birds of the sea that nested.

Where rock reached the water, old iron rings offered rope moorings for boat anchorage, serving fishing vessels. Larger vessels would doubtless stand off in deeper anchorage because the beach was shallow, high tide or low.

Sandra loved it. She found a bucket and shovel in the boat tackle, and began a digging campaign that left the beach looking like the habitat of prairie dogs. Mostly, she collected shells. She put them in her bucket and then filled the holes with them "So...der mommies can find them again..."she said, eyebrows knit together against the small striking breeze of sun and sea, fair curls in riot.

Adam was busy pulling at the iron rings to secure pirate ships.

Amanda was cooking breakfast on a stove not far beyond wood burning. But Amanda was thrilled. She rooted around in the kitchen for provisions and utensils, redolent with family memories, and the smell of bacon and egg permeated the tiny cottage by the sea.

She was in heaven, she said, pushing through the mosquito screened doors that squeaked in rusty protest. She lay breakfast tray on the porch table where Trevor was reading a newspaper and watching Sandra and Adam. She peered at him. The cottage had served his disposition well, she noticed. He was relaxed.

"Daddy!" yelled Adam, "I found a coin!" he said, holding up something.

"Log it in the record book!" Trevor returned from the hammock. "Make a note of where you found it!" he added,.

"...from the Barbary Coast Corsairs!" said Adam.

Trevor had to laugh. Adam was a scholar! Not just a coin, but a coin with a story to tell, he said, taking Amanda's hand and kissing it gently as she put down the food.

Ernesto had insisted on it. They were to stay with him and Anna until the Lady Vitoria finished with the repairs and plumbing in her house where they were staying…

Amanda asked about the beach house, and once they saw it, begged to be left there instead of the Guest quarters of the Main House.

Anna had it cleaned out the cobwebs for them, stocked it with basic supplies, and made it a family beach event for Trevor, Amanda, Adam and Sandra.

It was a long weekend, the bank holiday providing four full days for enjoyment.

Ernesto called. He had a plan.

He arranged for them to go fishing in a local dory vessel. They would catch sea bass and cook it over a fire that night on the beach, al fresco!

The fisherman that took them said was burly and muscular, a golden chain hanging from his neck.

He was normally an octopus catcher, he explained. He would dive deep, he said with his hands, to spot his prey on the bottom. And then proceeded to explain the wiggly scene on the bottom with marvelous gesticulation.

Only later did it come out that actually the Octopus was a shy creature with special defenses of camouflage. But as a fisherman, he got top money at the fish markets for his catch. People from all over asked for him especially: He was a man always booked for orders, he said. Go to any Restaurant with his wife... and he was on consignment from the Proprietor for a week's worth of calamari!

They laughed.

This week he was taking a break, he said. They had been asked to stop harvesting octopus, and in his broken English, he explained that that it was his desire to be always well informed about harvesting.

It came out that Laboratories in Europe discovered bacteria in the invertebrate's digestion column, mainly from the things they were eating, he explained. 'Amphipods' and 'copepods.' They were found to have suddenly too much chemo-autotrophic bacteria and hydrogen sulfide, a chemical highly toxic to most known organisms working through chemosynthesis.

Anyway, when *il Signore Ernesto* – who did most of the translating - asked him to entertain the house guests with a boat ride, he was pleased.

Today, the sea was a jeweled mystery of treasure.

Into the grottos they went, the water deep emerald in the shade, darker blue further in the caverns. Then with sunlight behind them and the tide turned, out came the Greek-colored aquamarine shadows of the sea. He pointed down to sea urchins; old anchors, and other obscurities lodged on the rocky bottom as they passed...

Adam and Trevor were going out again tomorrow, they announced.

Sandra was safely up at the house with Anna, thought Amanda thankfully. It was deeply intriguing, all this ocean going adventure...

But perhaps a little too much for young Sandra yet.

**

Four

The Fumarole lay deep within the heart of the fissure, its bubbles discounted as being within the band of the non-incidental.

The planet's sea floor was full of hydrothermal vents, natural features of the earth's crust that existed on many planets like Jupiter's moon Europa, and Mars.

Actually, it had only recently been noticed. Just 18 months ago. At 100m beneath the sea, it was little imaged yet. True, there had been subsea floor rift in the Mediterranean, shifting variably and in uneventful ways. But the nature of this fumarole was complex. It had sublevels of a highly saline character.

It's effluent had built up a ridge of deposits which obfuscated the vent itself. Being neither a black smoker, or a white smoker, it was invisible to the naked eye. Still, it was expelling 140°F brine effluent and delivering mealliferous muds.

Scientifically, it had been noted by two mining companies, Nautilus Minerals in partnership with Placer Dome, or Barrick Gold as it was now called, and Neptune Minerals. Both ventures discounted the substance as viable for yields for commercial returns. Plus its salinity was questionable. It did not warrant much markings on the chart.

Still, the saline character of this fumarole was puzzling. The vent was relentless in delivering its brine efflux, and the deposit created a steep ridge bench that grew to the size of a seafloor mound showing up as a 'shadow' on satellite imaging technologies.

When the shadow dispersed, it was thought that the ridge had simply re-dispersed itself along the bottom, the vent still finding its way to expiate its hot temperature effluent.

But the ridge had collapsed.

At the bottom of the sea, the movement was significant. It constituted a wave equal to tectonic creep, releasing its energy quite suddenly when the ridge collapsed. It generated a small impulse wave, displacing itself along the bottom and crawling along up to shallow waters.

It was unrecognized as a disturbance by highly sensitive instrumentation of the volcanologists along the coastlines.

The impulse wave was a less common result of hydrodynamic behavior. Almost like a lahar entering the sea, it was altered because of the small avalanches of its deposits, a lava bench displacing water. Once the waves coupled with atmospheric waves, they had fundamentally transformed themselves into a tsunami.

The danger, in human terms was the deadly nature of the kind of tsunami that would evolved. The height of tsunami waves heading for land were strongly influenced by the morphology of the coastline upon which they impinged.

** **

Sandra was sleepy and wanted her nap. So did Amanda. And by the evening sun of the third day, they were lost like the Swiss Family Robinson. Sandra had littered the porch with her tiny collections and piles. "For waiter… when…when Adam can come and see what I got…" she said, waving her arm in the air.

Amanda noticed that she hesitated less with her words when she was rested. And here she seemed to be in her element.

Anna periodically checked on them. As did Maria the maid. Trevor went up the house routinely to chat with Ernesto, found smoking after dinner by the veranda. Mostly they were left to themselves as they chatted about this - that or the other, Ernesto having retired from a long career at NATO.

It was on the fourth morning when it happened.

It was early - the air summer hot and humid. Adam was still asleep in the cottage hammock.

Sensing that their sojourn would soon end, both Trevor and Amanda took a stroll down the beach to herald a sparkling sea and fresh morning.

Sandra would not be left behind. Only this time, she added something else to her netted bag. A book about seashells: It would show the pictures that she saw last night on her mother's lap before bed. The shells she had, she said, were in the sea because they were in the book.

On the sand, Sandra ran out ahead of her parents, spotting one small exposed shape in the low tide that revealed itself. It was a large muscle.

Amanda turned to look back up at the cottage for any sign of Adam on the porch. Still sleeping!

Trevor followed Sandra.

A few feet away, in the wet surface beach sand, a shell larger than any other next appeared.

And beside it yet another.

Sandra was focused on her bucket and Trevor was catching up with her. She was squealing with delight at the things she was finding…

Trevor swooped her in the air with a big *hoopla* then set her down, running a few paces beyond. He turned and was squatted down, his pants rolled up for his bare feet, and he waited for her to reach him. "*Dis* … one" she was counting, "and *dis* one..and *dis* …and."

Trevor was watching her. Then looked beyond her. The bay was quiet really, not even any mate-calling. In fact it was strange, an eerie strange. Rising to full height and realizing with mounting incredulity, Trevor saw the landscape.

He and Amanda must have had the same sensation at the same instant. She stood, rooted to the spot.

No. Surely *not*…

Sandra was between them by a 100 feet or so, intent on her task.

Shells littered everywhere. Everywhere. They appeared suddenly, sitting on the sand.

The sea had recoiled.

That could mean only one thing. Trevor inhaled sharply and vaulted into action.

He swooped up Sandra and ran towards Amanda. "Run! Run! Run…."he screamed. "Up the cliff! Run Up! Up! Up!…."

It took Amanda a puzzled second to understand what was happening. The sea only drew back for one reason. A tidal tsunami was closing in their bay. They were exposed.

She calculated the strength of Trevor to run with Sandra, and together they aimed for a dead run towards the beach house.

That's when it became visible, just seconds later, in time for them to glance back. And even with Sandra now wailing, Trevor tugged her up the steps towards the cottage.

"Wait!" said Amanda, breathlessly following. "Stop!"

"No!" he said. Then he turned suddenly and delivered Sandra roughly into her arms with a fierce admonition "Keep climbing! Up! Up!...." and he was gone.

That's when it came upon Amanda that Trevor had no confidence in the strength of the oncoming rush of water. He had gone into the cottage to retrieve Adam, evidently still sleeping.

Amanda climbed the wooden flight of steps two at a time, Anna's voice now audible from the top of the cliff. She was pointing out to sea. Then with her hands beckoning them upwards…

Amanda looked down behind her. No Trevor. No Adam.

The rush of water that filled the bay entered with a Herculean roar and swamped the beach in an instant.

"Oh My God!" breathed Amanda, Sandra now wailing at the top of her lungs, her fierce grip in Amanda's hair.

Amanda paused only to breath, her lungs on fire for exertion. At the zigzag below them she hoped that Trevor was climbing the steps with Adam at his side. But she could not see.

Only way below she saw the wave that thundered against the cliff wall like a freight train. With leviathan swirling, the sea reached around the bay to re-gather itself into a thunderous assault that reached up the rock and tore the steps away from the cliff like matchsticks.

Up the cliff the water rose, tumbling upward against the rock and climbing up the cliff-side, absorbing anything manmade and tearing away in anger at the mountain that stood in its path.

Amanda, shrieking for Trevor, continued to climb. Higher! Higher! She puffed, Sandra screaming in her ear with fear and calling for Daddy.

Like splinters the wooden structures were dissipating into the water. Amanda turned another hairpin bend in her climb and saw down to the front of the cottage just beyond the reach of the gathering wave.

"Trevor!" she yelled.

It broke away, slowly at first, then crumbled like a clay castle, and the beach house was suddenly gone! Still she climbed, one last turn as she was at the top of the cliff, Anna's words of alarm now clear in the roar.

For the first time ever, Amanda felt fear like she had never felt it before. She felt almost certain that the sea had swept out Trevor and Adam before they could climb high enough to safety…Oh God!. She screamed, her hair soaking and Sandra now running blindly towards the house.

The wave was still climbing the cliff in surges and uplifting roots where it swirled into every crevice and drained out soil stratas. And just beyond its voracious reach was Trevor, pulling at Adam, the two of them loosing traction on slippery wood and broken railings giving way first to the mounting sea spray, then to the force of water coming in behind it.

"Oh My God!" yelled Amanda. "Trevor! Climb! Adam! Adam!"

Adam fell and Trevor almost lost his footing. Adam was clearly a victim of the sea had not Trevor stepped back into the advancing water and pulled at his shirt, heaving him up just enough for him to get a footing. Together they scrambled up the cliff in wretched fear of their lives.

They made it.

All of them sitting on the grass, panting. Exhausted. Relieved. And unbelieving.

It was several hours before they returned to normal. Most of the day was spent assuaging Anna and her household. But they had survived.

"I'm fine" repeated Amanda, all of them nursing blankets and drinks, now calm and tranquil inside the warm house. A sedative was administered to Sandra with a visit from the Pediatrician.

They were safe, at least. Thank God. No loss of life! But the damage was devastating. The cottage had gone.

An unbleached stain on the mountain side was all that remained of the cottage. On the beach, not so much as a plank was left. It had been swept out, as if nature had dwarfed the existence of man in one pass.

Everything manmade had been whirled out to sea. The iron mooring rings fastened to the Cliffside had been sucked away.

Nothing live had survived the wave, shrubs, topsoil, vines, trees hung from the cliff with their roots torn away.

Never had such an event been recorded by the family they declared, surveying the barren rockside.

Trevor gathered the family. He consoled them, comforting them all with assurances of a successful survival. He talked with his hosts, and they arrived at a plan, he, calming them of any self-recrimination. It was an act of nature, he remarked. Finally, as he started packing the car with whatever gear they had left up at the main House, Amanda felt sufficiently recovered to realize that they needed to be home now in Pozzuoli to complete their stay in Italy. Together, she and Trevor brought to bear all things necessary to take their leave from their hosts.

Trevor placed a slumbering Sandra on Amanda's lap. He hugged his son, and opened the rear door for him. Adam climbed in, quiet and afraid.

They drove home in silence, each with their thoughts to process their trauma.

They arrived after dark. A change of venue of sorts. The house in Pozzuoli was all lit up for them. There, several messages awaited them, as did the staff and hostess of the house.

A postcard from "Zio e Zia DeValois" lay in the mail. Distant relatives from her mother's family who had kept in touch over the years. They travelled a lot but had a vineyard estate not far from Marina di Carrera where they spent their winters.

It said simply *"Come Visit!"*

They settled in, coffee in the kitchen, the beds all turned down and the bath towels freshly laid out for all who wanted to clean.

Amanda thanked the hostess. Mainly, they needed rest and calm. Sandra had been mildly sedated by the physician, she explained. The trauma had taken its toll, and the child was sleeping.

All was well, assured Trevor, wanting to restore calm and peace. But it was hard to escape.

TV and news reports were everywhere blaring the incident as an Emergency Special Report. Government leaders assured viewers that calm had been restored. Police officials were interviewed. Media specialists and specialists explained the dynamics of the event, and the incident made for international news. In certain places of public exposure the damage was significant, imagery haunting and menacing as if showing what the sea could do.

Safely back in Pozzuoli, they had survived the ordeal privately and without public attention, all of them withdrawn, quiet, coping with the shock.

Trevor switched off the news.

The bay inundation at Anna's place was not mentioned. An isolated enclave owned by private citizens was largely unknown. Few knew of the tiny beach-hut perched halfway down the cliff. To circling overhead news channel helicopters, it went unnoticed.

But in their minds it was hard to reconcile. The good fortune that saved them was Trevor's quickness on the beach. Had it not been for Trevor's alertness to the condition developing and his strength that bought them just enough seconds to jump ahead of the tsunami, the family would have perished, if not there on the beach, certainly in the cottage!

The images swirled again in Amanda's thoughts. Adam, yanked from his bed by his father, the cliff steps falling away beneath them as they climbed, climbed, climbed before a thunderous roaring sea…

Barely had they escaped with their lives!

Trevor offered Amanda a scotch, but she declined, citing the children's need for her ministrations if they awoke during the night.

They sat in the front room, a lampshade their only lighting, contemplating the horrendous events of the day. Feeling suddenly overwhelmed, Amanda broke into tears. Trevor moved to sit beside her, and in the familiar surroundings of the quiet room, they gathered small measures of assurance, if only gradually.

What had happened? How?..

It was with some relief that Amanda sank into her bed that evening, knowing that they had survived a crisis that could have wiped out the family.

Amanda waited for Trevor to come to bed. She was intermittently dozing off…

Trevor had calls to make, he said. He would be up shortly. He had to call London..

Three of the messages, she noticed, had been written by the housekeeper.

"For Mr. Trevor, the message pad said. SUSAN."

She thought she heard Trevor say into the phone, the door had not quite closed behind him when he left the bedroom.

"God. I can only tell you how awful it was…"

Amanda slept, exhausted.

For days those words would surface in her consciousness.

"God. I can only tell you how awful it was…"

What was that about? OK. So he was talking privately to his many colleagues in London, of course.

But the message said SUSAN

"God. I can only tell you how awful it was…"

So, who was Susan?

** **

The Police were at the front door. The Lieutenant had a file that might identify the perpetrators. Could they please review them?

Trevor was preparing to leave town, Amanda and the children caught up in the arrangements of packing and the house was in a state of untidy disaster.

She invited them into the sitting room and asked Maria the maid to bring in a small service of coffee and tea for the lieutenant and his associates.

"Video camera shots from across the Street" said the lieutenant, pleased with the reconnaissance.

With the children out of the front room they sat and the images were laid out on the table before them.

Trevor and Amanda inspected them.

The photographs left them looking blank.

An assortment of blurred black and white images showed pedestrians moving about on a busy street. The picture was taken from above, and with little precision. Few faces could be clearly defined.

Trevor shook his head.

A second set of pictures came out showing the same crowd moving a few paces later. And another. None of the people in the images showed any alarm, just normal movements across a street and into shops.

For Trevor, there was little that registered anything remarkable.

Again he shook his head.

Trevor could find nothing here that resembled anyone he could point at. It was clearly frustrating. He looked up, his tired face finding little satisfaction to this exercise.

The Lieutenant was disappointed. After all, his appearance at their door with pictures looked so promising. The kind of evidence that would solicit praise from his superiors…

Try as they might, Amanda and Trevor could find nothing eventful in the images.

Nothing.

The Lieutenant persisted. Here might be someone responsible for his incarceration in the cellar? The bank was at least shut down…

The Lieutenant waited.

Amanda sensed that somehow, recognition was supposed to be the responsibility of his victims! "Here might be villains who stole treasure from the Banco di Tripoli" he said "all those precious items pictured here in Lobby on the Friday night - were now gone…And all stolen on the very weekend before Trevor was closed in the cellar!"

Trevor looked up, disliking the lieutenant's tone or suggestion. Amanda saw that he was beginning to show his impatience.

As Amanda procured first coffee, then brandy, she realized that this visit for the lieutenant was serving a purpose. It was helping the local police come to terms with what happened. Crime was something that was rarely solved in these parts of the country, she realized.

Today, with these images, they were at least they were doing something.

Finally, out came the last set of images with even less clarity. Another video from a traffic light intersection. More distant pedestrians crossing a street in the background. A background, presumably, that was in close proximity to the bank. *As if the thieves would wait at the light to be nicely photographed* thought Amanda.

She could sense Trevor's impatience. And when finally the meeting came to an end, Trevor explained that he was on his way to the Airport. He must return to London, he said. A situation had called him home early from the family vacation.

"Is there anything further that I could do to help?" he asked

The lieutenant looked at him gravely. "No. there is nothing further that we will need. We have your full report. And I'm glad we caught you before you departed Signore MacDonnell."

They left.

Amanda and Trevor took a moment. They considered nothing relevant in any of the photographs. And now Trevor was leaving them. The timing was bad.

Amanda felt disappointed.

"Daddy. Daddy…" said Sandra, bounding into the room. "Will you buy me a teddy?"

They resumed their packing.

Still, the timing was off. They had discussed the matter the night before. He must go, he said. Yes, *immediately*. Something important had come up!

Amanda could return to England at her leisure… when the children were finished at the summer school.

This visit with the Lieutenant had clearly delayed him. If not in terms of the clock but in ways of distraction from preparing for his trip. He had more calls to make…. Arrangements to confirm. Emails to answer.

Finally it was time for Trevor to leave. The phone would not stop ringing. Twice, the lieutenant called with a follow-up question.

Amanda had done all Trevor's personal packing, the housemaid helping. Finally, with all arrangements in order and the children buzzing about saying their goodbyes, the doorbell rang.

It was Yusef, Trevor's chauffeur.

"Good Afternoon Mrs. MacDonnell" he said. She hugged him. He had become a friend of the family. Good, wonderful chauffeur Yusef - now some years older, known to them since before they were married and now trusted friend of the children.

But clearly a personal escort for Trevor. Something was calling him home requiring special security.

That night Amanda lay alone in bed, puzzled.

Why did Trevor have to make his Exit so suddenly? What was it?

 The holiday was over, she understood. Still, he might have waited until the end of the week.

What was needing him with such urgency in London?

The English establishment were known to especially venerate family-time on vacation. And a vacation in Italy!

Amanda felt exhausted, and her nerves all out of patience. She lay on the bed, not fully prepared to go to sleep. She dozed off.

 When she got up, it was already dawn and the house was completely quiet. She took a shower, freshened up, and made coffee in the kitchen.

For September, the weather in Italy was glorious, a golden glow bathed the hot and dewy fields in luminous ruddiness, crickets everywhere adding to a full morning song. A yellow finch snatched a bug on the wing and settled n a vine trellis, its mate following.

Amanda strolled into the front room and picked up the images left by the Lieutenant. She held a second cup of coffee, her thoughts puzzled and distracted. But something began to agitate her, as if fiercely searching for something.

Suddenly she froze.

Something on the image had registered. It was met with horrific disbelief, even revulsion. But she could not avert her eyes.

There is was.

A figure on the Traffic Light Intersection image. How could she not remember that stoop, that neck-jutting chin posture? And those hanging arms, menacing, as if ready for action…

No. *Surely not!*

Walking, just walking away in the image with a dark cardinal's hat on and a large brown parcel wrapped in …*string?*

It was the way he carried it, under his arm. Just a view. A glanced moment as a black and white profile.

Yes?

No!

Her hand went to her mouth.

But for the fact that the man had a threatening demeanor when she first saw him.

She *knew him*! She recognized a man in the photos. It was the Priest. From the Cathedral.

Perhaps an innocent pedestrian… *Perhaps* just in the vicinity at the time of the bank heist.

Who should she call? Anna? Anna with her endless lecturing about Charles/Church/Cathedral – a séance that damned near got them both immured by the Hunchback of Notre Dame?

Yes. That was him!…

Or should she call Trevor, now half way to London?

Perhaps she was imagining things.

She would call the Lieutenant, she decided.

Yes.

Or not.

* *

"When will she be returning to class?" asked the teacher.

Ms. Prettyman was all smiles, even if she didn't like the woman. Still her position with the family gave her some license to speak for them.

"Little Sandra has had a rough time. Her parents are thoughtful and caring - the affair of surviving that incident at the beach was an ordeal."

The teacher was nodding.

"Sandra will be staying at home for at least another week or so with her mother before returning to pre-kindergarten."

"Adam?" asked Naatisha Suti.

"Well, he's the *bravest*!" smiled Prettyman. "He is very sociable. He wants to come back to school on Monday. And we think that might be alright. Mrs. MacDonnell has spoken with the Principle, and he concurs. Above all, Adam wants to be in the Summer Play, and missing another week might set him behind rather..."

Naatisha Suti smiled. "Of course, I understand"

As Prettyman left the school premises, she did not see the grey Mercedes across the street. It followed her slowly for a block, taking her image on multiple frames.

If Naatisha Suti planned well, this family would pay a handsome ransom! She would wait for the little one to return. Now *there* was a ripe one...

These days, Europe was full of rich families. Black market brokers didn't much care how their goods were acquired. It didn't much matter what services or human trafficking was being traded. Commodities were taken routinely. Smuggling was smuggling. At sea, on land, in private ways or public. The boundaries were endless.

There were opportunities *everywhere!*

* *

The Lieutenant couldn't quite believe it. Here, in his tiny office – more like a hallway Entry really, sat one of the most beautiful European women he had ever laid eyes on. And his boss the Superintendent was out!

So, the task lay before him.

"You are sure Signora?" he asked politely in his best police academy training voice

"Absolutely!" said Amanda Wells, pointing to the figure in the photograph. "When you first brought these photographs to us…we were still…well, getting over the beach disaster?"

"Oh Santo Dio!" he said "How can such a thing happen…And on *our* coast?"

"Yes!" she remarked.

"But you all are *ok*, the family, all the bambini? Si?…" he gesticulated.

Then he turned to the image, now preparing for business.

At last!

"So" he said soberly, pulling up his chair now. "You say you know this man?"

"Not exactly. But I *recognize* this man!"

He looked at her, as if inspecting her gravity.

"You see. It's hard to believe, and I say this with every respect. Out of deference for his position...." she hesitated.

He looked down at the photograph. "Si? Dove?"

"This man here...resembles the Priest from the Cathedral of Naples!"

"Come *'e*?" he asked again, looking aimlessly.

"This man. See here...*This* man, no. Yes! This one. He is the Priest from the Cathedral of Naples" she repeated.

He pressed the image between his fingers to look. His eyes searched closely, his head down as if his gaze could burn through the image.

He had stopped breathing, it seemed.

"*Impossibile!*" he rasped, glancing up.

But he did not see her. He did not really look up at her. For to look at her would be acknowledge that she was right somehow.

"Ma Non! Non!" he said, nodding his head.

Amanda sat quietly, waiting. But as the seconds became minutes, she realized something had happened here.

She was a little confused. He should have been pleased that she could identify someone. He should have ...

He was angry!

Mad a hell, in fact.

It occurred to her then that she had forced him into a contradiction in terms. How could he reconcile a *priest* in an image meant for a *criminal investigation?*

"Perhaps..." said Amanda, feeling that she had put him in a corner "...it's just a coincidence that he was....walking about at the time? Innocently?"

"Sì! …Innocente! *Certamente!*" he concluded, smiling hardly, harshly.

There was no resolution here, she realized. He was hostile. Somehow she had threatened him.

It didn't take long, her retreat from his office which she managed with as much grace as she could, suggesting that perhaps she was mistaken…

Outside she walked. She wanted air. Amanda felt alone. Frustrated.

Well that was a waste of time, she thought.

Innocente, my ass!

Still, she had the courtesy to stray no further into his cultural assumptions about priests in high places. She had done her duty. The rest of the deductions were *his* to make. Not hers.

She went home, a taxi ride though the coastal town was what she needed just now. It would gave her a chance to adjust.

She sat quietly, her nerves settling down.

She saw passing structures. She noticed bougainvillea draping from most balconies; roses peeping over the parapets and wild daisy at every stone crack. This was Italy at its most glorious. She took a deep breath.

They were going to be fine, she decided.

 It was hazy in the ocean glaze, and even if the sea had terrified them momentarily, the hospitality of the quaint Italian town brought nothing but love and longing to the heart.

Still, a small breath caught in her throat. *If only Trevor were with her…*

She disembarked at the bottom of the street.

Walking helped. It was a steep hill, and she was almost out of breath when she realized that the day had been long, the stress of multiple harrowing days. But neither had they been easy for anyone.

She made a decision. She would have an early lunch, then take a short nap.

Her next stop was at Anna's place to bolster the morale of her friend.

 Repeatedly, and with much distress, Anna was distraught. It was her fault, she said.

Anna was not in good health. Twice the doctor had had to visit her.

Finally Amanda persuaded her to come to come home with Amanda, and together with La Signora Vitoria, they would play Canasta on the Veranda, Sandra with them. A nice way to pass the afternoon together!

But as Amanda and Anna discovered, La Signora was beside herself. La Signora was still whining and explaining, her carapace hands rising to her face in disbelief and the headscarf falling off her graying hair that the workmen were leaving and it was a disaster. "Non va bene…"

 "What is it?" asked Amanda in English.

Anna went inside the house then reappeared. She looked at Amanda, her face in conflict between the beautiful dreamy world they lived, and the reality that faced her.

Along the perimeter of the floor tiles of the Maid's bathroom was a soft smoldering mold stain, as if the workers had just freshly covered it over in repairs.

The workmen claimed they had completed their task. They had poured lots of plaster, they said. And now they were leaving!

As they surveyed the damage, there realized that this was more complicated.

Amanda stared at the fissures. The others continued talking, one to assuage the other, each probing for a contractor's solutions. This was the foundation delivering a fetid and rancid odor of sulfur.

Amanda knew that this was a problem that would not easily be masked, and that it would be a matter of months before any solution rendered the place hospitable for human habitation.

This was a seeping acid from somewhere beneath the earth.

That night Amanda tossed about for hours.

Things were not going well. She had to make changes.

She decided she would arrange to visit Zio and Zia DeValois up the coastline. It would take some planning, but the summer was drawing to a close. And what might have been a two day visit would now be a two week stay with them.

* *

The silver face altered.

It might have blinked, rotating from the dark shadows into a sudden glint of sunlight before it turned purple, reddish and then blue cold steel again. Colors reflecting from the stained glass fenestration of the Cathedral gave the statue organic features as it rotated in its supernatural state.

And it was on the move again, doling out its blessings for the second time in the year for a citywide procession.

The town was enjoying the merry state of a religious Parade.

They wailed, the women in a row beneath the bust of St. Januarius. Historically they represented *parenti di San Gennaro.*

 More symbolically, they held the vial of blood that rested in their charge since the beginning of time. In ecstatic prayer they were to penetrated the veil of mystery to Absolutism. They pleaded for the blood of the holy Saint inside the vial to liquefy and assure safety from Vesuvius. That was their cherished prayer.

Outside, waiting in anticipation for the parade to commence, market stalls buffed up their festive wares. And Carabinieri polished trumpet, saxophone and drum to march in the parade.

A betting spree had begin. Who would come first out in the procession? The Saint Januarius, or the bust of the Holy Teresa? Lucia? Patricia? The excitement was palpable.

Youths were sent into the Cathedral by the bookies collecting money. They were to catch a glimpse of the processional sequence of Saints and spy for the betters.

The fever and festivity was growing in pitch.

At the Great Alter the incantation of prayers by the parenti di San Gennaro called for the miracle of blood liquefaction within the holy ampoule.

Spectators and visitors attending the feast cheered. Many of them University students in great humor. What was now the provenance of humanism had once been the medieval rite of redemption from the fires of the great volcano Vesuvius.

Saint Gennaro, it was told, was an early bishop of Benevento. He was martyred during the persecution of early Christians, beheaded by Diocletian, in 305 AD. Legend had it that the village women - in sacred anguish - kept a touch of the martyr's blood in an ampoule after he died.

Eight years later, a miracle occurred when the Saint's skeleton and the ampoule were brought to Naples. The blood liquefied. And every year since then, it did so again to assure the safety of Naples. When it did not, the city was in danger. Vesuvius erupted to bury them.

The skeleton had been placed to rest in the catacomb together with the ampoule where it had remained through the centuries of rebuilding. Straying never far from the original chapel of the 4th century. Today, it was the Cathedral of Naples. The bells rang out. Naples was safe… The Blood had liquefied.

A frenzy followed the procession now emerging.

Those pressing for bets surged, and those pressing to kiss the sacred vial also converged on the Cathedral. The silver face icon was first in line and resplendent in robes.

Many presented the Saint with their wishes of love and wellbeing. Above all, Vesuvius would remain calm because the blood in the ampoule had liquefied.

Everyone cheered.

Politicians wearing red sashes followed the clergy swinging incense goblets.

Behind them, prayers echoed through a megaphone, offered by the Cardinal as poll-bearers led out the saints.

With the bells still ringing, Saints borne on platforms and bedecked in gold, silver, jewels, and relics, the procession would thread its way around the town. Many would follow in festive frivolity. Here was the joy of spiritual affirmation. Today, love would seize the hearts of the sensible and lay cares of the world to the wind. The merry procession of the Saints, escorted by the triumphant Carabinieri, would splinter and be led through the city in various place. Spaccanapoli especially, then back to their repository at the Cathedral until the next bi-annual ceremony. Finally, the crowd subdued. A long weekend was to follow for a four day summer bank holiday. One platform made its way to the side street to bless the Via del Banco di Tripoli, it's platform well draped and beautifully decorated for the crowd. Everywhere the streets were festooned with garlands and streamers. More cheers and blessings. And the festivities would fill the restaurants with dinners and the streets with students, most of them non-believers. But all of them enthusiastic about the ritual nonetheless. It brought vibrancy to tradition, most said. And it brought money. Finally, the last of the Ferries departing for Capri and Ischia were leaving. And there, on the slopes of Mount Vesuvius all could rest quiet for another night.

Nobody would ever find out what happened here.

** *

The phone rang.

The Lieutenant's voice was distant and disconsolate. They had found the treasure of the Banco di Tripoli, he announced. Yes. It was all recovered...

"Really?" Amanda said in jubilant banter.

He had called to thank her for her information identification lead. But he went on to say that the collection was discovered sotto-terra in the cavernous foundation works of the Cathedral of Naples!

"Oh?"

Of course he was besides himself with relief, he said, the conclusions being many and too inconclusive just now. Vaguely along the concept of misunderstandings, you understand. But his Supervisor had insisted he find the courtesy to call il Signore and la Signora MacDonald to thank them for their observations...

"No problem" said Amanda on the telephone. "I am glad we could help!"

She closed her eyes, gratefully. Thank God...She was only too glad to wrap up this affair and leave the area. .

But what she heard next floored her. Because what *should* have been an affirmation of her suspicions was now turning into a mild threat *not to* interfere in local affairs of the community!

More.

"When was la Signora leaving?" he asked.

Amanda raised her hand to push back her hair, puzzling through the change of tone, and was about to recite a date and time plan to answer his question. But since she was in the process of formulating the details, she wasn't exactly sure yet. She suddenly felt that this question was inappropriate and peevish on the Lieutenant's part. She told him she wasn't sure yet, and ended the conversation.

It had miffed her a little.

Bloody hell, you'd think the Italians would be grateful for an ID. After all, Trevor had been holed up in that bank vault for the night because of the heist…And instead of expressing relief at finding resolution, they were *defensive!*

No wonder the Brits and the Italians had a prickly relationship.

She raced upstairs barefoot.

But on the other hand, she realized, to have something happen right under your nose and the culprit discovered by a *foreigner* was embarrassing for the locals.

She pulled at some boxes, earlier set aside.

Why? If is solved things?

Then she stopped suddenly.

Because in this case, the person in the picture that she had identified *did* put them on the trail of a person-of-interest: A priest on the staff of the Archbishop's offices, no less!

Directly connected to the Cathedral.

No.

That could not have been the Lieutenants brightest hour…And her waltzing into his office like that.

* *

Anna was fine, she said, and taking a nap for the afternoon. The telephone conversation said little else.

So Amanda went alone.

How she agreed to show up was beyond her.

She wore jeans, cork heels, a silk blouse and lightweight blazer. Comfortable… but in a jacket? Suitable? Yes. No!

She was no longer assured.

 In fact, she was tiring of the whole sojourn and wanted to get home.

Wrap it all up, she decided.

She closed the door behind her.

Trevor was gone and the children were in school for the day.

 Anna too busy to accompany her, and she had a note delivered to the home where she stayed…she had little choice but to accept. She went alone.

She would play tourist she decided, until the host arrived. Surely he would introduce himself.

The Archbishop's Palace was directly across from the Cathedral. That is, the Cathedral that had been commissioned by King Charles II of Anjou *-how could she forget those exhaustive details from Anna that afternoon about his father.*

She looked up.

As she stood there, she realized that for such a structure to be constructed it must have taken generations!

Further, Amanda noted with growing respect, even before continuing with the building of the Cathedral, Charles' son, that is, Charles II had to fight for every inch of his title!

She had to laugh as she imagined the event for a young adult: When finally declared king, he was still a prisoner! Even when released, he had to leave three of his sons and sixty Provencal nobles as hostages. Plus he had to repay 30,000 marks and return a prisoner if the conditions were not fulfilled within *three years*.

That's a high standard even by Wall Street today, she chuckled.

She looked around quietly and without Anna ringing in her ears. Painful years they must have been for the man who built this Cathedral.

Anyway, she was waiting. So far, he had not shown himself.

> *"Charles II went to Rieti where the new Pope Nicholas IV quickly absolved him from all the conditions he had sworn to observe as a prisoner and crowned him King of Sicily. It was 1289"*
> *Amanda looked up. This allowed the Pope to summarily excommunicating King Alfonso III of Aragon and leave another Charles of Valois in alliance with Castile — a man able to take Aragon and reopen the Aragonese Crusade!*

Valois was her Uncle's name. Zio and Zia in Carrera, with the Vineyard... What fun!

Anna had written notes with cute annotations.

"Now the Popes of the Holy Roman Catholic Church were on a course for dominion: Alfonso, being hard pressed by his awful excommunication. He agreed to the conditions of the Treaty of Tarascan.

"The terms of his negotiations were these: He promised to withdraw the troops he had sent to help his brother James in Sicily. He had to renounced all rights over the island. And he had to pay hither forth a never-ending tribute to the Holy See!"

Amanda now understood the growing power of the Church for the era.

"Alfonso died (childless) in 1291 before the treaty could be ratified and James his brother took possession of Aragon anyway, leaving the government of Sicily to the third brother Frederick.."

Anna added a picture of Frederick III of Sicily.

"Next, the new Pope Boniface VIII, (elected in 1294 at Naples under the auspices of King Charles II) mediated between him and James".

"They signed a Treaty of Anagni and agreed that James was to marry Charles's daughter, Bianca, known as Blanch of Anjou."

Amanda put her hand to her mouth. In this paper, Anna was evidently having a little fun. *It was an underhanded deal,* was in the margin.

"More importantly, he was given investiture by the pope of Sardinia and Corsica. And he was to leave the Angevins a free hand in Sicily"

Amanda was getting a little lost here. She put the paper away, thinking. Then looked up at the towering columns.

Well, his loan paid off…Must have been the coveted carrying trades and sea ports from the Orient and Arabia, teeming wealth and a means of conquest and dominion with no end in sight…
No wonder he built this Cathedral for the Popes and Archbishops of the Catholic Church!
Her thoughts were wandering.

Suddenly the realities of her circumstances threatened to engulf her. She looked around. *How naive had she been?* A man who had threatened them, a man she *identified* in the picture, and the subsequent *recovery* of the Banco treasures…
It was altogether too dangerous to be alone!
Jesus. What was she thinking?
Stupid, she muttered in the dark shadows of the crypt. She looked up and took a big breath.
Above all else, Amanda Wells was an historian. This, Anna must have seen. And as Amanda stood contemplating the artwork of masters held forward by Charles I and his son - both of whom had infused the medieval world with learning, she felt a draw to approach with a little more respect. There was something about this that could speak through its art. Rather, whose art was it? Did have vague vestiges of another…Or another culture?
It *was* wonderful to behold!
She inspected the workmanship. Stone carvings and effigies. Flying buttresswork. Filigree carvings. Mosaics. Floral decorative motifs. Crenellated pinions. Stained glass. Sculptured vestments.. How impossibly real it was - all those centuries ago, to carve life from stone marble.

Then it occurred to her suddenly. These kings had used the skills and talent of Jewish people in trades!. Of course…

In fact, that the real question that had drawn her to this place: Where did *Judas* fit into all this? Oh sure, he was occasionally depicted in the imagery designated the Holy Roman Catholic messaging of its autocratic theology. But there was more here that they just could not hide to the trained eye of historians.

The Jewish influence! Of course, it was *everywhere*…

In addition to Jewish scholars of the time…much of their culture was so intermingled as to advance the intellect of Europe at the turn of the first millennium. There was even the University of Salerno and Naples - employing translators: Men like Moses of Palermo – a man familiar with ancient classical Arab texts, no less.

That's what Anna had said. They had translated tons and dozens of medical treatises and practices were translated into Latin.

Much of it handed down from the Arab world.

So while beating off Popes and their voracious interests; deploying for conquest and dominion; the Charles' group *allowed* for Jewish scholars and tradesmen to shape their holy world!

Wow, she thought.

This then, was the nexus of ever expanding knowledge base. Here they had accumulated philosophical thinking and inculcated their ways into central Europeanism - appropriating classical antiquity and contemporary Muslim culture into pre-Renaissance Europe!

She was standing on the epi-center of the Medieval world. Right here, at the turn of the first millennium! If she were an MBA graduate, she would call this a mission to centralize and control the world…

She almost laughed out loud.

Except that, well…Not that she was much of a doctrinal thinker, but didn't Jesus of Nazareth advocate *individualism* to behold only one deity?

It puzzled her. She wandered a little.

What was all this decorative institutional centralizing, then?

Sure, the concept of acquiring cultural value and assimilation was neither new, nor pretty: 'Assimilation," routinely conducted by conquering warriors, had been the tradition for centuries.

But here the lines of identification were allowed to name their *originators*. Not entirely, and not without a good stroke of the world of Charles.

Still, he could not obscure occasional glimmers of *individuality*, as if the divine did encourage human excellence.

It was a masterful work of genius mixed with human individualism and Church *ambition!*

What an expression!

And to imagine the song of adulation rising through these choristers. The height and breadth of this Cathedral fairly took her breath away: It must have been awe inspiring.

The last of the choir was filing out, and those who sat at various aisles also left. At the great entrance doors, they walked out into the sunlight, their laughter lingering over the noise of an airplane overhead.

Amanda looked down at her watch. Oh what the hell, he isn't showing up.

She would call it all off. She would call Anna later...

She got up and side-stepped down the rest of her pew; nodded her head briefly to the alter for respect, and turned to walk out the Church.

By the time she looked back up the aisle, all entrance daylight had darkened, the great doors had sealed. The temperature dropped suddenly, and the air chilled.

* *

At school, the children were rapt. Adam was a donkey. Puck made him look amorous to Titania. *Mid-Summer's Night Dream* was going to be fun, the play Director told them.

Tomorrow, the entire cast was to come in costume for the final dress rehearsal. Then, just one more performance practice for the choir to coordinate with the play in song, and that was it. He smiled at them proudly.

They were jiggling with excitement.

At the School office, administrative details remained, arrangement underway. The school theater would be filled with parents: Ushers were laid on. Four school play performances in all.

The first performance was on Thursday at 5.00 PM for the school faculty, staff; board of Trustees and select officials of the NATO School.

Then Friday night's performance held enough seating for the actor's friends and family.

The Saturday evening performance was to follow a formal fundraising event on the premises of the school, and Sunday's matinee was open to the community wanting to see the school play with their children.

Adam was excited beyond measure that day. And while Ms Prettyman was busy collecting Sandra, he told this all to the child's teacher, Naatisha Suti

"Does your sister come to the play?"

"Yes. She's coming on the Sunday matinee, with Mommy and Miss Prettyman. And she will bring little friends…"

"How lovely!" said the African American.

** **

The voice from the shadows was clear, yet grave as a statue. It stepped into life from within a monk's cowl and robe. "Ms. Wells!"

Amanda jumped and turned suddenly, her hand cupping a small cry from her lips. How long had he been watching her?

It was the Priest alright. "Oh…Scuzi…" he said, repentantly, now lowering his cowl.

She would have liked to deliver a right jab into his monk's cowl for scaring her half to death. *Is that all the Italians ever do…say Scuzi?*

But one glimpse into his dark reddened eyes, and she saw a man deeply distressed.

She managed a smile, if pale and uncomfortable. After all, she did agree to meet him…*What was she thinking?*

He thanked her profusely for responding to his request, speaking only in Italian.

He had something to show her, he had said. "Please…*per favore?*" he offered direction, si? To approach and see, and follow him. "*Nel*

Palazzo…"he explained, turning down a circular stone stairway behind the holy enclave of the sacraments.

A barred elevator, evidently.

She followed.

And down they went, he leading the way, and she wondering why she hadn't told Anna where she was going to be for the afternoon.

After all, how bad could things get in a Cathedral?

They got out and turned down another flight of steps.

Very bad.

Evidently, as they passed through an underground passage where decorative plaster ended and cavernous arched stonework became their only overhead bulwark, they were entering deep infrastructure.

She tried to project the above ground spaces.

They were under the square *largo Donna Regina,* somewhere north of the foundation pillars of the Cathedral of Naples. Perhaps facing the church of the Donna Rgina Nuova. This was a vast and connected complex beneath ground, he said suddenly.

He talked, as a tour guide "…the original structure was been built in 1389 for a cardinal called Errico Capece Minutolo on the site of an earlier structure - the oldest Christian basilica" They moved deeper underground. "The building today" he pointing upward "is an expansion modernized under Scanio Filomarino in the middle of the 17th century" .

Amanda knew the period well, an era when the great naval expansionism and trade routes brought great wealth to the Holy Roman Empire.

"Il construzione…" he went on, leading her through the underground tunnels "il lavoro di Architetto Bonaventuri Presti" He paused "Per gli uffici della Chiesa…" *affairs of the Church*, was the euphemism he used, when it fact it was the extraordinary construction of the Archbishop's Palace.

Abruptly he stopped and pulled from his voluminous robes keys to a gate that guarded a room of granite blocks and encasements.

 It was an endless room, like a library, compartments in temperature controlled glass walls, an elongated shape that marked the perimeter of the Church structure with heavy foundation supporting columns for the three stone portals above ground.

He stopped at three different technology screens and encoded his entry. Then he turned, faced her, and simply folded his hands.

"You came in trust" he said, quietly. "And in trust I now come to you with materials that only the most sacred know about"

He waited for her response.

Amanda did not like caves. Closed security spaces. Or unknown priests. Let alone palavering with topics in which she had no business palavering.

But the answer was in her eyes. She was an historian. Someone he had decided to trust…

And time, he said, was not on his side! Just like that. Again he folded his hands and waited, giving her a chance to process the situation.

He was about to unfold something to her of some value. And whatever else she thought about him, it had come at a cost. A cost whose time had evidently arrived.

So she took a big breath, and waited for him to speak.

"I am the thief!" he said in perfect English.

* *

Trevor was barely disembarked from the plane when the car appeared on the tarmac, turbines still tearing wind across the landscape.

He seemed to hunch up his shoulders.

Two men got out and one went up to the plane to greet him.

They were in dark business suits. When the second man approached, they shook hands and all three walked back to the waiting car where Yusef, his chauffeur, held the door open for him.

In the thunder of engines, Trevor's hair was blowing wildly. He turned to the first man who gave him a brief case and envelope, and took from the second another file, folders and reading materials, all flapping. Trevor stopped and ducked down to address someone seated in the car.

 "I only want to talk about Susan"

"Of course!" came the response. "Everything is in readiness. A chopper will be waiting for you, Sir"

"Welcome back!" said Yusef.

"Thank you Yusef" said Trevor. "It's good to be going home!" Yusef stepped back.

Trevor paused, then turned to speak quietly to him. "Your mission here is as important to me as anything else. Please remember that Yusef. Do *not* engage! Stay under the radar. Let nobody know what you find… but me."

"Understood Sir"

**

"I denuded the Banco di Tripoli of all its precious possessions during the procession of St. Janaurius!" he said. .

Neither training in the academic world where scientific enquiry often defied belief, nor being a dignified married woman could erase the surprise on Amanda's face.

She could hardly register what he just said. And where he not deadly serious, the man might have laughed, perhaps. But he was not laughing. .

"You…err…*Stole*…?"

"Yes. You were right to identify me to the police!" Amanda took a step back.

Oh boy. *Oh boy… Damn.* It was getting hot.

She should have seen this coming: The ol' trick of every college campus newbie. 'Lure them below decks, sic 'em with the facts that *can't* be found and tell the campus about how-smart-they-be!' She knew a joke when she saw one. And dumbbell that she was, she'd walked right into it…*Dumb*!

So. Now wait for the real punch behind the joke.

"And you brought me here…to…?"

"Explain!" he said simply, pointing to a silver bust sitting on its platform. "Here is the good St Januarius – with his blood, which as you know is iron chloride found naturally in volcanic ground, mixed calcium carbonate and salt producing a solid substance which looks dried blood…" He lifted the glass encased ampoule and shook it violently "But if you shake it, it turns to liquid. Hence saving Naples from Vesuvius!"

"What… are you implying?" said Amanda, still not past the bust of St. Januarius' sitting down here instead of up in the Cathedral.

"The original…" he said, reading her thoughts "it is kept down here. Up there… is a replica"

"Oh" she nodded. *Of course.*

"And here… the original texts of Nostradamus and… St. James and… St. Judas and St…"

She followed him down an aisle of relics, manuscripts, parchments, rolled, encased, sleeved, labeled and wrapped.

"This, the Apocrypha"

"*The…?*"

Over here, he called, walking passed more collections, his voice deeper with physical effort.

"Jesus!" she uttered breathlessly without thought.

"Oh Yes. We *do* have a few letters of his own hand… by the way!"

She gulped. With the Catholic Church collecting relics and prized documents down through the centuries, anything was possible.

"Allow me to remind you that we have some of the original texts and writings collected by the Angevin Kings Charles I and his son…This was his seat, remember, and he it was that commissioned the buildings and repositories to honor the bishops and the Holy Roman Catholic Church…"

"*Here?…*"

"Yes. And why not? He is buried here! Why not keep him with his collections and contributions to humanity? Does not the Vatican have imagination too?" he asked, challenging her with the imponderable.

Sure, and the Egyptians believed in the afterlife too, she wanted to say, but didn't.

Anyway, nothing else mattered right now. Except for the delivery of the real punch behind the joke. She waited.

"You are probably wondering why I brought you here…" he paused, surveying her face with unblinking eyes.

She waited.

"Ecco!" he said triumphantly, pulling out a rolled parchment and luring it out of its casing. He unrolled a segment. She read the first few lines. It was the Epistle of Paul the Apostle to the Romans. Not nicely segmented in verses, but simply a manuscript, written like a letter, in a scroll. "Before we closed the cannon of the Bible" he grinned. He turned the first segment along its role. "Read this part" he said.

"For the invisible things of him from the creation of the world are clearly seen, being understood by the things that are made, even his eternal power and Godhead; so that they are without excuse:"

He rolled it up without patience once she finished those famous words. Words that would define Christianity for two millennium.

"Now come. We talk!" he said, delivering his marching orders.

She followed him partway down the hall to a small seating alcove. But they both stopped suddenly, the ground shaking beneath them.

They waited. Twice the movement returned, then ceased. The only disturbance was to small particles of dust. And the plaster from the ceiling dropped some chalky substance, like powder.

He had paused and held back a shelve. Smiling almost, like the plumbing had to be tolerated or something. But she noticed that at the back of his neck, a glistening moisture had developed. And by the time they sat down, he had to remove his eyeglasses and wipe them clear of perspiration.

The man was nervous. Or he was on a mission. And the urgency soon became clear.

"When I heard you would be in the area, I had to stage an event that would get your attention"

Amanda stared at him. *All you had to do was call,* she wanted to say.

"You see. It's not that easy…this dilemma. And only someone of your integrity and understanding could accommodate what I have to do!"

At this point, she was wondering if he had the Holy Grail down here too.

"It's…the Administration of the Church, you see. And we are about to lose it all…" he said, pulling out a large handkerchief to wipe his brow now.

"It's this damn place" he shot out, showing no respect. "They don't want to upgrade it…And..And…"

He was in turmoil.

"You see, when I saw you and your friend making a tour of the Cathedral, I knew that I was running out of time. I eavesdropped into your lives - found a way to get your attention.." he looked down "I hope that after I have explained everything, you will forgive me. And understand what I am doing…"

This didn't look good, decided Amanda.

* *

"Being a good medievalist academic, you would know that the language of religion is the language of politics. It shaped modern society" he said, looking at her directly..

" I *did* study Religious History…yes!" she smiled.

"No! I mean did you study *Theology?*" he asked.

Whatever remained of a smile was lost. God! This was *not* going to be easy…She cleared her throat. "Well. Alright. The study of theology does mean the study of God. The study of Religion does mean the study of a secular world understanding of religion not as a belief, but as a cultural system…"

"Va bene! And those words…eh…what you just read"

"They reflect the doctrine of Reform Theology. Def…" he came closer, his chin jutting out. She found her voice again "Definition for the Reform movement challenging the Holy Roman Catholic Church!"

He stepped back.

"Yes!" he said. "If Erasmus challenged the stomach of the church, it was Luther who challenged the doctrine of the Church: And to understand and interpret the very nature of God, Luther used the basic assertion made by Paul to explain him…in those words that you read!"

"They were an effort, in a long road, to centralize the faith of the biblical Christian on the First

Understanding of what God was when he made his very first Covenant with his Chosen Children. Man being in the *Image* of God, etc. etc. " recited Amanda.

"Yes. Because you see, every other religious doctrine posed a different image to worship, like what Joshua discovered in the Assembly singing for the praise of a Golden Calf..."

"So. Paul got it right in his Epistle to the Romans?" she asked, indulging him.

"Oh Absolutely! And the Lutherans did very good to challenge the Catholic Church...I say that as a scholar of course, not a Catholic priest you understand?"

"Yes. Of course"

"Except for one thing. St. Paul wrote Manuals!"

"What?"

"Manuals! How-to-books on how to be a Christian!"

Amanda nearly laughed. That's if all this was even laughable. Here she was in a crypt with a Catholic Priest who was hell bent and determined to argue the Truth of Gospels....Here? Now? Why?

He got up abruptly, grabbed St. Januarius' blood ampoule and shook. "Like this blood. Paul was a good Conjuring trickster!"

"I don't understand. Why would you say that?" she asked.

"I have all the evidence here...But we are about to be buried by Vesuvius!"

"What?" she said, alarmed

"And we will lose the truth *forever*! Bad enough that we kept the Truth hidden in this Vault for over a millennium. But that we should lose the evidence to a volcanic eruption that would make it ever unknown…is *unpardonable*" he squealed, now standing up in his fervor.

Amanda was still absorbing the part of being buried by Vesuvius. And frankly, she wanted to flee. She had had enough with this religious zealot, let alone rescuing the Truth for the World.

Her eyes went to the door. Or rather the gate. They were locked in.

"I see you want to go!" he said, the keys firmly in his pocket.

Oh God, she thought, her head spinning. Definitely not good.

* *

The minutes passed with heavy hands.

"Why is this so important?" he whispered suddenly. "Why must we save this evidence?" he asked again, pacing. "What was it that *so* mattered? Huh?"

He came closer. "It was the conquering of the heart, the mind, the power of the people by being a God, like the pagan gods of the Greeks, the Romans, the Egyptians…

"What is a theology that will bring the world to its knees?

"If you think of it in pagan terms, whereas death was a great enslaver, any man who could marginalize death was a theocrat worthy of a kingdom! And if a theocrat, like a Roman leader who was worshiped as a God.

"Add the elements of pagan justice…If a culture could embrace the sacrificial token of *One* that paid the ransom for the *many*, then it would survive as a doctrine!

"Such was the deity image in the ancient world of man-gods and territorial Emperors! This gave them supreme dominion in money, with deification, trade, influence and power over people, life and death!"

He paused, then peering at her said quietly "Christ was a powerful image. Yes?"

She nodded.

"This the Church knew! As did Paul…

"So the Holy Catholic Church of the first millennium closed the Cannon of the Bible to include the Letters of Paul – *as he saw it* – to inform their own ambitions: A Christian Image of God for the Catholic Order of *dominance*."

He walked about the room, looking down, perhaps choosing his words.

"But…when *Luther* came along in his Reform Theology, he challenged the veracity of the Catholic Church and *its meanings of what was the True God…*"

"What are you implying?" interrupted Amanda. "That God is all made up…?"

"Mmm…" he said, walking about with his finger held to his lips. "Clever girl!" he whispered.

"No!" Amanda held up her hand "We've had agnostics and atheists since the beginning…" she said, stepping back for space "Look. *I* have my Faith. *You* have your Faith. *We all* have our Faith…We make our choices."

"Mmm" he said, bowing his head. "So let me ask you this. What were the prevalent resources of the middle ages? Midwifery was what…the provenance of witches? What was the median age of mortality during that era?"

She looked at him carefully. Was he off the wall?

"Trade!" he laughed. "Trade meant the difference between success and failure. Survival? The Crusades? The Wars of the Angevin kings? How do you think Christianity was evangelized?"

"Well..." he said, answering his own question "The Romans understood this. And Paul....was a *Roman*!"

"So?"

"You see, Paul's letter was the First and Original citation that defined what the True Theology of God was!"

"And?"

"And it *wasn't what the Church had embraced!*" He moved close to a wall of metal shelves and placed both hands against it. "Trouble is, how many died in the process of fighting religious wars?"

Ok, she decided. Maybe he wasn't half mad.

That meant that she had to be mad. Sitting here listening to a half monk under the Cathedral re-examining his own convictions if not those of the early Church...At this point, she didn't much care which Church. If only she could get out of here!

She picked up her bag. He turned.

"Oh! I do apologize. I should not hold you here!"

She smiled gratefully.

He opened the door. "that Letter from Paul had an enclosure for another person within Paul's camp with the Romans. Read it! At the time it was to be read separately. It once had a seal...We keep it here in our secure repository. It came to this site from a third century monastery when there was only a

Basilica on this site. Then it travelled. Then it came back here. Yes. It is authenticated."

"I err…I couldn't possibly take it off the premises…" her thoughts flew to security and insurance amongst other issues. Holding a precious antiquity was a serious matter these days.

"No. No! You take it! Read it, please! Then you can return it to me in the Chancery Office in a few days!"

He looked at her. "Of, if you prefer…you have a safekeeping repository waiting for you to open…in…err… Roma?"

Anything to get out of here. "Yes" she said, and returned it to its sleeve, then put it in her bag.

Safely out the Vaults, back through the passages and up into the Cathedral again Amanda finally turned to him and asked "What is it you need me to examine and find, exactly?"

Surely the guy had a reason for all this…

"If the eruption of the Vesuvius buries us, it needs to be put in a safer place. This is a matter of history for the faithful to know the theology of Paul…" He looked tired and confused.

"You mean the theology of God?" she corrected helpfully.

"No. I mean the Theology of Paul that the Church chose to hide and recalculate for its own purpose.."

He entered the barred elevator and closed the gate.

"You see, Miss Amanda, it was Paul who wanted to be the King. He was a Herodian!"

Down he went.

** **

Anna called. Trevor called. The school called. And Santori called.

She answered the school first.

They wanted to confirm her seating arrangements for the Sunday matinee of the school play: Did she need any additional seats? Where would she like to sit? Could they place a Valet at the parking lot to escort her to her seat?

The play was to last well over an hour and a half. Then, after a generous Intermission for an Open-House tour, the new Faculty rooms would be on display.

She thanked them profusely. Their attention to detail was superlative, she assured them. And Adam was thrilled with his role. She and little Sandra were looking forward to see Mid Summer's Night Dream. Sandra might bring a friend or two. They understood.

Was there anything else that they could do?

Amanda thought a second and said yes, there was something more. Could they add to her donation account for a delivery by the Florist to give flowers for the performers?

"But of course" said the Administrator. "An added measure of elegance for the children's play"

and commerce for the local flower shop.

But in Amanda's view, for a youngster in a play, it was a small touch that might add to the experience, something that could stay with them all their life as they performed other challenges.

Next call was to Trevor. Unavailable. She would try later.

Finally it came down to Anna. "You'll never believe who I spent the afternoon with…" began Amanda. Anna came up with a few colorful suggestions as to who might be available in Naples…but never mind, she chuckled. So. Who?

"Guess!" insisted Amanda, and then she told her.

"That cretin!" yelled Anna "he's marginal sane, you know, but all heart they say"

Amanda gave Anna a fairly complete picture, if not the details. What transpired was stuff that would annoy her, she decided. So she said it more like a tour. Public relations like.

Anna explained that she and Ernesto were having the beach cottage rebuilt. The rudiments of the platform was now in place, but only for workmen.

They laughed, Amanda oticing that she was now reconciled with a natural disaster that "could not have been averted"

Still, Anna tired easily. And Amanda knew not to prolong the discussion.

"So, I send Mario over on Sunday for the Matinee with the two children, and you all enjoy the play. Then he drive you all back to my place for lunch, yes?"

"Yes, thank you!"

Amanda smiled. For someone who could hold forth for an hour and half in the Cathedral without coming up for air was pretty passionate stuff for a woman like Anna. Even if would take a little time for Anna to bounce back.

Amanda replaced the phone on its cradle.

Later that day, after a card game of Canasta on the porch with Signora Vittorina, she informed their hostess of her plans to leave at the end of the week.

"S'accommodo!" said the landlady. Trevor was a generous patrone for the Penzione, she said her two fingers cinched to gesture abundance. "Un gracie …per il Signore…che a pagato tutto in avanza!"

Amanda sent a message to have transportation available on Sunday for the play - to and from the School.

Prettyman was having the long weekend off in advance: She would return by Sunday for their school play, and help with the children.

After Adam came home that afternoon, he went out in the garden to make a mud pool of sorts, from the goldfish pond. Less than an hour later, Sandra came howling onto the porch.

Amanda swooped her up and popped her on her lap.

Adam came up to explain. Sandra could not play with him because she did not look after her chickens properly.

Disconsolate, Sandra had decided to change his mind. She had entered the chicken coop and sat on the eggs like a hen.

Amanda looked down under her frock.

The eggs had broken all over her lacy pants and were now dribbling down the back of Sandra's legs.

Sandra looked up at her mother, weeping and choking in horror.

Just then, the phone rang. "El Signore Trevor" announced Maria. Amanda looked down at Sandra's crestfallen face.

"Adam!" she called. "Speak to Daddy please!"

Amanda turned back to Sandra. She held the child tightly, and together clasped, Sandra stopped her wailing.

Sandra would make a perfect Mummy one day Amanda told her. A piece of broken eggshell was plucked from her tiny sock.

* *

It was already 9.00 AM Sunday morning and Prettyman had not yet showed up.

Nancy Prettyman, having been a flight attendant with a Medical degree surely understood advance planning and efficiency like no other. Yet today of all days, there was no sign of her at the house. Clearly, she would not be coming to the Matinee.

Amanda knocked on the door to her quarters. It had its own separate entrance from the main house. No answer. She opened up and walked in.

Inside the room of light pine and windows Amanda noticed that all was in order. Like a clean hotel room.

Amanda wondered about the undisturbed bed.

She was about to turn away when she hesitated. Could there be any sign as to her whereabouts? Even women had their ways of leaving clues when grooming…

Amanda walked into the bathroom and found nothing. She turned into the bedroom and opened the closet. It was empty. The drawers, cleared out.

How could this be?

In the trash there was little. Except for a tiny receipt. It was from an ATM machine showing a substantial withdrawal of cash.

This surprised Amanda. Not the cash amount withdrawn. After all, Trevor amply remunerated Prettyman with cash. Plus, she had a discretionary expense account when she had the children. No. What shocked Amanda was the amount of available balance left in the account at the bottom of the receipt.

Zero.

Amanda stood there a minute. When did people draw down their account to zero? Usually that showed intent of something. Or perhaps financial distress. God! Had she missed something? Was Nancy struggling with issues – and Amanda never even noticed?

 She pulled a cell phone and made a call. It was a recording. She left a message:

"Hello Nancy. It's Sunday morning and I see that you are, well, not here …"

You've let me down is what she wanted to say. Instead she cleared her throat and said in a soft but professional manner "I am sorry that you couldn't tell me about your plans…" Amanda looked up. "But that's ok. Just wondering. And err…I do expect to hear from you soon!"

Amanda was about to hang up. But she added "I hope you're alright Nancy, and that nothing is wrong. Let me know how you're doing, and how I can help if at all. We do care. So, please, please …*call*, ok?"

Amanda was about to walk out when a flash of metal on the floor between the desk and the sideboard caught her attention.

It was a computer stick drive for digital transfer of data from one computer port to another. Small and easily lost, it was something that people hated losing. Especially when setting up their desktop paraphernalia. Into her pocket it went to be returned to Nancy.

But as Amanda walked back to the house, she had the distinct feeling that Prettyman had left the premises. Quit even. Without notice.

Why? It wasn't Nancy's style to leave without an explanation at least. Even if difficult.

And she felt suddenly abandoned.

Ok, she breathed. Think. Regroup your planning!

The plans for the day progressed so fast that she was rushing. The car would be here in an hour to pick her up.

Maria, the landlady's daughter would take Adam directly to the school on her way to church in order to get him there early. It was the last performance, she told the recalcitrant boy. Yes, he was a superb actor. A hero of the play. But he had to be early nonetheless for make-up and costume.

Amanda was busy, if puzzled by Adam's irritability. Sandra's friends were coming along to the play. Anna's two grand-nieces, Dorothea and Alexandra were the same age. All of them afterwards returning to Anna's for a picnic.

"So pack for jeans!" is the way Anna said it, knowing that the day would be stressful with so many children about.

 And damned if Amanda didn't load two backpacks with towels, swimsuits, hats, toys and snacks and gifts.

Next, she would get dressed.

Amanda must have walked through the lobby at least three times rushing about before she noticed the blinking light on the central phone of the house that had a message.

It was short. And it was Trevor.

"Don't return to the premises!" was all it said.

She must have played it four times over.

Amanda stood there.

What?

By now most of the house was empty. Sandra came running through dangling her straw hat and trailing ribbons which the cat pounced. At least the child was ready and dressed.

There were few times when Amanda heard Trevor speak like that. She knew enough to understand the sounds of alarm in his voice.

Get Out! Trevor was telling her. No mistake.

How should she respond exactly?

In a sudden lurch back to basics, Amanda jumped into gear. *Stupid perhaps, but better safe than sorry.*

She grabbed the two backpacks and ran upstairs with them.

She threw out the towels, toys and beach trinkets and replaced them with extra jackets, jumpers and in a clean sweep of critical items. She flung opened the safe, took out a wad of money, grabbed passports, papers, banking documents and everything else stashed in the safe.

Out the door they flew. Just like that. But Mario the driver was alone in the car.

Anna called. The children, apparently, were a disastrous mess today. In no condition to be taken out to a play! Then with a sigh of despair at her daughter's management , Anna added "I've had it with them!"

They were a tight family of survivors, Amanda knew.

Mario at least did show up as promised. And off to the school they went for the Matinee, as planned.

Amanda was smart enough not to trip any alarms. She dressed predictably for appearances.

She stood there with her daughter at her side wearing a plumed Vivien Sheriff hat over a jacquard coat and dress. Prada heels and a Mulberry bag gave her a polished look. She had an image to maintain for the children, even if Trevor was not with her.

They loved her at the school. Parents, faculty and board members come forward to greet her.

Adam worked his way through the crowd and met her, his face coated in brown patches and wild green cuttings as headdress for the play. Sandra pointed and giggled.

But his eyes said it all "Mummy…" he began. "We have to go…" he said simply.

Definitely his father's son, thought Amanda. The boy had talked to his Dad. Clearly, there were instructions for him to follow.

Amanda didn't argue. She leveled her eyes "After the play?"

"During the …the…Intermission" he said, his troubled expression searching for words to say, and words not to say. "I have an…an…Understudy…I told Harry that he… that he… he would have to be in the play today. See there, his daddy is here…" he said, he face flushed.

Amanda nodded with understanding and touched his shoulder to steady her son's nervousness.

She looked up and smiled handsomely at other arriving guests. But then finessed her seating to the rear, adjacent to the hallway – not far from the entrance.

She sat, patiently. Sandra too. A steady force for Adam to observe from his quarters backstage.

And she guessed correctly.

There were many people backstage.

From the curtains on the stage another pair of eyes spotted her seated in the rear of the hall. Eyes that had been watching Adam's every move; noting now where his mother sat. And watching carefully the child beside her, Sandra.

Satisfied with the progression of things, Naatisha Sui made her call.

Outside, the grey Mercedes edged closer to the building of the school entrance. It moved around the corner and parked at the side exit of the faculty rooms.

The woman moved to the refreshments table, her cocktail ready to pour into someone's lemonade.

* *

As Anna's driver, Mario was determined to make himself useful for the event as an extension of his employer's hospitality.

He brought the car around the East entrance of the school building, and parked just beyond the playground.

He waited.

The building was all under construction, paid entirely by generous donations from happy parents

.

In the West wings of the school building, the theater, library, gym and new faculty rooms had been added recently. Masonry sand, cinderblocks and boards still dotted the construction area. But the complex of the premises was large. And being Sunday, the only Visitor's activity was related to the School Play Matinee Performance.

Their exit strategy had been well executed. Amanda had been agile about it all.

It happened during the Intermission, when the lights came up and all the audience stood up and applauded. They were all to proceed to the newly built Faculty Wing for a general viewing of the new construction before returning to their seats for the second half of the play, with refreshments on the break.

Adam had came up to his mother standing in the procession of parents making their way to view the new faculty rooms. He told her he had switched places with Harry. So he stood beside his mother, dressed normally, as the crowd propelled them slowly forward, approaching the entranceway that brought them into the auditorium.

A sudden need to go to the bathroom by Sandra — induced by Adam with a swift kick to her shinbone that sent her howling into her mother's skirt — and they ducked out of the crowd and down the entrance hallway into a side bathroom. Large windows easily let them out to the side Veranda.

Amanda, Adam and Sandra had climbed out of the bathroom window; walked the perimeter of the terrazzo, then ducked breezily across the low rail to the play yard.

When they reached the granite steps that marked the main school entrance, they ascended to the columned verandas.

From there they followed the porches that wrapped around the South end of the main building, and finally down a ramp that led to grade level on the East. Beyond the landscaped hedges, they reached the car.

Amanda had left Sandra's straw hat deliberately on their seat to suggest their return. And Adam had exchanged his laurel leaf head-dress with Harry so that the two heads in the fray of young actors could not be distinguished.

Amanda switched off her cell phone, and left it in the building.

By the time the Intermission ended and the second half of the play resumed, Mario had driven them half way out the city. Sandra had fallen asleep. Adam was quiet.

As the city gave way to la Campania, and Amanda stared out the open window, a warm wind offering silent assurance, she felt certain that she had escaped disaster with her two children.

So did Adam. That morning was a terrifying experience.

Evidently, he gathered materials fallen from the teacher's case when it opened up on the floor, and he went pale. He saw a file with his picture in it. Photographs of him at home; at the park in another shot. One, with his sister, his mother.

It was his sister, however, who was clearly the target. Her little image wearing the straw hat and ribbons was ringed with a large red marker, clearly for identification purposes.

All this he told his mother in the car.

She put her arm around him and thanked him for his diligence. He was distraught, she could see. But he had done what he was supposed to do.

Later, he told her that he knew what to do. He was told what to do.

"By whom?" she asked, curious.

"Daddy!" he grinned "When he talked to me on the telephone!"

God, thought Amanda closing her eyes. They had just averted a high-priced kidnapping!

How could Trevor have known in advance? Who was warning them? Was Trevor *unable* to reach her?

If so, she was on her own now.

"I kicked Sandra, didn't I?" Adam said after a while. He looked up at his mother.

She nodded.

 "I didn't mean to…" he said, then looked out the window "I am sorry" he said, finally.

She squeezed his arm. "You did good for us today Adam, Thank you!"

Yes, she decided. She was entirely on her own. The safety of her children was in her hands. And they were in danger. This she knew, instinctively. Travelling across Europe was difficult enough at best. But as a family on the run, it was frightening. Europe was an angry place to be in, right now.

Much depended upon where you stood, and when. Trevor's message, through Adam, was warning enough.

Mario had sensed their urgency evidently. He did not ask questions. But any friend of the family he served was his responsibility to aide. He only had to be told once to get out of the city. *Quickly!*

They flew up the road northbound, cars travelling with abandon.

What was happening to them? Amanda gazed out the open window, her thoughts flailing in the wind as if chased by Saint Seans' Egyptian.

Where to now? How to land safely on her feet with the children - away from Naples - so suddenly with so little preparation!

She thought of Prettyman. *Where was she?*

She thought of her last call to Trevor who was becoming increasingly *unavailable* to her. And then there was that lurking unanswered question. Who was Susan...

But the idea of having a child kidnapped was too awful to contemplate. It was altogether exhausting. Thank God a quick re-packing of their gear was possible! In it was a comfortable change of clothes for them all. Plus a few warm undies and pajamas. Plus, in her haste, all the contents of the Safe.

Finally Mario pulled over. He turned to look at her. "Mario.." she began, unsure of how to give her next instructions. Her chin came up, and she was about to speak. But her breath caught in her throat and her fiercely intense eyes became moist and uncertain.

The Italian people had been often mocked for their effusiveness. But they were good readers of the heart.

He looked down at his watch and with a steady gaze said simply "Would La Signora like for me to take the family to... *Roma?*" .

She looked at him. It was all she could do to nod.

He understood. He turned politely back to his driving and was in search of a gas station, he said to Adam, calmly.

A tear dropped to her lap, and Amanda dried her eyes.

In silence they drove for miles. It gave her a chance to clear her thinking. She must regroup.

When finally a green road-sign indicated Rome was ahead, she asked Mario to find a Ristorante for them all to stop and rest.

He agreed, and spotted a place less than four kilometers ahead - with an open area for eating augiardin. It would give them all an opportunity to stretch and refresh themselves.

* *

Five

Amanda would need to gather her things, some strewn in the car with her, some in the trunk of the car.

She wanted to reach for her cell phone, she felt lost without it, disconnected and isolated.

Amanda had left her phone on the school premises so that they could not be traced. But like a piece of jewelry, it felt missing, more like a confessional that contained her social contacts and deeply held sentiments, and it felt like more of as a loss than any valuable.

But at least she and the family were safe.

So get a grip!

She worried about the whereabouts of Prettyman. Had she received her message? At least she had tried to do something helpful, and she had left a message. Live every day as if it were the last, her mother once told her, so if you have something to say to someone, like I-love-you, *don't wait!*

She sighed. Now she was getting silly. Or maybe just tired.

Then there was Anna, and she was worried. How was she doing? Anna had a house full of family for a week. That was the best thing for her! Anna worked in linear progressions, one intense experience at a time. Anna would be fine, she decided.

The real anxiety that was lurking beneath her skin was beginning to surface, and she waved off her hair.

More road signs for Rome. Mario was approaching his stop for a Restaurant.

Her thoughts went back to the final moments before leaving the house. It was the morning of the school play, and they were rushing about to leave.

Still, the call she got from the Lieutenant was most disturbing. It was a pedantic phone call, as if he were *measuring* her responses. She remembered thinking that there was something menacing about his tone. What was her intuition telling her? *Why?*

She thought about it. What had he said exactly?

Yes. He had told her that they had recovered the stolen goods from the Banco di Tripoli.

Well, that is…it appeared they recovered *most* of the missing inventory. Si.

La Signora, as he addressed her, had given them a "lead" with the photograph when she identified the Priest…of course! Si! But he called her identification an "aviso".

No more New York Police jargon now, she observed.

He was driving at something.

Evidently, there had been a *misunderstanding*, is what he had said. Some kind of private *arrangement* with the Bank officials that had been made apparently, all of whom were unknowns.

He lingered on the topic. How had he phrased it? A *longstanding trust* that had evolved between the Banco and the Cathedral of Naples lending out exhibits, *discuzione di fudicia*. Meaning, prior assumptions and tacit understandings between them.

Amanda remembered being a little surprised at this new revelation since the investigation had turned up nothing until he met with the Church. But she said nothing.

It had crossed her mind that this might be a cover-up? No. The Lieutenant was not finished. She remembered how he proceeded. "Except for *one* thing" he had said, purposefully.

His tone was deliberative and he was taking his time. There was something curious that Priest had added.

A *Text*, of some sort. A scroll of religious importance to the ancient doctrines of the Church… from ancient Rome.

Somehow, the priest had explained, he did not have it with him! That, plus and a few other items, perhaps that Amanda might shed light on?

Amanda listened intently. No, she had said. There was nothing else she could remember.

"Perche…" continued the Lieutenant, when he asked the Priest about the nature of object that was missing, he said he had no idea. Again, only that it was a Sacred Artifact… A treasure of the State. And it was part of the whole collection from the Banco di Tripoli.

He waited.

"Oh" said Amanda, transfixed.

He was chewing gum. And she could hear him breathing as he waited for her response.

What did want?

How could she have explained to him that weird and creepy encounter beneath the crypt of the Cathedral in the Collections Room with the Priest? How to explain all this with the truth…

No. The Lieutenant was chewing, enjoying toying with a mouse. Because he was still toying with her.

"How should I know' the Priest said to me?" repeated the Lieutenant.

Amanda played it cool. She let out a chortle and tried to sound casual and relaxed.

"What was it he referring to?" she had asked.

Amanda was caught off stride. Her hair was all fixed up for an exotic hat pin and Sandra was heading out the front door in a muslin frock.

The Lieutenant did not answer immediately.

"'Ask la Signora' said the Priest to me. She has it!" said the Lieutenant.

Amanda's thoughts jumbled, rushing. What was he implying? What just happened there?

She had thanked him and quickly ended the telephone conversation.

Within minutes she flew out the house as the car pulled up.

She has it

He had dropped a small bomb. The Lieutenant knew exactly what he was doing: It was payback for embroiling him in a nasty little local affair.

Of course none of this made any sense to her. Until now.

She has it

The implication was clear. She was accused of stealing the sacred text foisted upon her by the Priest!

The duplicity of what had transpired between them appalled her. There was no way that she could explain the circumstances of how she was given the text. Her credibility, when weighed against the words of a Priest would be considered tenuous at best.

She was angry.

She walked to the trunk of the car at the Ristorante, opened her knapsack and froze. There was the *Epistle of Paul to the Romans.*

She stared at it.

It had been placed in the Security Vault of the house. And because of her sudden change of plans *not* to return to the house, she had emptied the Safe of all valuables and put them into the backpack before leaving.

She has it

A breeze rushed upon them, tossing her hair into her face. Yes, she did have it.

She straightened up. If it weren't so serious, she would have laughed. Or cry. She felt almost overwhelmed by the turmoil of the past few days.

"Are you ok Mum?" asked Adam.

"Yes" she said, smiling lamely.

Regaining her resolve she added "I'm ok. We're going to be fine. All of us!" and she gathered a distracted Sandra to her side.

Resolutely she took Paul's Epistle in her bag and walked into the Restaurant.

They ate spaghetti and meatballs, followed by tiramisu and cappuccino with biscotti.

Mario was a good companion after all. He sat with them and entertained them with stories about Roma. He laughed with the children and Sandra was all giggles and tickles.

A few times the Italian Polizia, *Carrabinieri,* came buzzing by, and Amanda's elbow clutched her bag a little closer.

This was absurd! *Bloody man, that Lieutenant!*

She was getting angry.

But by the second cup of coffee, she had relaxed sufficiently to make a plan.

She explained to Mario that she and the children would make their way north to visit family in Marina di Carrara. Zia e Zio diValois. But that she would take a day or two in Rome first. Could he leave her near the Central Train station? She was familiar with a lovely little Penzione there, she assured him.

Mario was happy to oblige. But later that afternoon, as he pulled away from the train station, Amanda was getting nervous.

Was Rome full of busy Carabinieri, or was she counting too many sirens? Either way, it felt scary. Having the Epistle of St. Paul under her arm as an unauthorized possession of Roman antiquity was not good.

Sacred Artifact was the way the bastard described it, as if to emphasize the severity of the infraction…

Amanda understood the penalties for absconding with a national treasure. They were serious. She almost panicked, considering her professional standing as an Antiquities Specialist!

The police, she decided, where decidedly after her now. How to hide from the obvious? *God! What was she doing?*

"Now children…" she announced with a calm grin "We are going to take a tour of the City, like tourists!"

Mercifully, and just in time, a horse carriage for tourists came trotting by.

They had several ours before the Penzione would admit them for a fresh room: So this would be a convenient time-passing promenade through Rome. No one would search a horse and buggy for a theft.

After dark, they would spend the night at the Penzione near the train station. Then leave first thing in the morning.

The sun was soon to set. It was hard to remain unmoved.

The sheer force of Rome as a city was too much to ignore. Its history spanned two and half thousand years. It was capital to the Roman Kingdom; the Republic and the Empire, a model of Western Civilization. It's lands defined the character of the Mediterranean sea from the first century BC to the 7th century AD, having been the Seat of the Papacy and Byzantine Empires before becoming the center of all Papal states. Only later did become the capital city of Italy. This she explained to the children.

If Sandra was entirely preoccupied with the two beautiful greys trotting ahead, Adam was captivated.

The Italian Renaissance moved to Rome from Florence in the 15th century. Here, the Papacy created churches, bridges, town squares and public spaces, she explained.

She pointed out Saint Peter's Basilica, the Sistine Chapel, Pone Sisto, and Piazza Navona.

Adam was told of artists like Michelangelo, Perugino Raphael, Ghirlandaio, Luca Signorelli, Botticelli, and Rossellini. And somehow, her enthusiasm was contagious.

It was fun, trotting through the streets.

Clip, clop.

Some passengers came on, some got off. But they all became friendly.

Clip, clop…

One lady, who discovered that this was also the place of conflict during the Reformation that took from the Popes a large part of their authority at the Council of Trent mentioned that here were the precepts of the Protestant movement.

"I'm from Georgia" she said. "An Episcopalian"

Finally, the carriage passed the Tiber River one more time, and they got off at the door of their Penzione near the Rail Termini. From there Amanda knew they would surely be able to get to their next destination. And without being noticed.

They dismounted, thanked the Groom and Amanda realized how exhausted they all were. Sandra was getting cranky, and Adam glad to be at the end of the day.

To go to the vault or not to go to the vault? That was the question that plagued her. She had maybe two days left before the password changed. Who else knew that?

It was the designated repository for the original Judas manuscript from Turkey lodged at the Bank.

What was it that Hadid *implied?*

There was no way to tell for sure. She could be walking into an unknown.

What if the vault contained only that which she had put into it? Thus, checkout would leave her standing there alone...

Yet Hadid urged her to move on?

Why?

Whom did he so distrust? He didn't say.

She looked out at the soft yellowing landscape under a setting sun. The sun and terra here turned everything a golden dusty haze at dusk, like the field color of a fresco painting, as it had for so many centuries.

Hadid didn't have to say whom he distrusted. *The priest in Naples did!*

He wanted her accessing that vault for the Judas manuscript - suggesting that it might equally serve as a good place to leave the *Epistle of Paul* scroll which he had given her.

Why?

No! Definitively. She was sure. The priest *wanted* her to go to that vault...He *intended* for her to go!

If she had walked in and claimed what? They would inspect her bag. Of course!

Why?

The answer came to her.

By impugning her professional credibility, the Judas Manuscript would be disbarred from her management and sub vent once again into the margins of history for the Holy Roman Catholic Church.

No wonder Bob James was so averse to religious fervor. It took the academic objectivity out of the historical perspective!

Then again, Shirley did warn her of the dangers associated with antiquities…

For her to be accused of stealing *the Epistle of Paul scroll*, a manuscript which, because of its absence from Naples, could be construed as purloined or illegally transported, even somehow manipulated, was sufficient to damage her reputation!

She could explain that she no longer had the Judas Manuscript.

… Why return to the vacant vault unless you had dishonest intentions, they could ask…

Either way, it would cause an enquiry.

Again, it would sub vent the Judas manuscript from public view…

Hadid *had* implied danger, perhaps pointing to a path to futility.

Yes, she decided. They had laid a trap! She should *not* go to the vault.

Clearly, they were waiting.

Someone did not want that manuscript to see the light of day.

All she had to do now was find a way to dispose of the damned *Epistle of Paul* scroll foisted on her by the Priest.

How to do that in a professional manner?

They did get an early start. And just as well. As the train pulled out, the station was populating with Carabinieri.

Amanda had to stay calm. She got up and closed the blinds besides them in their compartment. . This, the children had not to see.

* *

London

The room was dark.

A table-spread desk screen with touch digital options splayed before them in the gloom. Surrounded by digital wall screens reflecting different milieus and different discussion groups, they had reviewed data for hours.

Seated on comfortable swivel office chairs, and listening to the brief on the overhead monitor delivered by a team of experts, the scientists were making their assessments.

"We have amongst us the greatest talent pool of knowledge related to this event" said the Director, pausing. "But we are clueless!" he said, a favorite expression of the learned.

It was a soft approach.

"And that's the good news!"

He shuffled through a few notes.

"Here is what we know. And please understand that any effort to mitigate this impact is naïve at best, stupid at worst. So, be patient as we proceed with our presentation!"

"There are a number of hypothesis. We should examine each one carefully. The first to address is a Super-Volcanic Eruption."

They shifted through Notes to the data sheet.

"In scientific terms, a super volcano eruption with an ejecta greater than 1,000 cubic kilometers (240 cubic miles) is almost indefinable in terms of our quantifying.

"Generally thought to be about a thousand times greater than normal eruptions. This is because the magma has risen to the earth's crust from a hotspot but cannot break through, and creates a pressure buildup like a large lake. It blows the crust off the earth like a sunspot eruption. There are several known "super volcanoes" sitting beneath the earth's surface. Here is the standard map used by most scientists: Yellowstone, Long Valley, Valles Caldera, Lake Toba…etc."

He paused.

"The basis for our studies cover some favorite sites for analysis because history has been kind to reveal some of its secrets. These sites include this, the Phlegraean Fields.

"In this chart, we see Campi Flegrei, (from the ancient word, if my Power Point software will show. It is generally acknowledged as being a caldera some 13 kilometers (8.1 mi) wide, and comprising of some 24 craters and volcanic edifices beneath the sea. There is evidence of a gas crater, featured by the phenomenon also at the boreholes left by marine mollusks. There, the sea level has varied, we know…

"This you all know from the Report."

He waited.

"There are two major threats. The one in the mechanism of the "super volcano." This is a volcanic type within large igneous provinces and massive eruptions. Here's the picture" his monitored pointed to something labelled the LIP.

"Of the First kind, such as Iceland, the Siberian Traps, Deccan Traps, and the Ontong Java Plateau are extensive regions of basalts on a continental scale resulting from flood basalt eruptions.

"But the Second Eruption - with a VEI 8 - are colossal events that throw out at least 1,000 km^3 Dense Rock Equivalent (DRE) of ejecta; VEI-7 events eject at least 100 km^3 (DRE). Such eruptions are so vast that they create circular calderas , not cones because the downward withdrawal of magma causes the overlying mass to collapse and fill the voided magma chamber beneath like an emptying of the lake."

He paused " Any questions?"

Trevor dialed in: "The scenario of any pending disaster that worries you most is ….?"

"The *Phlegraean Fields*…not because of the natural disaster and eruption, which will wipe out most of Italy and Europe as we know it, but the consequences to the planet…"

The room fell strangely silent.

"Worst case scenario?" The speaker drank some water "This results in an immediate global ice age. And…" he paused "I'm sorry to say it…perhaps an Extinction Event."

Some whispered, others muttered. The room fairly took a break to absorb the momentum of his words. Gradually the collective mumble settled down to silence in gloomy foreboding. .

"When should we expect this?" asked Trevor, as incredulous as the question sounded, and only as he could ask it.

"Well…it depends…" He lapsed.

"How long?" repeated Trevor

"It's not as if we have accuracy for history…"

"Outside maybe 17 years or less…Or…"

Trevor got up and walked about. This was almost too much to absorb. He sat down again.

"Continue" he said.

"It could be…imminent. Even 17 years would not allow sufficient time for precautionary planning … Scientists feel that an ice age may, repeat may — recover over a few decades such as that induced by the Toba eruption."

They waited.

"Naturally, these numbers will differ in today's global population. Plus there is some scientific evidence, from tools found in the Southern Indian Ocean region above and below a thick layer of ash from the Toba eruption that show the eruption *did not* wipe out a local population of people…Or so it is suggested in the record…"

"In other words, *whoever* was there …seems to have survived the eruption. This we need to examine as to why and how."

He sat down, finding this a good place to leave the discussion. And the room fell silent.

Trevor stood up. "So…what is the *Strategic Planning and Conditional Expectation* recommended?'

The answer, which he had been prepared for came easily enough, if without details. A unanimous decision was expected amongst the panel of scientists.

Sustainable Underground Survival Analysis Network: SUSAN.

Trevor stood there, and said nothing, waiting.

They started debating, and the discussion was not without some stress. Finally Trevor had to ask

"Where does that leave England?"

The discussions continued. Today, he knew, there would be no consensus of option.

He adjourned the meeting.

The crowd thinned, then dissipated in distracted fashion.

"Thank God" said Sir Reynolds as they passed outside the room "that this is only a drill!"

"Right" said Trevor.

With his hand combing through his hair, he exited quietly, other things on his mind. Like his family stranded somewhere in Europe.

Trevor received the message from his Assitant. It was in code, suggesting a matter that he already knew. He called in.

Apparently, there was a breach of security. The message was being routed through NATO, a dangerous place to have spies. Amanda his wife had become a "Person of Interest" to foreign interests. Amanda was being followed, her life in danger.

Ernesto had warned him. "Amanda and the children need to be safely secured Trevor"

Trevor could not respond. To respond to Amanda was to close the tracking loop for any potential perpetuators.

Trevor's meeting of scientists was being held under the tightest security as a matter of national defense. Trevor picked opened his cell and dialed the Americans. They would know.

The trick was to uncover the motive before unveiling the intelligence link.

Who were the foreign interests?

** **

They were moving north, and with some privacy.
A train was transporting them in relative comfort.
Bathrooms. Gelato and a coffee bar. In fact, a full
dining car if they needed it.
So far, Amanda had managed to keep things on an
even keel. A tourist stop in Rome; a scheduled visit
to Zio and Zia DeValois up north…And the train
ride to get them there.
Never mind that they foiled a full scale abduction
event. Or that the police were after her for theft of
a seminal scripture of some valuation…*Nor* the
terror of a tsunami on the beaches of the bay…
She was beginning to wonder how much more
stress she was supposed to handle before foaming
at the mouth.
Come to think of it, was there any connection to all
this?
Ok. Maybe not the natural disaster on the beach.
But Prettyman had disappeared. Anna was
distracted. Trevor was out of touch. And as for that
subterranean-freak that cornered her with totally
unbelievable stuff about relics that needed to be
rescued…*Give me a break!*
She was beginning to sound like a conspiracy
theorist. Something not known to enhance a
scholar's reputation. Still, what started out as a
sublime summer in Italy was un-winding very
suddenly. Why?
Fortunately, she had had the presence of mind to
respond quickly… as if she were a pro or
something! With little warning, she had packed
swiftly and wisely.

Further, with disarming agility she managed to slip away during a school play without detection while under full view! *Tell me if that isn't the sign of a polished fugitive!*

But she had no choice, she decided. The children were in danger. Sandra…

Stay Calm.

She looked at the children, both of them comfortably relaxed and settled in for the rain ride, and she smiled at them.

She took advantage of the moment to pull out her laptop which never left her bag, and she checked her e-mail. Not having a cell phone took her back to basics.

Nothing from Trevor!

Santori however, had asked her how her Assessment was coming along. He was dismayed at the report of a theft and wanted to know if…

She was terse.

"No theft, Santori, What is the real motive behind wanting to move your collections?"

Normally, she would not respond with acerbic comments. But she was tired and losing patience with Italians who had an agenda. Their reluctance to share archaeological findings with the world was legendary. Especially history related to the first century and earlier, notably from Pompeii and Herculeum - much of which remained buried by the eruption of Vesuvius still. And frankly, he had not been specific.

This first century period was acutely sensitive to Paul's early Church foundation when he wrote his Epistle to the Romans…

Santori was fishing!

She had been played. She felt like she had been set up.

A message came in from someone she recognized. Of all people, it was Jacques de Torraine. He enjoyed their dinner together, he said. Unaware of anything amiss, he bantered on about their possible next meeting.

Amanda looked up. Perhaps she had misjudged him? Perhaps her fears had been groundless.

Or perhaps she had averted disaster.

She opened more mail, one in particular was a response to hers of a few days ago. It was sent to her by someone she trusted.

Amanda had asked the question: *"Someone from an Institution I respect, presented me with incredulous information about St. Paul being Herodian. Is there any scholarship to support this assertion?"*

Amanda checked on the children. They were playing cards. She had time to read it.

Shirley came back with the answer, and it did surprise her. Not the kind of stuff people normally digested about these figures of antiquity or theology. But reviewing it was not an option. Not as long as she was carrying around one of the world's most controversial and sacred documents!

"Paul's Doctrine is a prickly issue. First, here are the fundamentals. And I need hardly say scriptural questions have been analyzed for centuries:

This matter threatened to undermine the authority of the Church. And it was debated.

Remember, the Church was a central power in the middle ages. The future of civilization would rest upon it...So judge accordingly.

As author of most of the New Testament, the content of Paul's doctrine has been examined by modern scholars as well as old: Augustine of Hippo, for example defined Paul's ideas of salvation as being based on faith and not "Works of the Law" This is significant because for centuries it just hung there, uncontested...until Martin Luther split the world in two with his interpretation of Paul's writings in his Lutheran doctrine of *Sola fide*. Meaning, belief in God by "faith alone"

By the turn of the millennium, the Catholic Church was in its formative stages. It had gained social acceptance; territorial control and commercial credence. But it struggled within the confines of the Roman Empire. Paul was a problem.

In conceptual terms, how to reconcile his teachings with the Faith now that the Bible Cannon was closed – And his books constituted most of the New Testament.

The prevailing wisdom of the time went something like this: Resources were precious, men *chosen* for their leadership; and even in a slave society with an occupation force, social acceptance had to include judgment by a logic of the intellect. If you wished to rule, you had to be an iconic symbol of power.

The notion of *ownership* meant entitlement to human capital and all resources - That was the dominion of a conquering force. This gave the territorial ruler power over people's labor, life and cultural legacy.

Paul was born a free man. This was extraordinary by itself…

** **

She was being watched.

From above, somewhere around the luggage rack, Amanda looked like a sheepdog peering down at content in her hand. Across from her, her children could be seen, sleepy.

Amanda was oblivious to any observation, her mind clearly preoccupied with reading the content before her.

Overhead imagery captured her every movement. Hidden within the folds of a passenger's pocket-satchel above her, the device was not much more than a smart phone.

The transmission actually was tied into a laptop belonging to someone seated several places behind her. It sent the relay tracking and observation feed to a NATO terminal digital link.

A message was sent with the feed. *The target has been acquired…*

Shirley was persistent.

Her analysis was critical to the museum's assessment. It was Amanda's duty to be informed, lest a public microphone be thrust before her for answers to a museum publicity campaign. Besides, she had not kept up with her readings.

Shirley was sharing with Amanda some background scholarship that she knew Amanda was qualified to handle. Certainly, it might help with public relations, to say nothing of fundraising from corporate donors.

But there was more than that here. The material sounded more critical. It was Shirley establishing credibility in the face of resistance.

Why?

Amanda read on.

"To be an independent individual meant a great deal, and was a valued commodity bought at high price. Not being a slave implied freedom of self will. Or self determination and redemption. (See Acts 22:29)

Paul, who claimed that the Knowledge of God came through nature, presented the notion of Natural Theology.

But Aquinas, a church man, qualified the knowledge of God as being incomplete and coming indirectly through Creation, asserted that there was no contingency to understanding God. (God was Eternal, and Self-Existing. No causal connections to man necessary).

This is a highly controvertial element to scholars, and it might shape the public perceptions given to the Judas Mansucript, "Evolving from the heritage of the Greeks, Phoenicians and Egyptians, the Romans were not an Empire by accident! They embodied the very finest of resource allocations, military organization and social thinking! Remember, theirs was a reputation of strength built on elemental justice - notwithstanding the means of achieving that goal.

"Judea was clearly within their jurisdiction, as were the cultures within it. The Jews had both place and nation status within the Roman Empire, as Caiaphas the high priest articulated.

"Paul was a Christian, rather a Roman Citizen of the Hebrew culture. But first and foremost, he was a Roman Citizen.

Here atheism re-introduced the thinking of Aristotle's First Cause, and re-cemented the foundation of Nature providing for God's authorship of the Universe: Man was rational enough with his understanding of Truth to reach a consensus about God .

"The prevailing thinking of the era still held with the classical traditions of Aristotle, Socrates and Hippocrates.. (Even In Judea Paul argued his case before Pharisees, a sect in doctrinal divisiveness with the Sadducees.) Hence from the philosophy of Aristotle, currency was given to the First Cause, or <u>original sin</u> that must equal a doctrine if it was to gain traction.

"So the Christian Faith had to survive the field of scrutiny that scholars of the scriptures presented through the first millennium. The draw of Epistemology had to hold up with rational arguments that expressed the understanding of God through Reason and Faith."

This was the point of departure for the Protestant faith from the biblical interpretation of the Existence of God…

"St. Augustine was the first to ask the unutterable: Per Deum Homo? In a rational argument for a Messiah, he asked Why was it necessary to have Atonement?

What constituted the argument that provided a satisfactory view of Atonement? Why did "God" have to become a "Man"?

How does it make this religion unique. And was it what Judas had in mind?

This informed the questions about Justice, including vicarious sacrifice offering atonement… thinking of accountability still in the Augustine era.

Indeed, It was even voiced by Caiaphas the Priest when presented with the dilemma of what to do with Jesus Christ after he raised Lazarus from the dead "…that one man should die for the people, and that the whole nation perish not. He…prophesied that Jesus should die for the nation. And not for that nation only, but that also he should gather together in one the children of God that were scattered abroad. " (John 11: 50-52).

"Mommy, I have to go to the bathroom" said Sandra as the train slowed down.

In bringing rational argument to the existence of God, Augustine explained that 'believing' was an intellectual process of the human mind chosen to better understand God. Inversely, understanding God was not just left to blind and mindless faith.

Does this square with Judas who implied self-agency? Or were the agnostics seeding the soil for a Catholic doctrine to *appropriate* the Jewish belief system?

But, in his official Confession of Credo ut Intelligan, he also expounded that God was incomprehensible, or beyond the complete understanding of man. Thus man could only use, at best, an Apprehensive knowledge enabling intellectual understanding God:...

Now 'Enter' the Church for intermediary interpretation of what the ancient texts said - or didn't say?

Amanda was puzzled. She would continue later and logged out. But as the motion coaxed her thoughts, she wrapped up her reading on her iphone in a matter of minutes. Perhaps now would come the explanation for it all in literature.

... to be satisfied with the simpler child-like faith uttered by Paul, was inadequate. Men were obligated to grow up and learn more because the scripture "Word of God" was designed to aid in understanding. If man was found moored by blind truth, duty or understanding of God, then he remained negligent.

Amanda could not reconcile the argument. She was ending her reading, and felt strangely unsatisfied. This was all very well, but the real question was the question of Judas?

...In this way, Augustine gave the Christian Faith Rationale. He adorned it with moral accountability and judgment of God. But in so doing, he opened the argument for Reason vs Divine Revelation. Especially in the Doctrine of Creation.

Still, as far as Amanda could tell, the Church had found a good way to manage a medieval society into subjugation. Faith or no faith!

The point was, who was Judas?

Why, over time, had he become such a threat to doctrinal values?

"…Hence the central question for the Church to solve was that the Existence of God either existed through something, or it existed through nothing at all.

Ontological Argument for the Existence of God held in the cosmological argument that went back to the Aristotelian question of First Cause vs. the Theological argument: And this went back to the first design - and the Designer. (Creator)" she read.

The dilemma for the Church was gaping, not closing. Credibility was the danger.

….St. Anselem (root of the Western Philosophical History) framed the argument around the concept of "Being": In his ontology, he claimed that "God is that, than which, no greater can be conceived" In other words, God had to be a pre-existing reality as well as being discovered in the mind.

St. Aquinas, holding a central concept adopted by the Catholic Church laid out the logic in ontological terms about the "necessity" of being — that something could not be its opposite, hence God was in existence at the core and foundational of reality.

She felt tired. Tired of it all. This was not her cause! - Neither was it her problem to negotiate; nor hers to judge… It was not her business *at all,* period.

Especially if it put in jeopardy the safety of her children. She looked around.

She shuddered, not with cold, but with the uncomfortable feeling that she was being watched.

** *

The reception that Amanda and the children received in Marina di Carrera was one of welcome. And it came not a minute too soon for Amanda's frayed nerves.

Daughter to her mother's Aunt, Zia Rita of the DeValois family has kept up with Amanda Wells over the years.

Zia Rita had been a European linguist and interpreter, sustaining a career through many international events that often eclipsed her husband's career as a diplomat and Industrialist.

And she was overjoyed at the family reunion.

Now reaping the fruits of their labor as retirees, they lived in considerable comfort. Here they occupied a modern apartment building at Marina di Carerra.

A buffet was set up for them as house-guests. The gathering was a fabulous reunion of laughter and chatter unending.

It was a commodious place. From white marble floors and generous fenestration, the vista from the penthouse was spectacular.

"From here, we can see the world" explained Zia Rita as she led them out to the veranda for coffee and dessert.

Before them, the Adriatic sea met with the blue mountains of Carrera, mountains that had provided marble for architecture and sculptures for civilized man.

"The Greeks, the Romans, Phoenicians, Chinese and Arabians come to mine the marble blocks" she gesticulated, "bringing ships and barges to this sea port. And with that marble, they inscribed artistic statements to shape their world."

Together they stood on the Veranda, and Amanda faced her aunt.

Zia Rita had softly undulating white hair and blue twinkling eyes. She had never had a chance to meet Adam and the twins, she said. Only by voice, photographs and video. The children took to her instantly.

Sandra lifted her arms up to her. They looked at each other gravely, and slowly Zia Rita smiled at the child. Sandra smiled back, and yawned.

Zio discovered that Adam not only played chess but billiards! So by the time Adam was shown books on Armor, Amanda knew that he and Zio they were off and away like a band in comraderies.

Their guest quarters were more than adequate. Staff attended to housekeeping, and there was enough space to give them each their own bedroom.

By the second day, Amanda was relieved to have some time to herself.

She had a new cell phone, and had left messages for Trevor.

When she finally opened her laptop and lay on a white King-sized bedspread, she felt sufficiently recovered to consider the scroll she had on her possession. Amanda had not had a minute to herself. Yet she was a professional interested in its historical integrity. She thought about it, rested enough to think about with some discrimination.

As a Researcher, she was curious about its provenance, its history, its influence on society and those religions of Western Civilization.

Even the Islamic culture, ever vigilant about sacred writings of the ancients, knew of its venerated contribution as a seminal text.

Yet, why was it was considered an orphan somehow, like some Addendum to the Gospels, even removed from the debate of scholarship if not viewed rather disparagingly.

She knew that it had been included in the cannon of the Bible in the fifth century. But there was something about it that was considered…well, somehow, *off…?*

Surely, it added to the precepts of "doctrinal proselytization," as Bob would have called it…

Amanda sighed. She lay back on the bed.

Tinkling sounds of toys, laughter and music filtered through the noise, and she shut her eyes gratefully for the respite it afforded her.

Later that night she turned to her mail. There was, after all, if she searched for it, more to read on Paul. It came in an email from a fellow scholar "H"

And now she was in a dilemma. She had a decision to make. She had better know what she was doing. Or undoing. She had to make a bet.

Neither a theologian nor a doctrinal expert, she was now *de facto* a Conservator. She hoped it was the bet of centuries!

She read on.

…"You must understand that the story of Paul is critical to the validation of the Church. Again, he wrote most of the New Testament. His biography is rich and full of articulated prophetic understanding and declaration of doctrine.

So how to explain his *political* posture?

Acts recounts that on the way to Rome Paul was shipwrecked on "Melite" Malta, where he was met by Publius and the islanders, who showed him "unusual kindness". (See Acts 28: 2)

"He arrived in Rome c 60; apparently witnessed the great eruption of Vesuvius, whose crater was Somma…

"There are various accounts of his influence on the Church: Ireaeus of Lyons in the second century believed that Peter and Paul had been the founders of the Church in Rome. (The Catholic Church believes that to Peter the keys to the Kingdom of Heaver were given by Jesus - making him the first Pope)

"But Paul was neither a bishop of Rome nor the founder of Christianity since it was already developed there. It is assumed he did shape the early church of Rome.

But it is also suggested that he had *appropriated* the cultural story of the Messiah and wanted it for himself because of his own interests. He had positions of candidacy and lineage himself.

He was in fact, related to Herod.

He was possessed of the professional skills and insight of the workings of a Christianity that could make a man a Roman-God: In that era, such a thing was not remarkable.

This theory has been implied by recent atheist-centered scholarship that Paul was a God-seeker himself.:"

Amanda paused. This was not what she expected from the author of ancient scripture!

"Such a concept was not unusual. The Herodian Dynasty, The Early Christian Church and the shaping of a future with Crusades and kingly crowns…allows many to read his words in a *different* light.

"Remember, in a slave society, this concept fit nicely with the prevailing social hunger of the time: The *"Grace of God"* was like a commodity, dispensed to humans wanting independence from slavery, as if liberating them from moral bondage as slaves, and making them free choice individuals. It had a power allure.

This kind of dispensation was like an agency, managed by an "enabler" who promised spiritual absolution and atonement. It gave people freedom and status. It gave them redemption from an authority of ownership. Many scriptures allude to this: *"Give to Caesar what is Caesar's, and to God what is Gods."*

Christ, remember, had a Hebrew lineage, an authority of his own, even before he gave his spiritual power to others to assume.

Paul did not fail to observe this power.

Neither did the Church fail to observe this power. Especially as it would proceed for the next millennium to dispense moral justice and power, like choosing and anointing kings to rule people by divine power, puppets for dominion over kingdoms, society, trade, taxes, tithes and armies.

"To reveal that is self-interest is to *unravel* the Church history of the first millennium. They would rather die with any such evidence than rewrite the foundations of the Church legacy!
So, if buried, then understandably so...
Be careful if you have any knowledge of it. And remember, even Luther believed in the foundations of the Holy Roman Catholic Church. He advocated Reform (especially of the church "indulgences" which he claimed misled the faithful into believing that faith could be bought) He did *not* intend for redevelopment...
 He embraced the basic tenants of the Holy Roman Catholic Church, as do most Christian Protestants of today.
So, Heresy might be an apt word, here. Basically, this is not a sect or doctrinal argument. Rather, it is all that holds the world together, including perhaps, the bonds of honor that upholds contract law, sovereign rights etc etc... So, tread carefully: A door never to be unlocked, if you will.

Amanda paused. And here she was absconding with the keys to unlock the door to the Kingdom of Heaven!
God, how to put things back?

* *

Carrera, Italy.

Sightseeing became a family event. Something Amanda relishe.

In the front seat of a blue vintage antique car was Zio Paulo wearing a dapper panama hat, nodding here and smiling there as he pointed out one nifty corner shop after another. Here, a bicycle shop to take the Tour de France. There, a pet shop that sold elephants, setting the children giggling with his outlook.

And beside him sat Zia Rita in a sea-colored raw-silk dress and pearl necklace, reminding them of a garden park here; a museum there. Nicely confusing elephants with bicycles until everyone was laughing riotously.

 They stopped for lunch, and later walked for sightseeing.

Adam and Sandra did very well on their tours of the Cathedral; Ducal Palace; Fine Arts Academy and baroque church of San Francesco. Zia Rita spoiled them at every turn with gifts, clearly having fun herself.

Amanda was thrilled - relieved to share the charge of children with relatives and family, if too worn out to keep up. Zio Paulo noticed. Not that they were any more vigorous with the children. Later, he ascribed to his chauffeur the duty of delivering them around, at times the car casually advancing in the background as they all perambulated, but he knew he was helping Amanda unburden her anxiety. And he was pleased for the opportunity, he told her.

"Even at a young age, children should be exposed to great art and architecture" he said, striding beside her. She concurred.
"Scholarship might follow at a later age…" he said "But for now, it was all about colors and shapes and funny hats and silly human statues. And that was fine. Here was plenty of it!"
She smiled at him.
Finally, when Zio volunteered to take the children to Luni the next day for rides on the Ferris wheels at the Luna Park.
"Who wants candy fluff, duck shooting and spinning rides?" he asked.
It was all they could do to race through the rest of the day and get back home.
On the way back, Amanda did get a glimpse of Monte Sagro near the quarries, and as the Autostrade A12 motored them along the Tuscany coast and past the Cave di Marmot, she felt as if she were on hallowed ground.
Tomorrow, with the children preoccupied with Zio, she would return here by herself for a tour. This she explained to Zio.
He understood.

* *

That night, when she opened her laptop, she found an email message from Santori.

" I have an official request to make.
We have just had another earthquake here, and we are increasingly alarmed. From a

cultural standpoint, the stability of our sublevels of historical record...as well as the curated collections that we have may be compromised...

Forgive me Amanda, but at the first sign of security failure and distress, looting becomes a common thing. It was my hope to bring *theft* to your attention in focusing on one particular collection. And whatever may have happened in Naples – and I am told that things are still under investigation since it appears some valuables have been purloined from the Cathedral's collections – is only a sampling of what might happen region-wide.

 As you know Amanda, historical integrity is a thing to be valued as a social asset. For us in particular, it represents a large share of our economy. Without it, we are financially depressed.

"So, now is the time for frankness. I was hoping that I could talk you and your husband into considering a national transport of our collections to your safer repositories in Great Britain. We trust few governments as we do England, and we know of your technological advances in preservation, security and insurance.

This will come at some expense, I know. So it is no small thing. But it has and will become a national plea in official channels soon from our country to yours...

Please give us your endorsement. And forgive my initial opaqueness.
Best,
Ernest Santori "

Amanda thought about the email and realized that it must have come at some effort.

True, the United States and Great Britain had harbored many collections from other nations for temporary safe-keeping in recent history, chiefly because of high standards in museum management. Especially for collections on loan.

But Amanda also knew that those days of collection transfers were over: For one thing the costs of moving, insuring and preserving valuables was astronomical.

More critically, the repositories themselves where not in abundance. Security had taken its toll in updates and outdates. Manpower and museum budgets were keenly guarded within England's communities of curators. And risk aversion had seized financial decision-makers by the throat.

She would answer his email in a few days, she decided. This needed some thought and investigation.

What alarmed her most - and kept her up all night, was the inference he made to something which had gone "missing"…as in item or items which *have been purloined from the Cathedrals collections*.

The priest had implicated her with this Paul Epistle. Certainly, she understood his motive once it became known that she was the Courrier for the Judas manuscript. He could easily combine the purposes.

Except that, at the time he gave her the Paul Espistle, he could not have known of her mission to deliver the Judas Manuscript.

Hadid had made sure of that!

In fact, even when he anticipated that she should show up in Rome, later, his intelligence was misinformed.

What was he doing then? Why?

He fairly foisted it upon her for the purpose of examining it. Of course with the assumption that it be returned: Yet he told the police that it was ...*missing?*

What a rat! What was he doing?

He was making a public issue. At her expense!

Still, she had the thing in her possession! Even if she had not had a chance to open it - given the circumstances of her sudden rush from Naples.

She could explain everything, she told herself. *"Right..."* they would say.

She calmed her runaway thinking. Surely there was a better way to handle this situation.

Then a thought came to her, and she looked up incredulously.

Had the priest planted it on her *purposefully?* Surely not... And if so, why?

If there was one thing Amanda would not be is a patsy for other people's schemes: Naïve, perhaps. And clearly too trusting.

True, she *was* a little afraid of engaging with the thing. But she was not insincere. And her motives were pure.

Twice she switched on the light during the night.

Damn it to hell.

The third time she got out of bed, opened her back pack and took the ancient scroll out of its sleeve.

She must have sat there for an hour.

Yes. It was a letter. *To the Romans.*

It took her breath away, the penmanship that articulated the famous lettering; admonitions known all over the world by the Christian faithful.

"The just shall live by faith alone" words that triggered the great Lutheran Protestant movement of the 16th century.

"…For the promise, that he should be the heir of the world, was not to Abraham, or to his seed, through the law, but through the righteousness of faith.."

She could hardly believe eyes.

A scripture redolent with the doctrine of Atonement - that one should absorb the sin for the many.

Amanda, herself of the Christian faith, read those original words with tears in her eyes. The parchment was old, the ink oxidized. But legible still, thanks to centuries of safekeeping.

She softened on her opinion of the Priest. After all, these documents had been kept and housed safely in the vaults of the Church for how long now? They had been kept safe, a conservatorship of sorts. Even if hidden deep within the vaults…

Amanda looked at the document reverently. It was ancient. Old. A most beautiful rolled text letter.

Then suddenly she froze.

There, at the end, were unpublished words - words not found in the Gospel.

What were these words?

Signs of a seal, long gone. A salutary suffix of parting, a signatory authority…

How did St. Paul sign his name?

Was he not caught up in the newly forming Christian movement? Was he not to defend himself before Casesar? Had he not been imprisoned? And was he not about to be imprisoned again? Did he not swear his allegiance to the Apostles in various churches across the Mediterranean?

How did Paul sign his name?

She looked carefully.

In the Bible he closed with the Blessings of God…

But here?

What?

"Herodias?"

She looked again.

Paul signed himself the scribe for the mission of his relative and Patriarchal Master, *Herodias* - in whose service he dedicated his labor. And he set his seal on it...

Surely not!

This meant that Paul had been commissioned *not* for the Apostles, but …but…to propagate the message for the purpose of trade and enrichment for his Master and Family name!

Surely not!

Amanda put on her clothes and went up to the terrace for air. There was little breeze that night.

She could outline a darkened sea unrepentant before great mountains. She searched the heavens. Had the shadows of humanity defined themselves through the centuries?

Back in her room she replaced the scroll back into its sleeve and restored the burlap bundle into her knapsack.

Today, she needed freshness. She needed to be alone. With time to think. She decided, above all else, that she needed to be rid of the scroll. And absolved, somehow.

How?

* *

Zia offered to accompany her more than once at breakfast. When it became clear there might be an issue, Amanda asked her directly if there was a problem.

"No. Niente" said her aunt, eyes calm. But then she hesitated. "E bene, c'e l'istoria d' anarchisti…li jiu, e sono un po…." She waved her hand dubiously "Besognia fare attenzion…" she said finally.

Amanda laughed, then kissed her on the cheek. And although it had been several days before Amanda was able to return to the Marble Mountains of Carrara as a tourist, she appreciated the lovely days spent sampling food in restaurants and viewing high couture shops with her Aunt who told her that she came to Florence once a year to restock her wardrobe.

"Nice!"

She loved the wandering through colorful vegetable and fish markets with Zio.

Even one night dressed up for a soiree with them both. Those few days together infused them all with relaxation and enjoyment, Amanda told her.

Still, Amanda had to get on with her agenda, especially with two children in tow: That was obvious, obvious in the conditions under which they arrived - unplanned, unannounced and very fatigued and stressed.

Zia Rita looked down and smiled thoughtfully. "This is all about making a situation easier for the children."

Her Aunt sensed that there was more. Some unfinished business… And for that Amanda truly appreciated the support of another woman, a woman who had seen much in her own career as a professional interpreter. It was said in her deep blue eyes.

So this was also her way of saying B*e Careful.* Here was a haven of socialist anarchists who had been known to infiltrate the ranks of the miners working the mines of Carrarra…

Amanda got it.

So in a small Fiat Amanda approached her destination with care. On the Alpi Auane as the sign said, she spotted the town of Colonatta. There she would find the Fantiscritti marble quarry — a place where Michelangelo apparently selected source material for his greatest works.

At first, souvenir shops littered the zig-zag approach, but the higher she climbed the smaller the roads and tunnels, all shared precariously by hauling vehicles and marble moving machinery.

The mountain slopes looked snow-white with marble dust and tailings that fell from block quarrying.

She parked the car and took the railway that showed the process of marble mining, then she followed the viewing platforms to see a working mine.

By the time she reached La Piana Marble Quarry, the Fantiscritti; the Carrara Mable Museum and the colonnata, she felt she had seen it all.

She considered calling it a day.

That was before she was saddled with a holy sacred text. So no. *This* Amanda Wells - alone as she was - would wander about some more…

Angry, she was. Hurt and slighted by those who abused her graciousness, taking liberties that served their agendas…

Yes she was angry, she realized. She moved into the shadows of the mines. To Explore. To discover.

What the hell?.. How could you go wrong with St. Paul in your bag?

Nor was she the first to feel anti-social down here: The Commune was in the province of Massa-Carrara, in Tuscany Italy near the Carrion River, some 100 kilometers west of Florence, the leaflet said.

And as she entered the vast complex of subterranean caves and tunnels, she saw the mediaeval emblem that marked the famed inscription amongst the ancient guilds "Fortitudo mea in rota" *my force is in the wheel* — a force that remained unchanged since before the first millennium!

Even today she knew of surprises still under discovery deep within recesses of the mountain that confounded archeologists. Pictorals, sculptures, artifacts telling stories about events… like secrets that predated the chart of known activity by humans. Where? What were their endeavors?

In the cavernous spaces of the mine, the earliest date so far recorded was the 9th century BC when the Apuan Ligures lived in the region.

Nine centuries before Christ!

Like the Children of Israel who were known to have carved the pyramids for the Egyptians, these elements were made by the hands of workers within these marble quarries!

Who were they?

Exploited after the conquest of Liguria by the Romans in the early 2nd century BC, they remained through the fall in the middle Ages to the Byzantine, then saw Lombards in possession of German territorial lineages. And it was Catholic Bishops of Luni who were assigned to oversee the Port from which the quarried marble and transported by sea.

Clearly, this was source of enormous classical wealth. Perhaps even the cause of such malcontent and abuse down here.

Struggles were known to have endured in this vibrant and cash- rich community. Abandoned even as an autonomous and unruly commune in the 13th century during the disputations of the Guelphs and Ghibelllines. Only later were these mines given recognition as the Renaissance builders of the Republics of Pisa, Lucca and Florence.

Amanda had to wonder at the territorial claims that fed the ambitions of early modern European dominated by princes and principles seeking economic advantage. She knew of a few:

There was Filippo Siconti of Milan in 1477, then Tommaso Campofregosos, Lord of Sarzana and the Malaspine family during the 16th century who by marriage made up the famed d'Este estate before it became a Duchy of Modena. Certainly these mines and mints had filled catholic coffers and provided for royal anointed princes in treasure, fertility and foot-soldiers.

Amanda paused, amazed at it all. As if gazing down the long halls of history much like a portrait gallery of patrons and patronage.

But neither were checks and balance entirely absent…features never far behind in the face of God through the ages: Here it was not land that was contested. It was labor.

Down here, it was easy to think about things…to make things…to shape society, even.

Above all, and treasured more than a gold mine, the marble mines developed over the centuries a reputation for skilled quarry workers, especially stone carvers:

In a world of figurative and ornamental art, the image was the face of power, wealth and governance. The public message of social following came in public art, works and architecture that defined the social hierarchy of legendary imperial power and control. It was a world beyond the hoards of the unskilled and laboring masses: It was the window through which workers passed to perform their wonders. And to receive some acclaim as artists and artisans, even through their chiefs and foremen.

Yet they returned from such exposure with thoughts of injustice and exploitation: They harbored radical beliefs that set them apart from others. They embraced reformers, thinkers, designers and artisans, even reflecting the spirit of the anarchist in their fiercely realistic work, critics claimed. Over the years, revolutionists had come from here. Communists, unionists, organized labor that would later spread across Europe and infiltrate states of patronage.

Sculptured marble monuments, carved from the hands of workers with poetry in their hearts; dreams in their heads and anger in their voice were dotted all over Europe.

Down here, observed many, were no engraved edifices to the nobles and empires they served, but to the human spirit of *individualism* in its most distilled form.

Amanda Wells paused.

 She looked at her pathways.

She approached an underground working shed and noted the tools there. Further down, a full exhibit, even handle-worn saws used to carve the great blocks…Signs of hard labor was everywhere. Recognizable easily, through centuries of social development. And Amanda felt a deep sense of appreciation for their hard work.

"Can I help you?" came so suddenly that she jumped.

Not a monster. Nor a policeman. Nor an elder.

But a closely shaven technician in a lab coat with techy protective eyewear.

"Scuzi" she said, throat parched "Sono…perdita?"
He laughed.

"Aren't we all?" responded the American voice.

He led her down a tunnel of motorized carts and side chambers where she saw young interns wearing insulated overalls, if plugged into ipods and nodding to music. They moved in and out of temperature controlled glass rooms.

Clearly, dust was a problem to their environment. She identified herself.

He gave her a short tour as a nod to her profession, explaining that access was limited to the sciences and high technology analogy development. Computer modeling, geology and forensics was served by graphics, he explained. This was research-and-management-central, he laughed.

Casual as he was, there was an underlying awareness that University educated scholars now engaged in what was once the provenance of laborers and journeymen.

Amanda showed interest in their work and presented her own credentials, the Project Director came over. Happy to introduce himself and to give her the full tour of their work mission, he said.

* *

"It's a honeycomb structure" explained the young technician "It holds structural integrity as interlocking cubed cages, built originally in heavy timbers for the gold mines of San Francisco" He pointed to three dimensional graphics on the screen.

"Supporting them are the feed lines of supply, power, ventilation, exchange and discharge…" he said changing the grid to a network of channeling and flow design.

He looked up at her and grinned with an admission "I was inspired by the spaceship Enterprise in Star Trek…"

Amanda smiled. "Of course!"

"These are cracks in the mountain fissures large enough to house an infrastructure the size of small buildings below the surface" added the Director.

"This is the prototype of a smaller opening in section 898. It's old and has not been mined for a couple centuries. But its walls need stabilizing if lower levels are to proceed excavating…"

"How will you manage human thresholds…?" asked Amanda, fascinated by their work.

"Actually, it's quite interpretive…" said the young technician. "It's all I can do to get a Grant to proceed with the drawings…But actually, if this thing were to be built, it would give new meaning to building Rome, right here inside the marble mountains of Italy!"

She chuckled.

"Here, there are openings to sunlight in the higher reaches of the Alps that would allow for green survival, human habitability, and glass enclosures for giant interlocking chambers. We could house entire museums while at the same time offer storage …Complete with thermal vents, ultra violet lighting, exhausts, road and access ways for small vehicles…and you might even have tree-growing rock-parks for the kiddies!"

Amanda smiled. "That's very inventive!"

"That's very expensive!" admonished the Director, leading her on. He completed her tour with a visit to the main vaults and repositories of statuary and prize marble collections of antiquity.

She was shown a large vault door that opened like a bank vault of stainless steel bolts, and in they walked with small rooms branching out in many directions. The boxes and crates were all carefully marked. In one room were artworks lines up in wheeled carts.

"My God" she said.

"Works in progress under restoration…" he explained. "So, as you can see, we are turning the mine into a working community of reclamation and restoration. It is, after all, a valuable resource to the nation… And it holds the right natural temperature thresholds!"

She knew of course that he was referring to the centuries of battle that had occurred over this resource in one way or another. Or, as he put it, to own this section of the world, was to own the economies of Empires!

Anna would be proud of her Charles.

"And here…because of the electrostatic compressors and humidity control, we keep the records and collections of books".

Tall stacks, protected by glass sliders, allowed covered wooden steps to roll down aisles for access to boxes and books and records.

And it was at precisely that moment that Amanda made her decision.

Not that she had been not been patted down at the entrance for hard objects, but her soft pouch for a handbag was of little interest to the Entrance Guards.

She had brought the scroll in it.

Finally, if somewhat unexpectedly, she found relief in resolution.

"Dr. Phillipo…" she looked down, uncertain as to how to proceed exactly. But the tour had given her courage, if not redemption. "I am in possession of a scroll that should be under safekeeping. Will you please allow me to leave it with you here until I complete… my err…findings?"

"But of course!" he said, without hesitation. "Your reputation precedes you. I have read your papers. And I would be honored to keep something here for you…How shall I catalogue it?"

Now this could get interesting, she thought.

"A Letter to the Romans" she said, looking at him straight.

He took it in his stride without blinking an eye. This was Italy. There were lots of letters, treatises and scrolls written by the Romans, for the Romans and to the Romans over the centuries. Why not?

Very clever.

He gave her a receipt, and placed the sleeve with the scroll carefully inside one of the glass enclosed working cabinets of the Books collections. He even noted the shelf on the receipt, she noticed.

Thank You!

"I can assure you that once we shut this vault, there is no chance of security compromise, *that I promise you!*" he was saying.

She could have kissed him. She left her card and promised to follow through with further correspondence.

Right now, all she wanted to do was flee the premises. Flee the document that could rob so many of their faith. Flee the notions of religious manipulation, indoctrination and deceit by the righteous…the thinkers…the…the…*whatever* …

She wanted to run! Security be damned. The content of those words left her cold and betrayed.

* *

London

"There are basically three stages for all critical path items. Each with immediate, medium and long range projections. The first elements will be those of National survival and continuation. The second will be social infrastructure and integration. The third will be development, reconstruction and expansion"

Trevor paused, waiting for it all to sink in, and for those taking notes.

He was briefing several government Ministers, and he had to allow them to adjust to the shocking new realities of a demolished Europe.

The conference table was long, and every branch of government and civil service had been invited to attend. Those that did not have Clearances would be briefed later.

"England has to survive!" he said definitively "First and foremost. And as fearful and catastrophic an event as it might be, we have advanced sufficiently to expect a sustainable transition. I leave it to the experts to brief us, but we will each have to show courage, leadership and strength as the population goes through this. We may show the way to others. Or we may stand alone. But either way, plan we must!"

Again he paused, and finding no questions, continued.

"Once we accept the possibilities of what might happen if we neglect to make preparations, then we can proceed with calm and with planning".

"How certain of this can we be?" asked one fearful hand that lifted off the table.

"Positive enough to consider the risks of "doing-nothing" unacceptable." answered Trevor.

Some humphed audibly, a few choice words muttered. Others looked down at their notes. No one was comfortable. No one was comfortable. But one thing was clearly on everyone's mind.

The cost.

How do you explain to a Nation with limited resources; a relatively small geographic footprint but a large global influence that they should lead the way? By example?

Or perish… There was no alternative.

He cleared his throat. "I need hardly explain the costs; the consequences and the conditions that follow…They are staggering realities to build for. But frankly, they are moot considering that the world will may no longer be the same. And while entire populations and regions may lay in ruin, we can, and should count ourselves fortunate for the options that we do have at our disposal. We must, at the very least, maintain our cultural identity!"

"What do you mean?"

"I mean, count this to be a four-hundred-year-ice-age Diaspora Gentlemen. And when it hits, it's all over and too late. So plan we *must*…"

The room went silent. But not for long.

"This is impossible!" blustered one elderly statesman. He got up abruptly and walked to the side wall where he patted his brow with a white handkerchief.

"Yes" adjoined Trevor quietly "Truly. If this is a Quasi-Extinction Event - the likes of which is writ only in rock fossils. May God be with us, indeed. Because at the end of the day, our faith and beliefs may be the only lasting elements that define us as a culture!"

The room fell silent.

He went over the generalities with them again, and many left the room with their eyes swollen and their heads bowed in utter demoralization. But not before someone asked what the operation should be called.

"The Modern Ice Age" said Trevor without thinking. It seemed a logical analogy. The details would come later, he decided. Enough for one day. "Even if we are wrong, not to consider the possibilities and not to plan for such a contingency is folly. That is what we shall exercise!"

* *

Six

Amanda called them at the Park.

"Mummy. I did de…Fewis wheel fwee times wif Uncle Zio" said Sandra's voice on the cell phone.

Amanda smiled. The word Zio in Italian was uncle, but for Sandra, that was all she would call him.

Adam came on "And he bought me lots of turns with the guns…(*not now!*)" he added, as if batting off a pesky bug "and guess what, I rode in the Bumper Cars and SMASHED into all the ….*no. No!..*" Finally Amanda heard him say "(*Oh all right…here!*)"

"Mummy, I got a dolly anna …a..a. ponyhead on a tic…"

"A stick" said Amanda.

"Yes and…" she was interrupted brusquely by Adam.

"Mummy, there is something wrong" he said firmly, no longer hesitating with chatter.

"(*Come on!*)" he was saying to his companions, his voice changing direction "(*Now!*)"

As afterthought he said into the phone "It's the woman… Naatisha Suti. She's here!"

**

Amanda arrived in a taxi.

They had kept busy, walking about between the carousels, balloons and deepening lights.

The bushes in the Luna Park offered little shelter, but just enough to get them through the passageway of the rear entrance to the Park. Amanda had waited to join them in the gathering dusk.

She hushed them all…

She could see that Zio had a car waiting, and she behaved as normally as she could – as if nothing were wrong, somehow managing to usher the children into the vehicle.

Until she felt a hand on her shoulder.

It was the Lieutenant from Napoli.

Yes, he apologized for frightening her. And yes he was pleasant enough.

He explained that when he got a call from the school who found her cell phone and discovered that she was missing, a search was mounted for her and her children. Of course, the teacher, Naatisha Suti there. Most kind and helpful. She had offered to help in the search, and somehow spotted the children for identification. A tip, he said, that he got from a waiter who saw them on the way to Rome, he said.

He was talking to her, but not seeing her. Not even remembering their context in Naples where he and his Superintendant came to visit them at Pozzuoli. Somehow, the connections with Trevor, Anna, the school were lost to him. He was on Auto-pilot, evidently. His mind had another agenda.

She tried to look at him. But he would not look into her eyes.

He moved forward. Would she and her family please get into their car and kindly follow him to the police station? He had some questions...

What happened to him?

Amanda knew trouble when she saw it. But she smiled gamely, and joined the children into Uncle Zio's waiting car.

This was not the same Lieutenant. Sure, he was the same man, but his disposition had changed. He would not look at her. And while she promised to cooperate, she felt certain that there was more to this event than she could trust.

For one thing, the missing script, reported by the priest was *unmentioned*. Clearly, it was known that the Priest had been identified by Amanda. And a connection had most certainly been made. It was a glaring omission.

Perhaps the embarrassment to the establishment by a local police officer...reported by a foreigner was something that required heavy retaliation?

He returned to his waiting police car.

The woman got in behind them and sat in the rear with the children. There was only one comment she made, and it was directed at Amanda less than two feet away in a quiet voice.

"If you wish to see your children grow up...you will produce the script from the Cathedral to *me*..."

There was no misunderstanding.

Foiled once and deprived of a good kidnapping by foreign white people, here was another opportunity for reward.,,

Amanda knew that if this woman got her hands on the ancient manuscript it would disappear on the black market for years. Let alone the consequences of an inquest about the disappearance of a seminal Christian parchment scroll of the Roman Empire that was priceless. She would have no answers!

Amanda was now glad of her deception in depositing the scroll with Dr. Phillip at the Mines: The sacred scripture was at least safe in the Mountain Vault, if under false pretences.

That did not mitigate her present situation. Nor where there explanations that needed understanding. Like Prettyman's disappearance for example…

Amanda stayed focused on the dramatic unfolding at hand with one eye on the children. If they saw her panic, there was not telling how it would go. She remained calm.

This Suti was not a woman to underestimate. She was dangerous as hell. Of that she was certain.

Uncle Zio climbed in the front seat, besides his chauffeur. He said very little. As if observing.

It was dark as they moved down the road and left the decorative lights of the Amusement Park, Sandra now softly whimpering..

Zio began to speak to Amanda in a general voice, as if for conversation. He asked her to stay calm.

The last thing Amanda felt like doing was have a chat. Did he even have an idea about her predicament, exactly? Or was he oblivious to the fundamental need for shelter that had brought her to his door?

Perhaps she should have showed him more respect and explained everything in the first place. That first night in their apartment would have been an ideal opportunity. With the exhausted children tucked in bed, and the three of them having drinks together in the library, sharing pictures and memories and family connections…

But so overwhelmed was she from her escape trip that she almost dared not breath. She would wait until things normalized, is how she had rationalized things.

This was not a good time. She looked out and saw the town lights twinkle unmercifully. And she felt so isolated, her eyes lost and disoriented.

Then she felt a sharp nudge in the ribs, and looked down.   Zio was holding a card over her lap, discretely.

She remained steady.

With the two of them sitting in the front seat there was nothing to alarm those sitting behind them.

The street light intersection gave them a very slow light change. That was when Amanda saw the card with the crest and emblem of his boat name *Ligura*. Not a word was uttered.

Amanda paused, looked up calmly, then looked down again. With his hands still on his lap, Zio pointed to the door, and then to his watch, marking five minutes.

She understood.

Distance now darkened the road of the coast. Traffic moved about in dark strains and shiny reflections from faraway lights. As far as her captor was concerned, this was a cage now secured.

Evidently the driver to Zio's left was gestured to slow down, calmly.

Amanda turned back to face the seat behind her and noted that Sandra was sleepy. Would she like to come and sleep on Mummy's lap?

Over the seat the child came, in her pretty dress and socks and black shoes.

That left Adam all alone on the rear seat with the woman. He looked at his mother anxiously. And as Amanda was lifting Sandra, her eyes beckoned to him and pointed fixedly to the door of the car at his side: With a small jerk of her head and eyes, she made it clear he must exit the door with the handlebar..

It happened at the next intersection.

 Amanda held Sandra tightly in her arms, and as a siren of polizia roared up the street with commotion, noise and lights, Amanda knew that was her moment for distraction.

The door snapped open, Amanda popped out, banging Sandra's little head on the bulkhead, but *out* nonetheless…

Adam got out in a flash, and without a word, the doors of the vehicle were all locked in unison by the driver who pushed off at full speed.

From the rear window, the woman could be seen looking back at them in utter consternation. She had been the one trapped in the car. Zio would proceed directly to the police station as the Lieutenant had directed. He would answer the questions.

Amanda could call on no help. But she knew what to do.

Amanda and Adam moved swiftly across the street and into a taxi. She asked for *LaSpezia*.

That is where she would find the Yacht. At the Marina where Zio kept the *Ligura*. It was not a short trip. Her thoughts threatened to abandon her. But as she thought about it, the topic of her Uncle's yacht did came up during the conversation on that very first night of their arrival, and she remembered now.

Finally she appeared at the Gate of the marina. A Gentleman in official white marine dress came forward.

"Signora MacDonald?" he asked.

"Si."

"I am the Captain of the *Ligura*"

She followed.

"I have instructions from Signore DiValois to sail you to Nice. Is that alright Madam?"

She nodded, fatigue and gratitude in her eyes.

A large recreational sailboat, the *Ligura* had originally been sailed down from Nice France several week ago, scheduled to return in two days.

They walked down to the dockside. Again she nodded, afraid to awaken Sandra fast asleep on her shoulder.

There it was. An eighty foot yacht, moored off the docks at anchorage in LaSpezia. Evidently, complete with a full compliment of crew and captain, waiting for their Master's instructions.

As they were raised onboard, she wondered if her Zia could envision their movements from their Veranda. She looked back into the night sky, and could see nothing.

Her eyes welled with tears. Tears that nobody saw. This event, she explained to the children as they drowsily asked why they were on a boat, was the plan!

Adam took it well, Sandra having slept through the launch ride that took them out across the harbor in the dark, waves lapping precipitously near the gunwale.

And in less than two hours, the yacht had cut lose from her moorings and was sailing out to sea with them all settled in warm and comfortable stateroom accommodations.

Again she cast up another prayer of thanks.

Thank you Zio!

* *

London

The Speaker was one of several who came for a three day symposium at the request of London's chief Ministers. The topics were to include explanations, preparations and sustainability of an ice age.

The first, a physicist who specialized in the Earth geodynamics showed how the earth's magnetic fields were weakening: While ample evidence showed that this was not new, the *rate* of change and consequences of that change was not fully understood.

"We have a number of scenarios. What we have in this chart, is a simply schematic showing how the solar system flares deliver bolts of magnetism to the earth, if you will. Scientists believe the magnetic field is generated deep inside the Earth where the heat of the planet's solid inner core churns a liquid outer core of iron and nickel.

"The solid inner core is thought to be a mass of iron about the size of the moon that is heated to several thousand degrees Fahrenheit. Heat radiated by this inner core builds up at its boundary with Earth's liquid outer core, causing the fluid there to expand.

As it expands, and becomes less dense (or more buoyant) it rises. This is the standard convection when hot fluid rises, then cools off and sinks again. It is this action that generates an electrical current, with its magnetic field.

We do see a sudden decrease in magnetic fields. And yes, we are alarmed. If the trend continues, the field may collapse altogether and then reverse. Compasses would point south instead of north.

What will that mean? The dilemma then is to figure out what's happening, from where and why.

Evidence is abundant for reversals, especially in the fossil record. But who can figure out the earth's thermo-calendar, right?

Sources of study are multiple, and the reasons many: The first, are solar flares.

A sunspot is a place on the Sun's surface which is characterized by a very strong magnetic field. Therefore, the number of the sunspots on the Sun is a good indicator of the intensity of the overall Sun's magnetic activity. It is well-known that the magnetic field of the Sun peaks every eleven years, a cycle known as the sunspot cycle. In simple terms, the speeds of the equatorial and the two polar speeds (North and South polar speeds of rotation) have the most similar values during the period when a maximal number of sunspots are recorded Recent flares are alarming. The low sunspot activity from this sunspot cycle has baffled solar physicists. However, a switch in the magnetic field of the sun is inducing this. A 'Killer Flare' will be the result.

By the end of next year, the next polar reversal will take place on earth. This means that the North Pole will be changed into the South Pole. Scientifically this can only be explained by the fact that the earth will start rotating in the opposite direction, together with a huge disaster of unknown proportions.

My readings are clear on three things. Firstly, with clock-like regularity, reversals and pole shifts are natural to the Earth. Secondly, the result is a possible worldwide destruction – and this is supported by paleo-magnetic evidence and early manuscripts. And thirdly, the reversal of the poles is attributed to the harmonic cycle of the magnetic fields of the sun!

I would therefore suggest to you that you must consider the following in our exercises: The earth will be subjected to extremities unimaginable, near total destruction.

Expect hunger, cold, no recourse for many and no hope of recovery for others. This is because all conventions, knowledge and resources normally driven by information will not be available to isolated pockets of the populations. And it is in this scenario you will may have to survive….

On the other hand in the greater scheme of things, it is a re-generation for the earth, if you will. Remember, the magnetic field of the earth is no accident of natural science. Its primary task is to protect us against cosmic and solar radiation. So, while we examine the sun spots to register our magnetism, we must also evaluate other factors. And for that we have a host of other scientists and experts…"

Lunch came none too soon for Trevor. He walked about everywhere. Unable to settle anywhere, or with anyone. It was grim, expensive, incomprehensible and daunting. Plus he was exhausted.

His thoughts ran frequently to Amanda. And tight as security was, he wanted a way to get word to her. He had no idea what she was coping with, or why. Except that he wanted her back, with the children. He managed to make arrangements through a third party to send an email message to her general box address.

Come Home. Keep moving, North…

* *

"In this scenario, we have other considerations for the earth's magnetic field deteriorating" said the next speaker for the afternoon, a geophysisyt from Berkley California.

"Evidence is all pointing towards enormous volcanic activity on its way: In our exercise, we must imagine a Geomagnetic reversal over the life of the Earth is the orientation of Earth's magnetic field that is known to have reversed several times, with magnetic north becoming magnetic south and vice versa — an event known as a geomagnetic reversal. Evidence of geomagnetic reversals can be seen at mid-ocean ridges where tectonic plates move apart and the seabed is filled-in with magma. As the magma seeps out of the mantle the magnetic particles contained within it are oriented in the direction of the magnetic field at the time the magma cools and solidifies.

"Bear in mind that in this case, we are talking about Yellowstone Super Volcano here and thus signs of awakening can be huge such as we are experiencing now.

"In particular, four major scientific developments spurred the formulation of the plate-tectonics theory: This demonstrated the ruggedness and youth of the ocean floor; and secondly, it confirmed the advent of repeated reversals of the Earth's magnetic field in the geologic past; Thirdly, it showed the emergence of the seafloor-spreading hypothesis and associated recycling of oceanic crust; and finally provided precise documentation that the world's earthquake and volcanic activity is concentrated along oceanic trenches and submarine mountain ranges…" He paused and reached for a glass of water.

It was an hour before he was done with his talk, and Trevor called a short Recess.

"What kind of time schedule do you hold, Trevor?" asked the Minister of Interior, Davie Thomas.

 The two of them stood outside the conference room. Thomas was holding a silver monogrammed flask and having a stiff drink, he said, offering Trevor a shot.

Trevor shook his head and declined.

"I'm not sure…"

"Well you'd better be sure my boy... We need to start setting money, plans and contingencies on the table next"

Trevor took a big breath. "I agree"

He looked at the attendees around him. "But I had to make sure the facts were understood…by all"

Trevor drained the last of his water "That is, before I start making decisions. Otherwise, they'll accuse me of delivering Apocalyptic Prophecies!"

"Quite Right!" said Thomas, waving his flask. "So be certain, for God's sake!"

They opened the door to walk in and heard the speaker at his podium.

"Here…you see on this chart… the magnetic variations turned out *not t*o be random or isolated occurrences, but instead revealed recognizable patterns. When these magnetic patterns were mapped over a wide region, the ocean floor showed a zebra-like patterns. Alternating stripes of magnetically different rock were laid out in rows on either side of the mid-ocean ridge: one stripe with normal polarity and the adjoining stripe with reversed polarity. The overall pattern, defined by these alternating bands of normally and reversly polarized rock, became known as magnetic striping."

The evidence was piling on, thought Trevor.

What he wanted was a good skeptic!

* *

"We are stopping at Santa Margherita Ligure, Signora… For provisions.." said the Captain, interrupting her sun-tanning on the foredeck of the Yacht.

The water sparkled. It was a glorious day on the ocean.

The children had been entertained by the crew and knew of every nook and cranny in the ship to crawl into or pop out of. Amanda had relaxed. After all, as Trevor would say, how could they get lost? It's a boat!

Oh how she missed him!

"Tonight, under cover of darkness, we sail into Geneva, silently through the night in deep water channels. Then we anchor so that we remain standing and invisible as moving night targets on the radar…"

"Thank you Alberto for you help and attention! You and your crew have made my children very welcome on your ship…"

"Nothing at all Signora" he bowed. "It is our Director who employs us, Signore DiValois: He is a great man, your Uncle. He do great works for our *industria* here in Italy…"

Zio had called her that night on a cell phone number that he knew she had in her pocket. He said he had information about the trip. "You will stay within sight of land, you'll see the markers for Arenzano, heading west, then southwest to Celle Ligure, Savona…."

She would have liked to speak, but she sensed his urgency, and let him flow. He told her to stay calm. To listen.

"…Then you'll be sailing due south almost, past Finale Ligure, Pietra Ligure, passed Albenga, San Bartolomeo al Mare. There you can rest a day or two. There is a captain on board you can trust, with a very reliable crew.. You will keep following the Ligurian Sea coastline, and by the time you get to Sanremo, Bordighera you're almost to France" he explained.

She would not rush him, and waited for him to continue.

"If you anchor in Saint-Jean-Cap-Ferrat, its only a bay away from Nice. There you will be put on Le Var Route de Grenoble, up the Alpine pass and be on the train rails to travel north in relative comfort. There are very simple border crossings, in case they have your passport on the grid…"

"Zio, thank you so much for all this…"

"I'll have a flight waiting for you in Frankfurt to London. It'll be on my corporate jet. Trevor will be waiting for you in Heathrow. *Now I say GoodBye..*"

The conversation ended abruptly.

* *

London

The next day's crop of Speakers were no more cheerful than the first, thought Trevor. But exhaustive they must be… nonetheless.

"We are witnessing Cosmic rays, high-energy particles. These are components that we suggest are radiant energy accelerant fostering planetary changes on Earth. This, added to weak solar activity and a fledging solar wind is allowing more radiation into the solar system as the solar heliosphere acquiesces. We should expect more chaotic planetary system fluxes on Earth in the next eighteen months or so."

God, thought Trevor.

"We understand, as one our chief scientists says "It's not a question of *if* the Earth is going to reverse the magnetic field, but *when..*"

The data was relentless. When the final panel came up, it was well attended by all.

Volcanologists could only show that future apocalypse is inevitable with the increased activity of magma chambers beneath the crust of the earth.

"In conclusion, we know that there are several hot spots, and we have covered them amply, including their recent restlessness and warnings.

"They are stable items, it would seem, as the tectonic plates pass over them and make them appear to be moving.

"But perhaps they are showing signs of a need to erupt and induce an ice age. Clearly, they are the cyclic thermostat that regenerates the earth's function and surface evolutions.

"What we need to focus on now, is the *preparedness* issue for what is known generally as the volcanic winter: An ice age that follows a super volcanic eruptions that could well be an extinction event all by itself.

"While some date show alarming signs of degradation, others say we should expect a super volcanic eruption certainly within our lifetimes. To be unprepared, this time, will be a record for history to judge"

Well, thought Trevor. There is was. No one could have put it more bluntly.

He consulted his watch.

Now he should be calling Ernesto.

* *

The ship was well supplied. It had every possible onboard amenity, including a small office for routine business. She knew not to call out. But she could use the internet.

Amanda took the opportunity to write to Santori.

"It may not be feasible to lean on the resources of other governments for your cultural collections" she wrote.

"But I have a wonderful solution: Fund a Scientist Dr Phillipo and his team working at the Technical Labs in Carrarra. He could build you an underground repository for all your treasure and collections that would survive any catastrophic event"

She read her words again and giggled. Ideas, for academians was one thing. Funding, another.

"You have perhaps one of the world's most secure places there, deep within the Marble Mountains of Carrara. And what a fitting place! Right there, in the heart of your own country…"

"Build a honeycomb city underground" she continued. . Then repeating what the technician told her.." Using the highest technological advances in temperature control and ventilation, complete with overhead vents and chimneys for natural sunlight and spring water! Build glass encased chambers for habitability; work and curating, and there is your heritage!"

To Send or not to Send, she wondered. Perhaps she was being too frivolous?

"Mummy, Mummy…" called Adam "I can drive a boat!" She hit SEND, closed the computer, and joined them.

* *

The small fissures had opened up.

Warm water bubbled up from the bottom of the seabed in columns of suspended nutrients. The water column had widened to 8 meters and anything that was caught in its vortex died quickly, floating upward. The sulfuric content was toxic.

An algae bloom had spread across the ocean floor at an even faster rate.

What was soft blue and transparent had turned into a rich green, spreading across the bottom like a sea carpet, covering and blooming over every surface, crevice and sandy seabed it could find, and altering it to a fuzzy mucus.

Neither was the water temperature stable nor the salinity. At the bottom of the Tyrrhenian Sea, the earth's crust was opening up.

* *

Amanda was painting her toenails on the deck of the yacht. The children had just finished their breakfast of fresh fruit, juice and bacon topside, and the view of harbor in the distance was brilliant with morning sun.

Beneath them the transparent water glistened in shades of blue, green and silver, bringing into contrast the rocky bottom characterized by crags and caves that lined the Mediterranean sea.

They were anchored calmly in a bay, and Amanda knew that for their last morning on board, she had much to do before for the journey ahead.

For now, Adam was having his last swim, and Sandra was playing in a sandbox arranged just for her at midships. There she was determined to finish building her sandcastle.

The more rested the children, the less strain at transitions...

They had been entertained, the children, for three days by the crew aboard the boat. There was no space on the boat they had not explored. The Captain had given them whistles, like trains arriving in stations, he explained, to mark where they were, and on which deck! Sandra of course followed Adam everywhere. And Adam was at times capricious with ship spaces into which he sent his sister.

But with the whistles blowing at all points and for all reasons, it was hard *not* to know about the presence of children onboard… all day long!

Amanda worried that it was causing a disruption to the ship's routine. The Captain smiled. He had three children of his own, he said. And he would rather have their noise than quiet, he assured her.

Even in the ship's galley, the Cook has festooned a small swinging hammock for Sandra to sit in as she watching him drum up exotic meals and toss up pizza. Once, the Captain had to awake her up from a deep slumber where she had been rocked to sleep by the ship's motion, clutching her doll.

For Adam, a raft had been rigged for aft towing when the boat was at half speed and in safe waters. But his favorite place, Amanda observed, was at the helm of the ship where the Captain allowed him to sit occasionally.

A good sign, she thought. A tradition found through and through the generations of her own family! Every man should learn know how to steer a vessel. Trevor would be proud of him, she concluded.

For Amanda, the use of the onboard office facilities had come in handy. She caught up with her thoughts, her communications. And it had given her a few days of rest.

But mainly, she had unburdened herself with a decision that had to be made. The issue of the Letter to the Romans had remained. And she had to solve it.

But had she made the right decision?

The priest, it seemed to Amanda, wanted the truth buried, he was of the conviction that it detracted from the effectiveness and history of the Catholic Church.

True, it turned out that there actually *was* some scholarship supporting the theory that Paul was a Herodian.

And she had to wonder: Was Paul perhaps using the cultural following of Christ to re-direct such allegiance toward the prevailing theocratic deity, *Herod?*

Or was it possible that Paul's written words had been appropriated by a church wanting those privileges for themselves?

Was the word and wonder of Christ's following something to be harvested like a market commodity?

Amanda groaned. She was a historian, true. This was way beyond her to absorb, let alone explain and disseminate. It would take worldwide review to reconcile. It would take…

Yes. It was definitely beyond her capacity. Besides, only Biblical scholars could decide. It was not her specialty.

For now, it was not even within her state of mind to respond to.

Moreover, anthropologically speaking, it was entirely possible that Paul was merely working within the paradigms of his era?

More importantly, why was the Priest at the Cathedral trying to suppress this Letter to the Romans?

 He held that it was incriminating to the Church – doctrines already tested, he had told her, by Protestantism using the very words of Paul…

Perhaps he considered it unacceptable to have such a prospect aired.

And now that the valuable collections had to be relocated from the premises of obscurity…What was he trying to do? Keep this from surfacing in the cataloguing process?

Somehow, she had been set up!

When she identified him in the photograph to the police officer, he then came forward to accuse *her of stealing!*

Never mind that he had pushed it upon her to Review? Worse, he led her out of the Church…holding a relic that was a valuable possession of the State to incur an egregious offense.

Why *her*? When had he decided to make such a plan?

Amanda thought about it.

He had followed them around the Cathedral on the day Anna was giving her the tour…that endless account about Charles.

What was his thinking? What was his motive?

 He had implemented the heist from the Banco just to get the collections moved. Alright. She got that. Certainly, he could have destroyed the scroll himself. Except that no, the item had been doubtless recorded, copied and lay elsewhere catalogued. Perhaps at the Vatican itself even…

Paul was his obsession. Whatever revelation came out about Paul and his Letters to the Romans would be considered social manipulation by the first century Church? History, others would claim, could not be rewritten.

The answer dawned on Amanda.

When she was under duress and questioned by police who implied she had *stolen* an item…That was it! This was a world rife with suspicion about authenticity, antiquities and insurance scams.

He wanted to destroy her professional *credibility*. Anything related to Amanda might be connected to would become *suspect*.

Worse, that god-awful woman Naatisha Suti who worked at the NATO school had seized upon it…

And yes, it must have taken a day or two for the Principle of the School to receive her letter, a letter explaining their early withdrawal with many thanks - and a large donation to the school. But even so, the circumstances should have been explainable.

Naatisha Suti knew that the stakes were higher now

For Amanda, the two issues had merged into one: Thank God for the events of Carrara…and for her chance encounter with Dr. Phillipo!

Further, Amanda was getting concerned about Prettyman: She had heard nothing since she left the house that Sunday. It was unlike Prettyman not to explain herself…

Amanda had decided to come clean to Phillipo. The scroll was in his vault, after all. She told him everything in an email. That is, everything related to the scroll from Naples.

And just last night, he responded with a short email.

"I thank you for your earnest effort to reveal the facts, and your professional integrity to explain how it is that you have this document.

"Of course I will keep it secure. This is something that neither the Church nor the Government should subvert. Rather, biblical scholars world-over will want to review it. It may retell the story of our faith, it may not. I leave it specialists to consider.

Meantime, thank you for your concern. I have sent a copy of this email to the Director of our Research Institute for your protection and for verification purposes…"

Amanda would have preferred to handle the matter in a cleaner way. But she had been set up. And she did the best she could given the compromising position she was in.

Moreover, she had the safety of her children to consider, made worse by a kidnapper using the event to herd her into a corner…

So, until the scroll was officially recognized, she and the children were still in the sights of the police and that woman Naatisha Suti.

No, she affirmed. This was far too dangerous to carry alone. Telling Phillipo was her only choice.

And she was glad she made it.

She was still thinking about it all when the Captain came up. The expression on the Captain's face was grave. "La Signora has made preparations for the children's travelling?"

Yes, she said, all was packed and under control.

"Passport, papers, maps, tickets and schedules were here on hand for her journey, he announced. Arrangements made for car rentals, in advance, and a new pre-paid cell in the car for her convenience…I continue to place a call through to Signore Trevor MacDonald on the Ship-to-Shore transmission channels, signora…"

She thanked him profusely.

"I will have the launch ready to take you ashore at 1.30 PM. Signora, va bene?"

An hour later he reappeared with confirmation that she would have a taxi cab waiting at the dock. And since her train was not until 4 PM, he recommended that she stop in Zone Pietonne where they could find a little shopping area with cafes with gelato and food for the children. Yes, she agreed. They did need a sweater or two to travel into the cooler regions. She thanked him for his thoughtfulness.

Finally, he looked up and heard Adam splashing off the swim ladder. "Please, Signora, I ask that the boy come aboard. We see a sudden rise in sea temperature that I am not familiar with…Perhaps niente…" he trailed. Then be bowed abruptly, and retreated.

Amanda looked down at Adam still in the water. She noticed, imperceptibly, a subtle change in the color of the seawater. It was nutrient rich and greener, a slim having obfuscated its translucency.

"Adam!" she said abruptly. "Get out of the water now!"

* *

Amanda was shutting down her laptop to put into her luggage when she noticed a new email.

It came from Prettyman: "I am so sorry to have skipped the job.

" …I met this man and, well I hope you will forgive me, and especially Sandra. …More than anything, I so want to apologize to you"

Amanda nearly cried out with relief!

She responded in full, accepted her apology with complete absolution. Her own experiences, she said, had been harrowing…

Anyway, she'd be in touch when she got back to London.

* *

With her bags packed, Amanda followed the children down the gangplank that lay between the yacht and her dockside berth. It bounced a little, and the children flexed it to make it wobble.

They ran ahead, and Amanda's bags and belongings were being stowed in the trunk. She was about to get in when the Captain called out to her

"Signora! A call was connected for you …from Signore MacDonald" he held up the receiver for her to see.

The tide had gone out and the gangplank had slacked to maximum capacity. But nothing could have stopped Amanda from bounding back across and up to the wheelhouse where the Captain stood. She told Trevor all she could, and more. He would be waiting he said, and their plans quickly made before the call ended.

It was an hour before Amanda came down to earth again. And somehow, it made the world go away.

 Hearing Trevor's voice grounded her in a way that brought sense and stability back into a very tenuous expedition. She had so needed to hear from him, especially now as she swam in a sea of doubt about…about… *everything*, really. Especially with the children on hand. She had reached almost to the end of her resources, she told him.

What a *relief* to receive Trevor's call…She was on her way home now!

In the taxi she was telling Adam and Sandra how Daddy said *this*, and Daddy said *that*. Sandra wanted to know everything. And before Amanda knew it, they had arrived at their destination and were sitting in the Pedestrian Zone of Nice eating antipasta before going to the train station.

In fact, she even neglected to visit the near-by shops for warm gear as she had intended to do for the children. They were happy, if not *excited*. Surrounded by market tables, umbrellas and mobs of pedestrians with pets and children, there was little not to giggle at…

It was perhaps because of her dreamy state that Amanda had let her guard down. She was in fact paying the waiter for their refreshments with some frivolity.

It was Adam who saw her first. "Mummy…" he began

Sandra was pointing.

The grey Mercedes had stopped less than twenty meters away. Out stepped two men and Naatisha Suti. She looked straight at Amanda and began to advance with both men across the piazza.

A Tourism Trolley stopped and obstructed them from view. It was pinging its bell and waiting for pedestrians to cross.

* *

It didn't take Amanda a split second to respond. She swooped up Sandra, and with Adam, dove into a cluster of shoppers.

They merged, slowing down, the side-walks obfuscated by flags, awnings, beach hats and umbrellas. Tourists were thick everywhere.

"Mommy.." began Sandra.

Amanda darted into a small side street parallel to the *Promenade des Anglais.* She walked on, then stopped.

For a minute she thought she had lost them. But in the reflections of the shop windows across from her, it was clear the form of one pursuer was moving systematically down the street, searching.

They wanted their loot, cursed Amanda. As far as they were concerned, she was still in possession of a very valuable property.

Amanda was pressed against the glass of a small shop. She shifted her position and entered the door she was leaning against.

It sold children's shoes.

She sat Sandra down, and had the attendant bring a pair of white party sandals for her. This way they could lean over the child, and stay low down, which would hide their profiles. She had Adam sit beside his sister. She watched carefully, her breath uneven.

And as Sandra giggled when the attendant ticked her foot before placing the shoe on, Amanda was aware of time ticking. She glanced at her watch.

How would they reach the train station in time, let alone evade these assailants, now fanning out. She and the children had little chance. The train station was an even greater liability.

"I will buy these" she said to the Attendant. "And I wonder if you could tell me from where I might be able to call a taxi, close by?."

He was more than delighted to help. He offered to call a Taxi for them in advance, he said. He was used to tourists, he said. He would have one waiting at the corner of the promenade along the Baie des Anges. The Taxi driver was Giuseppe, his brother. She thanked him, and with Sandra in her arms, left the store and weaved directly to the Promenade through back streets.

The taxi did take them to the train station. But as Amanda knew, it would expose them too long in view before boarding a train without being spotted by this gang of wits…

She had the driver stop just outside the train station and asked him to wait. She opened the door to the Rent-a-Car Agency and used her Executive Account to rent an older Sedan convertible. Within minutes, she was taken to the car depot around back, and had the Taxi cab deliver the children inside the depot, along with all their belongings.

It was all Amanda could do to get out of Nice fast enough. She took a left off the Promenade des Anglais and onto Avenue des Phoceens and proceeded on Tunn. Du Paillon where she hit the gas and moved at 70 miles per hour. At the fork she veered left onto Boulevard Jean-Baptiste Verany from which she continued onto Penetrante du Paillon D2204B and finally the ramp to A8/Saint-Andre/LAriane.

Fortunately, the Rental Agency did not have any questions about her International Driver's License. Nor her intention to take children across the Alps. But hell, she had driven buses up the Lebanese Mountains for Sister Theresa on many occasions. That was before seat belts and laws checking for children. With a GPS and a mobile phone in the car, she'd find her way.

This, she would have to do alone.

 She kept an eye on Sandra, Adam was helpful in his silent strength and understanding. He could be very grown-up, she decided, when he need to be.

But it riled her that those thugs were still after her! No wonder Italy was often considered a lawless state.

And there was something else that bothered her even more. How did they *know* where to find her? How did they know she was in Nice, France?

Clearly, reporting her position to the police was not the solution.

* *

Seven

On the screen of the car's dashboard was a Global Positioning System. Amanda knew that at some point she would be re-entering Italy, then up north to Strasbourg. She would stay off the main auto-routes, and change up for another car rental - at least twice. That is, if she could.

 She mapped a plan that would take them to Frankfurt through various countries.

She decided that she would find some hostelries outside the cities since she was travelling en famille. The question, fortunately, that the Rental Agency did not ask was what route she was taking.

Still, as she peered repeatedly into the rear view mirror, Sandra had made the car her home and was napping peacefully. Adam was a good travelling companion. So, as long as she could remain calm, they too would feel no panic. If anything, it was an adventure.

For Amanda Wells, however, it was a flight from abductors whose plan to kidnap her daughter had been foiled.

Not only could she identify them as criminals, but they now knew she was in possession of a valuable antiquity...

Worse, she was in a rented sedan suitable for sunny rides down the beach promenade. Ahead of them was a climb of six thousand feet into the Alps.

For that she would need to be equipped and able to traverse the Alps in a rented car.

To do that was no small task! What she needed to do was equip herself.

With an eye on the GPS, she turned right onto *Pont Carigliano-le Tigre* then left onto *Route de Turin*. At the traffic circle she took the first exit onto the A8 ramp to *Genes/Monaco/Menton* and passed through the tolls with her credit card.

She merged onto the A8 and was already entering Italy when she knew she was in the Piedmont stages of the Alpine terrain.

Once on the road towards Milano, she took an exit for a small side town and found what she was looking for.

She paused.

Both children had to pee, they said.

She bought herself coffee.

She needed to focus. To stay alert.

It was a small side Ski Shop. A tourist stop on the roadway to Alpine skiing for weekenders.

She bought a warning triangle, shovel, tow rope, torch and a pair of heavy duty gloves for chains. Chains she would buy further up the road, she decided.

However, she added two spare car light bulbs, and a set of skis which she placed on a jury rigged ski rack. She sized up some Parka clothing for them all, and extra wool socks and booties.

She paid with her credit card. Expenses, she realized, that she must deduct from her travel voucher ...that is, if she ever came through this alive.

Finally, coat plastic tags which she labeled and pinned grimly to the coats of the children for identification purposes. In case something happened.

By the time she was approaching Como on E35, she knew her next stop was a toll road on the A9 entering Switzerland. Once over the border, she would survey her tires. She would need chains. And hopefully, have them installed by a mechanic.

If she broke up the trip into two days, she would have plenty of time to arrive in Frankfurt, "like a champion coming in from La Mans" she said to the children. Making a connection for the Airport would be easy, she thought.

Next, she turned to the children behind her and said "We must find an old Medieval Castle to spend the night..."

They laughed, their eyes wide with excitement.

She turned on the radio, and they sang to Swiss songs for miles.

* *

Trevor was beside himself.

He had no idea where his wife was, he said to his secretary.

She should inform the Italian Embassy that if the police were to locate her, then they should report it directly to him before questioning her.

"Yes Sir"

"…And Irene, please cancel my engagements for this afternoon. I have work to do upstairs that cannot wait…"

There was something else that bothered Trevor.

After a short and wonderful conversation with Amanda, he had had time to think: She mentioned everything that occurred, especially the debt she owed to her Uncle for his resourcefulness in Italy, and she thinly covered the context of her escape from Naples with the children...

What remained unexplained, though, was the item of value that she claimed *was now safe.*

What did she mean by that? *What* item?

Trevor was summoned.

The heavy gates preceding large medieval iron-studded oak doors closed behind him. He entered the Court Chamber in the deepest parts of the palace, passing beneath the stone arch carved with the words of seated watchman *Eternal Vigilance is the Price of Liberty.*

The center table was dark and shiny. Only two were seated. The chandelier was bright, as if they had just recently been assembled. Trevor knew the rules.

Here, they could speak, and nothing from this chamber was repeated or overheard on the outside of the medieval structure. And he didn't care.

"You have placed my wife and children in jeopardy!"

They watched him, mutely weighing his words, and waiting for the impact of his accusation to fill the air.

He stood resolute. He knew the ways of these men. The moon and sun could revolve around them, and their quest would not be moved. But they were quite human, he knew.

"We regret, Trevor, that we had to exclude you from our proceedings. We know you to be in a position of responsibility and you bear the burden of many upon your shoulders."

"You could have warned me... Told me of your plans..." he glowered.

"We look beyond the here and the now. We are warriors, if you will. Your wife, Amanda, is to be commended. She is a person of integrity and she is well informed."

"You *used* us!"

"We did.." They paused, the echo chamber deep and cavernous. "...But as even the Israeli Antiquities Authority knows, there are some things that supersede ordinary channels of procedures. There are cultural values, the values of a people. We are Keepers of values that transcend the now..."

"Explain, please!"

"We have diverted the Judas Manuscript directly to London where is it kept in safekeeping. It is password-protected, and date sensitive. Only your wife will be able to open the secure repository. It will then be transported to America, its intended destination for the museum. Only then she will have dispensed her duties, and is free to come home and enjoy her family…"

"You sound as if she signed up for this…?" said Trevor incredulously.

"Oh, but she did! The minute she touched the manuscript, hers was a commitment unto death if need be. But no! She did not know it at the time. And we apologize for trespassing upon her right to know."

"They are in trouble."

"Yes. And we shall place all our resources at the disposal of this situation for their safety. Again, forgive us our duty…"

"And once the artifact is in America?" demanded Trevor, his chin jutting out.

"Oh, be assured my dear man, that we have guardians in places that you cannot imagine!"

He was furious.

Trevor was already walking out. He knew of their resolve. Once they decided that they were duty-bound, they would stop at nothing to ensure a complete and satisfactory resolution.

Unless, of course, they had waited too late! And he had a suspicion that they had.

This, he would explain to Amanda when he saw her. The will of those who saw 'Vigilance' as their motto for cultural preservation…If in the greater things of importance, also as in the smallest things of life that held value."

The danger now was her safety.

He would need to reach Ernesto. But how secure was the back door?

He thought about it. There was much she did not know.

Amanda was no fool, regardless.

But she needed his help. The time for vigilance and exercises was over. He would need action now.

Plus, in all of that, as he recalled her conversation, she never mentioned the whereabouts of Prettyman. Either the fact simply remained unimportant to her, or was happily explained somewhere. But it was absent from her conversation.

Trevor knew his wife. She cared deeply about the things…and people. She would have responded proactively had she known about Prettyman.

Something was wrong. Definitely, he concluded.

Prettyman was found dead by the police in the Bay of Naples, her body identified. How could Amanda *not* mention that?

Unless she did not know!

He decided to use his own resources for an investigation. Amanda needed to be found. If he had to fly her out of Germany himself.

Apparently, there was a plan standing by for her in Frankfurt. Thank God! But where was she *now*?

"There is a message from your wife's family, Sir" said Irene, his secretary. "A Mr.DeValois from Italy, Sir"

"Si. Hello Trevor!" said Paulo DeValois, the uncle Amanda referred to as Zio.

"I cannot tell you how much we enjoyed having the children with us for a few days! They are wonderful,

Rita and I felt young again with all that noise and activity around us again"

"I'm very glad to hear it" said Trevor. "Amanda speaks often of you with much warmth and affection. I do wish I could persuade you to spend a summer in Scotland with us"

"We would very much like that, thank you. Perhaps next year. If I am not too old…" he laughed

"Nonsense!" said Trevor knowing that this was a man who changed the economy of Italy with his drive and energy as head of a major manufacturing corporation.

"Anyway, Trevor, I call to tell you some information that may be of interest to you indirectly.." He took his time with small telltale coughing on the side "I wish to inform you that while Amanda was safely delivered to Nice, France, the yacht *Ligura* sank with all hands onboard shortly thereafter."

It took Trevor by surprise.

"We have had a chance to process this loss" he continued "but in light of what Amanda and the children are going through, this might be of some concern. I don't have to tell you how dangerous these waters can be" he said, alluding to the increase in criminal activity.

Both he and Trevor were aware there was much instability and rebellion roiled Europe. Something that attended financial meltdowns as Europe was now experiencing. Especially for high profile bankers, investors and corporate executives.

"You see" said Paulo in his calm Italianate accent "The ship was blown up by explosives!"

"Oh God" said Trevor "I am so sorry Paulo…"

"Well, I call not to add to *your* troubles, my friend, but to alert you to danger…Your wife could be in serious trouble. And you too!"

"Yes. I can appreciate that. And I do thank you" said Trevor, running his hand through his hair.

Paulo waited a second before finishing up "And of course you are in a position of leadership in England. Something that might have world-wide implications, you understand. So please, Trevor, be careful for yourself as well…"

"Yes Uncle" smiled Trevor.

" In any event. I have a corporate jet in Frankfurt, fueled up and ready to take her to England…part of those privileges that I received from the corporation, you know…" he coughed again "they actually gave me two by the way, the other is in a hangar in Paris! Anyway, you must let me know if you need anything from us. And give our warmest affection to that beautiful wife of yours! *Arrivader'à*" he finished.

Trevor knew danger when he saw it. Someone was close on the heels of his wife and children.

He picked up the phone to Frankfurt US Air Base. There existed few people who could do that.

* *

Trevor had called for Proposals on how to deal with the sustainability of life during a volcanic winter, as it was called. The building of infrastructure and planning was enormous.

The diagnosis was dire and the timetable short.

One of the greatest priorities he knew, was securing energy. In Scotland there was much he had to attend to.

"Whereas the onset of the last glacial period attracted most attention" said one prominent scientist, "the eruption actually only caused a brief, dramatic cooling or volcanic winter. The temperatures only dropped 3-5°C and accelerated the glacial age…This is what the Greenland Ice core samples suggest. But on the other hand, what followed was 1,000 years of a cool period"

Trevor looked at his watch.
The next scientist to speak cited the Toba stratosphere loading. The sessions for reconstruction and preservation were drawing near. He had to speed this up.
 His first chore, it seemed, was to get the scientists to agree upon degrees of severity and fall out of a super eruption. Several hot spots around had been identified as potential areas for an impending disaster, including Yellow Stone in the United States and several on the Pacific Rim.
But his objective was to focus on how Britain might survive geographically, if one were to occur in Europe, and the consequences of the volcanic winter that would envelop the entire plant following. What concerned him most were the essentials needed for survival: Energy. Food. Light and Infrastructure. Britain had many resources.
Firstly, he decided, he would need to set up the kind of legislation that defines the new rules of

engagement for accessing and prioritizing the nation's need.

He was mindful of one thing, if people were to perish without having taken care to preserved the *value* of life, then *all* would have died as animals. To uphold the Republic and the principles of human values was *essential* to him.

After that, how to manage and conserve without throwing a doomsday scenario on the lives of people suddenly.

He noted the sequence of events as they were explained by scientific models and scenarios:

"The eruption pumps dust and chemicals into the atmosphere for years, screening the Sun and cooling the planet. Earth goes into a perpetual winter, plant and animal species disappear…"

The future should be arrived at with these considerations in mind…

* *

 Amanda was driving through the night.

The children were fast asleep in the back of the car, and so far, the weather had held.

Alpine roads had a way of responding instantly to a change in weather conditions. So far, little had changed, except for plunging temperatures.

Was ice a problem, she wondered.

With the headlights on, and the car warm, she was pushing forward. At her side was a flask of hot coffee. She stopped occasionally for a ten minute break. Usually a reconfiguration of her chart and directions.

Somehow, she had managed to keep the children searching for hidden castles until they fell asleep in exhaustion.

What she would love, she decided, was a castle to appear at about dawn. Complete with a hot breakfast, juice and place to rest for a couple of hours before pressing on!

No chance. The map was bleak and devoid of human hamlets!

The mountains soared ahead and behind her.

Across the ravines a roadway could be seen occasionally threaded. Consistently, it was rugged going, and required careful driving.

So by the time they found a roadside restaurant in the morning she was exhausted.

"Look!" shrieked Adam, pointing.

It brought her to a halt.

There in the air, several thousand feet above sea level flew a cow tethered from a helicopter. They all fairly squealed with amazement.

As it was, the cow was being air-lifted to the farm behind them. So excited were the children at this airborne cow, that it was all she could do to keep them from running forward to the field where the operation was underway. In Switzerland, home of cheese-making, cows and their deliveries to dairy farms was of preeminent importance.

The farmer was a generous old man.

Seeing their unabated interest in the business, he encouraged them to come over and view the transition from a safe distance. Amanda managed a sallow smile of gratitude, and he assured her it was alright. He had children here all the time, he said.

So Amanda gave Adam strict instructions not to

trespass on the farmer's hospitality. Sandra was to stick to his side like glue.

Amanda re-parked the car, as she was invited to do, closer to the barn where the dairy operation took place. And yes, based on the sign at the Entrance of the driveway, they did take visitors.

She accepted a room there, an end unit. With Adam and Sandra cheerfully following the cow patrol about the dairy barn, Amanda was able to oversee them from the veranda of the small chalet where she sat in a chaise-long, wrapped in a thermal sleeping bag.

It felt wonderful, with the warm sun on her face.

Above her stood an array of mountains topped by snow that fairly glistened. She was close to six thousand feet up. Pillars of strength they had been, through centuries of conquest and human struggle. Those who understood their language of shadow, shape and towering background against the sky warned of weather that could come suddenly, and dominate with such force that humans had little choice but to take shelter. Even for those that knew the conditions and understood the consequences. Those that did not perished.

For the people who claimed them as home, they were a sanctuary of freedom. Those close to these stunning Alpine peaks understood they could never be tamed. From far away, they stood as a beacon for those who could see them. The Alps were the grandfathers who validated Europe.

She closed her eyes.

And she also realized they were the destination of play and recreation.

Visitors teemed here. Bikers. Skiers. Hikers. Trekkers and hardy tourists.

It was an adventure in the extreme. Not for the initiates. Or for the unprepared, she groaned.

Amanda opened her eyes casually. She took in a deep breath of mountain air. It was a rest well appreciated. Only she had fallen asleep, and it was Adam who came nudging for attention with Sandra a muddy mess beside him.

Amanda ushered them all into their room, ran hot baths for each one in turn, and got them all ready for a wonderful country meal at the Main House Inn.

The two hours nap did her wonders. And while she took the rest of the day to stay easy and relax, she was counting her lucky stars at the occasion of the stop.

It was after the meal however, when she had paid with her card, that she was approached by the Maître.

He informed her that the Main desk had been approached by an African lady asking if they had seen her and her children.

She stiffened suddenly, half listening to his explanation:

"Since the desk thought you were guests of the farmer, and did not have your car tags recorded and signed into the Central Hotel Register, they had no way of knowing your name!.." He apologized.

Amanda could hardly believe her ears. He was still talking, actually repeating himself. ..The desk mistook the request altogether, he said, and said they did not know of you... Would she like him to recall them and inform them of her whereabouts, he wondered.

No, she said graciously. She appreciated his information.

Those assailants…that Naashti woman were in pursuit!

OMG. They were following her tenaciously!

Amanda had to move on immediately.

She could not afford to be trapped behind them. Nor could she be found by them. Somehow, she had to get *ahead* and evade them.

Night driving was the answer.

. Whoever was searching for her clearly had digital and computer aides to locate her whereabouts. This was almost a certainty. Once her credit card appeared on the grid, they would know where she was, too.

To Frankfurt.

She moved with an almost automated mechanical precision. She settled her accounts at the desk. And in the darkening evening light, after a few deliberate hours of rest in the room with her children, she re-packed the car, gathered Sandra from her bed in her pajamas and settled her gently on the rear seat of the car with her dolly. Adam, she aided quietly to the front seat where he settled his head against a pillow, and snoozed.

She climbed into the driver's seat, peered up at the forbidding peaks against the night sky, and switched on the headlights. It would be a long night ahead. This was a decision she had to make.

One last commercial stop at an ATM machine, she decided. After that, it must be cash all the way back…

"Mummy" said Adam, gripping the dashboard "Must you rush so…"

"I must" she pleaded.

** *

Trevor was wearing down, and getting frustrated. How could all this be happening at once?

He walked into his office. On his desk was a picture of Amanda Wells. He picked it up, and sat down. If there was one thing he found in her smile, it was a cheery hope…

He returned to the trauma of the conference rooms. Everyone was in a daze of disbelief.

He shook off his fatigue.

"…Neither could the models predict locations" said one weary presenter.

Trevor looked at his watch. At least they were moving on with the agenda. The plans for survival, next.

At last!

He found his place and sat down, his translator's earplugs on. This Teleconference was being attended by a global community listening worldwide between scientists.

Neither could they agree on the location "The whole of a continent might be covered by ash, which might take many years -- possibly decades -- to erode away for vegetation to recover" Nor could they agree on the timing.

Only one British team pronounced that "the odds of a globally destructive volcano explosion in any given century are extremely low. No scientist can say when the next one will occur. But the chances are five to 10 times greater than a globally destructive asteroid impact…"

Yet it came from the next scientist who warned for preparations when he said "A super volcano capable of producing an eruption with an ejecta greater than 1,000 cubic kilometers (240 cubic miles) will mean that life on earth will have to be underground."

The room fell silent.

"We should plan with early stages of fixed geographic Grids and Nodes that function independently as well as inter-connectedly, even if under ice age conditions. They should have independent and integral units and resources built within them to sustain life on a long term basis including provisions for energy, water, food, light, communications.

"Our oil and coal reserves need to be evaluated…"

"Our infrastructure- byways including roads, rails and canals for passage, albeit *altered* in extreme weather, should be recognized as connectors to Nodes because they are known and easily recognizable…

"Early stage building materials and design for honeycomb-interlocking structures with flexible design will be the new models of shelter…"

Yes, thought Trevor. He recommended the idea after he read Amanda's email about subterranean mining operations. A place she visited when in Cararra!

"…Amassing of our storage capacity and research facilities must be ongoing. Our critical functions must be organized for distribution to nodes. Centers of function and operation must be planned out… if civilization is to go on…"

"The Americans are accelerating their research and infrastructure planning, including space and communications; flight research and oceanographic possibilities; including underwater domains. Defense and protection *might* become very important for preservation and sustainability" he added "but plan for them we must!" he was saying.

Trevor could take no more. He got up and walked about, his thoughts flying to his family.

Amanda, where are you now?

** **

Pakistani born, he was a handsome man by Western standards. Money was not an objective.

The loss of life was.

He collected his ticket and picked up his baggage. The plane was not entirely full. Europe was feeling the stress of economic changes, and many families were returning from vacation and re-grouping for the end of summer plans. This he found amusing. Wait till *he* was done!

He saw an Iraqi woman in a burke pick her seat at the rear of the plane. She had two children. He might learn something about protective care from a mother on travel, who knows. So he chose the seat in front of them, and would spend the flight listening in on them. Her tongue was familiar to him.

He had been a child once, centuries ago.

He assessed his own agenda as he looked out the window. The plane was preparing to lift off the runway.

 There was only one thing remaining for him to do, apparently, on this mission.

Killing the woman in Naples was not so difficult really. Neither the sinking of the vessel. But if his instructions were to take down a party that threatened the very cause he had dedicated his life to, then he would do it, regardless. Even without money.

He drove about Europe, he laughed, with a missile launcher in his trunk! That is, as long as he did not have to pass any inspection point, or was stopped by police for a spot check of vehicles. So he drove like an angel, he said. He wore Hawaiian shirts and a Panama Jack happy-hat. Oh yes, he could be as saintly as any monk if it helped his cause, he said. The men that gathered with him at cafes all over the Mediterranean always laughed at that.

Presently, no cause could suit him better than this one.

This was not an instruction from his superiors to target individuals for abduction, piracy or ransom, but to damage the influence of a high profile leader that had public visibility, travelling with his wife and children in Europe! Regardless, *his* cause was global disruption. Western. Eastern. Jewish. Muslim. Christian.

Anarchy, of any kind.

And who would know him? Educated amongst the very best at the London School of Economics no less. So he understood the basic principles that could undermine society. Create enough havoc and instability in an economic system, and society would be altered, if not broken down completely.

Further, the more confidence that one could erode from leadership, the more encouragement for ground roots rebellion and dislocation, let alone sustainability and planning.

Amanda Wells was the prime target because she was vulnerable with her children. The wife of a highly visible leader in Great Britain with ties to all banks of long standing credibility. Plus, she had connections with the authorities in various countries about valuables and antiquities. A woman!

Only now, having exposed one of his prime cells of operation in Italy, Naatisha Suti, *he* was on a mission to eradicate her.

A stupid, inconsequential operative as she was, this Naashti Suti, passing off as some African American teacher, but an Operative nonetheless. Something that might have long term payoff, he decided.

So, Frankfurt it was, said the information he had.

It was unfortunate. He had to do this because the others had failed to locate and capture the target after they disembarked the yacht.

Nor did he like the message he got from the Operative following his execution of the sinking.

"Failed mission!" As if *he* were the culprit of *their* mess!

That's because no one was prepared for them to disembark so suddenly in Nice! The yacht was following the coastline south. Trains heading north were in abundance…

What he liked even less their excuse for their debacle: After the target was spotted in Nice, it vanished! They had searched every venue of exit, train, airport, auto-strada. Everywhere that a god-fearing family woman would attempt with children. Someone, he decided, was giving her shelter. Or, she was clever. Very clever, this Amanda Wells woman.

So, when the call came in that she was in all probability heading north by now, he instructed them to meet him in Strasburg by taking the high road northward.

And they should keep their eyes open…

* *

Dawn was just peaking over the horizon, setting ablaze the snowy peaks of the mountains in a glow of pink and purple luminescence.

She glanced behind her. Both children were fast asleep.

She had driven like a fiend all night.

Thinking. Computing. Counting the miles. Planning her Exit-Strategy, as they called it in business.

One thing came to her mind in the middle of the night. Her assailants had bigger fish to fry! She was certain.

Their tenacity and laser focus to *manipulate* her children at the school implied that they had been a target for a while. And for a reason.

The reason was doubtless…Trevor.

Filled now with self-doubt she wondered: Had she been careless somehow? Had she made herself vulnerable? What was it that drove these people?

Trevor was in England. Why could she not access him?

The road was long, her nerves steady but testy.

Bloody hell, what was he doing?

You'd think the world was going to end the way he was behaving, she thought. And she was irritated beyond measure, following the cliff side of the road with her headlights, mile after mile after mile.

Suddenly one of her headlights gave out in the middle of the night. She stopped to inspect the damage. Debris from falling rock had pierced the cupping that protected the bulb.

Fortunately, she had a spare bulb. And for that she was parked on the side of the road at two in the morning. She took the opportunity to refill the tank with gas from an extra container stowed cleanly in the back of the car: Not exactly regulation driving, she thought, but a precaution she had taken by buying an extra container at the supply store when she bought chains.

There she stood, covered in her parka, wooly hat and gloves in the middle of the night on the side of the road in the Alps. How lucky they had been with the weather! No so much as a stir of wind. Just icy cold.

She took a moment and surveyed her surroundings. They were silent, these mountains, having been pushed up from the bottom of the sea in subvention by the movement of tectonic plates. How incredible!

Yet as formidable as these elements were, she was surrounded by silence.

These were the moments, she decided, that the local people must cherish. The assumption of timelessness in all the natural force that was represented around them. In day or dark, these

Alps served as steadfast assurance. It took her breath away.

If Trevor were with her, he would observe this as one of her poetic moments; laughing with her often to view beauty in every creation. At every juncture. He could embarrass her sometimes with his teasing. Even as she turned every road trip into an adventure, he remarked. But once he took her hand gently and said softly "…and that is why I so love you Amanda!"

It fed her soul. It gave meaning to her life.

Only now she was freezing her ass off, she decided. She quickly returned to the warmth of the car, checked on the children, and drank water. She turned on the ignition and kept going.

But as she moved forward down the road, she noticed icy rock-falling with increasing frequency. She sped up, rather than slow down. And how relieved she was that she did so.

Only half a mile ahead, with the road curvature safely contoured into the side of the mountain she looked back. The road behind her buried in snow. A small avalanche had coursed its way down the slopes as she travelled. It would take a day to clear. Had she not passed it, she would be behind it.

She heaved a sigh of relief. Because if the truth be known, she wasn't sure how much more pushing they could all take without feeling severe duress.

Yet tired as she was, she felt invigorated. Her plans were straightforward now. To reach Frankfurt and make a communication connection with Zio DeValois' arrangements. She could envision them waiting for her at the airport.

She consulted her map and GPS.

She was entering Germany on the Toll road A2 and would continue on the A5. She would take exit 26, then take exit 21-Frankfurt a. Main-Niederrad toward F-Niedarrad.

** **

Amanda revised her plan to change up the Rental Car in Strasbourg. The rationale behind her decision was getting a little foggy, exhausted as she was from the driving.

She decided to make a run for it directly to Frankfurt, find a way to communicate with either Trevor or her Uncle and get herself safely on the jet waiting in Frankfurt. It would take her to London. That was the plan. That was the only clarity that she could manage right now…

 She pulled off to the side of the road. At least it was a commercial Gas Station. She topped the tank with fuel, refilled her coffee flask and managing to stretch her legs in the brisk morning air. Back in the driver's seat, she spotted a Rest Stop a few hundred yards down and coasted into it, parking the car between a stand of blue spruce and fir trees. There she turned the engine off, pausing quietly not to arouse the children from their travelling slumber.

Without knowing it, she fell asleep.

It was Adam who woke her. To her dismay she realized she had slept for almost an hour!

He was looking at her, her son, and simply stared, finding no cause for alarm, as if this were the mountain way of things.

Evidently, they had crept out of the car, the two of them, and enjoyed the Rest Stop: The bathrooms were good. There was the children's swing set. Water fountains. Juice from the nice Attendant within the hospitality hut, hosting tourists. Even a short movie to watch in the Visitors Center, Adam said.

No problem!

She smiled at him vaguely, and his brow furrowed suddenly "You alright, mummy?" he said. "You needed some rest"

How lucky she was to have such a family!

*** ***

Eight

Trevor was seated at the table's edge, waiting for the call.

When it came, he told Amanda exactly where she should go and at what Gate of Entry into the Airport - the location of the Hangar. There, a waiting Jet was located.

A special Para-military unit out of Manheim was to pick her up at the Gate and drive her through. From there, she and the children were to get on a small commercial plane marked as a *EuroZoner* manufacture plane AZ 645.

The plane would fly them home, he assured her.

He could still hear the sound of her voice as he paced down the hallways of his offices in London and approached the Officers waiting in his chambers.

He requested a British unit of training cadets to be on standby in Frankfurt for a cooperative exercise with the Americans, he said.

It should remain quiet.

Of course he should have anticipated that his family would be easy prey for enemies of the state…His role in the survival plans of a country were precisely the kind of potency that anarchists sought: Emergency planning was often a target for chaos.

This was made worse by a relic event that held some cultural significance to the Italian government. How that issue blossomed into a full scale request by them, citing worsening conditions, to the Government of England regarding a *cultural treasure*....

God, he thought.

He walked the full length of the hallway, furious.

If they can't even receive a Banker without locking him up in their vault, how in the hell did they expect a smooth transition of Treasure transport? Moreover, it sounded more like a moving wagon-train. This would be a beacon for thieves, looters, black-market racketeers and antiquities dealers!

Besides, it was the last thing Britain could take on right now. The liabilities and costs of guarantees and preservation packaging were beyond present budgetary constraints.

This he would have to deal with later.

"Thank you Gentlemen!" he said, greeting them each by handshake.

These were a Unit of Sandhurst Officer Training Personnel that could handle Special Assignments. They were to work with the American base personnel and create a filter across an area that would let them net an anarchist preparing to make an assault on a corporate jet. *EuroZoner* manufacture plane AZ 645.

The Operation was assigned by their commissioning officer. And when they asked Trevor what the nature of the cargo was on the plane he told them.

"My wife and children" he said plainly. And if she was abducted, he said, his effectiveness as a leader would be diminished to carry out pressing tasks at hand.

Further, it was their goal to identify the *source* of the assault. Who were these people? Who was behind it? What had they planned? Where did they come from and what was their ultimate mission.... These were all as important as the rescue of his family, he said.

He left the room with a heart of lead. The last time he set up a target he was on a military mission.

He all but flew down the hallway to return to his office quarters. He looked at her photograph, a glass of Scotch in hand, and sat heavily into his chair.

He should feel distressed. But actually, he laughed out loud at the angry words out of his wife's mouth when she called him.

"Who is Susan?" she wanted to know.

He had managed to get through the entire conversation without informing her of Prettyman. That was an unnecessary burden just now. But how to impress upon her the danger, without frightening her to death, was a balance he had to weigh. Especially with two children on her hands. He had to do more, he felt.

* *

Amanda had turned onto Schwanheimer Ufer/K809 and continued driving onto Niederradeer Ufer.

The car, which was blue, had turned into a grimy grey. It bothered her. She had to get the chains off the tires, and somehow get it looking respectable before she became too noticeable at the Toll booths.

She turned off the highway, and found a garage that filled up the gas tank; checked her oil, and took off her chains - which they offered to dispose of. Meaning, they could be re-sold. She agreed.

She bought snacks and a city map. She was within sixty miles and the flight was scheduled to leave at 6PM tonight.

Trevor had given her instructions, and the notion of getting safely onto an airplane without being noticed presented her with doubts.

What were they thinking?

How was she supposed to maneuver all these logistics without being *detected*? And how was she supposed to return the Rental Car without being checked?

If the police were still after her, she was easily registered. If her assailants were looking… she was easily seen. It the Rental Car was alerted, she was a targeted.

Still, even if it was a long shot, at least they aiming for the safety of a Terminal. She could be early enough to elude detection of any kind. Especially if the Rental Agency were… inattentive.

She continued onto *Theodor-Stern-Kai* and went onto *Gartenstrabe*. From there she turned left onto *Stresemannallee/B44*.

There was supposed to be a car rental agency on Wilhelm-Leuschner_Strabe/K818, she noted from her map. There she would return the Rental car, then take a taxi to the airport. Just like that.

So she took a deep breath, and walked in.

The fee for returning the car would be astronomical, she noticed. But because she was in cash, the attendant was impressed. And not reading her computer…

Amanda made for easy conversation. Travelers of all kinds came to these Alps to ski.

"Oh yeah?"

These were the signs of the privileged, said the attendant. Amanda knew that much of her cash would be pocketed by the attendant after she was gone.

When inspected, the Rental Agency was gracious enough not to remark on the crumbs inside the car. Or the finger stained windows. Nor the grime on the headlights and bumpers that were the signs of hard alpine travel. There was no deduction for the lack of gas in the tank. Clearly, this was a rickety and old car picked up in Nice. Hell, it didn't even register of the fleet of their company! So, as long as the car was running, they seemed satisfied.

But barely so. And there was a moment of hesitancy.

It was not that Amanda appeared inelegant, or suspect, it was just that jeans and a sailor-striped Tee within an excursion quilted jacket gave her the resemblance of a wilderness hiker rather than a caring mother. Amanda did not look very responsible at the moment, her backpack was an Army issue duffle bag and her eyes dark, hostile and hidden by hair.

Especially with Adam looking worn, and Sandra downright bundled up in an Alpine parka. Not that the Germans had less respect for the adventurous sort, but when it came to children, they held the highest expectations for respectable responsibility.

It was all in the cashier's eyes, she could read it. Still, she conceded.

As for getting to the Airport, yes, there was a mini-bus that took passengers from their depot. She could wait, they said. And there was a small Restaurant for the children, they said.

Next door. There they could wait for the Shuttle.

What she needed was a bath and good night's sleep, she decided.

No. What she really needed was a drink!

She looked at the children. They were fine. And that strengthened her resolve.

The meal was rustic and designed for adults. A small lamb chop and gravy gave the children the mashed potatoes and hot apple cider they needed. And they ate bread rolls.

Amanda's thoughts were already elsewhere.

Ahead was the trickiest part of the journey. She was to enter by the East Gate, and she would have to show her passport.

Sandra was getting tired and cranky. "Daddy?..." she was asking, her eyes imploring.

"Be quiet!" said Adam, perhaps too coarsely.

Tears welled up into Sandra's eyes. It was getting to be too much for her, Amanda knew.

Amanda looked out the window of the Restaurant, and surveyed the conditions they were going out in. It had started to drizzle. The traffic was ruthless and the weather icy-edged. Most of all, they were alone in a strange town.

When the Airport Shuttle Bus arrived, it was a mini-bus in bright designs. They piled in, tired, grateful and happy to find seats in the rear.

It was only when she peeled off her Sandra's hoodie to roll up and stuff it into the backpack that Amanda glanced out the rear window. She could not be sure. But she thought she saw a grey vehicle pull out behind them some three hundred yards. They had paused, waiting.

The mini-bus lumbered down the boulevard, as did the car. It stopped at the traffic lights, then approached the exit ramp towards the Airport, now visible with its Control Tower, and made a left turn, easy as any slow Shuttle bus with passengers.

Amanda moved forward towards the driver. She held her map. Would they be passing the East Gate of the Airport by chance?

He shrugged his shoulders, nodding at the same time. A harmless gesture. But one less worthy of a trusted employee of an Airport Shuttle bus, lacking somewhat it courtesy.

* *

The Airport Shuttle was painted dark blue with yellow signage all over it. Flights all over the world, said the logo, Airport deliveries from the city for passengers travelling. ..

Inside the bus, wall paper maps showed the logo of the Airport Shuttle behind two happy faced Asian

travelers: Reliable as an airplane, steady as a ship -
in three different languages.

Amanda held on to the chrome poles as it lurched
down the highway, and veered abruptly for a stop
to pick up passengers.

Nobody came onboard.

On it jostled, progressing routinely toward the
Airport. As tired as she was, there was a certain
cadence to the driver's way of driving that she
noticed. He was not bored.

Nor was he the customary driver of this bus.

For one thing, he was clumsy on the brakes,
sending them into sudden lurches rather than a
smooth transition into a stop. Something that
seasoned bus drivers learned to attain once they
knew the capacity and performance of the vehicle
they piloted.

This, Amanda knew from her experience as the
driver of a diesel school-bus. Children could go
flying. Here, it would be luggage that would go
flying!

She looked about her. While there was little luggage
in the bus, there were plenty of luggage racks,
luggage straps and lines and netting for a full load
of passengers!

He stopped again, the driver.

One passenger came onboard, stayed for two stops,
then disembarked.

Plus this driver was revving the engines into r.p.ms
that were higher than the normal threshold, she
thought. This was *definitely* not the normal bus
driver.

A small suspicion began to creep up her back. She
looked behind them suddenly.

The grey car was gone!

The driver maybe knew the passenger that had come onboard. Judging from the look they exchanged when he came onboard, it was suspicious. But with no words spoken, it was hard to tell.

She was getting paranoid.

Still, Amanda moved forward again, the bus being completely empty. And she put on her sunglasses, as if preparing her defenses.

Clearly, the bus driver could see her peering about, clueless. But in actual fact, Amanda had her eyes trained sideways. She wanted to observe the driver. There was something about him that had caught her attention.

He was good looking by Western standards, and calm. But unfamiliar with the driving. Why did this bother her?

Amanda started to survey the interior of the bus. At mid-section, there was a passenger door with two steps and chrome bars as rail.

The children were chatting in the rear. Adam having found some bungee cord that had entwined itself around the chrome handle bars. They appended from every seat, and he was testing them all.

The bus stopped again, routinely, and the driver opened the two doors by an automatic mechanism that he operated in the front by his seat.

Nothing could have prepared Amanda and the children for the passenger that stepped on board by the mid-section doors of the bus, with a long back pack.

It was a Airport personnel, complete with para-military security badge and uniform. But it was someone they knew.

Naashti Suti, grinning like an old friend and responding to the children, stood there. The children were surprised. Sandra grinning, but Adam froze.

Suti's eyes remained calm, but as she turned to Amanda wildly, a darker recklessness came to her face.

Amanda Wells would not elude her again.

The bus kept rolling, giving her moments to measure her position of strength.

Adam put out his arm suddenly and shoved little Sandra behind him just as the woman opened her backpack and pulled out a snub nose firearm.

She stood up slowly, and looked more than black-faced and disconnected. She looked like a savage having cornered her prey. And in that instant, Amanda could tell there was collusion between her and the driver.

Amanda gripped the bars tightly, the bus lurching still.

"You have a prize that I want!" said the woman.

Amanda said nothing.

"You eluded me in Naples. But I am no fool!" she spat, edging backward. She turned suddenly and pushed the butt of the gun against Adam's face as she reached for Sandra.

"Adam!" cried Amanda

Adam ducked. Sandra squealed out, and sank suddenly out of sight.

Amanda jumped up, knowing danger when she saw it. The instrument they called a field operational rig gun was aimed at her chest, a soft trigger to pull.

But then settled down. The woman had her game, and she was not about to lose her platform.

Amanda calculated that she would use her head against an untrained and stupid woman focused no further than that little trigger on a man-sized weapon.

Amanda feigned fear and froze, her mind racing through options.

From peripheral vision, she could tell Adam and Sandra was below the seat.

The driver looked back, squelched on the brakes and barked at her in a harsh guttural language.

Suti pointed forward, implying that Amanda should keep her eyes forward if she wanted the child alive.

Amanda turned slightly towards Suti.

"What is it you want Naashti" she said calmly, her nerves and brain working on full cylinders now.

"You know what I want…*Where is it*?" she rasped

Amanda had to play for time, but carefully "Oh, you mean the scroll from the Cathedral…?"

As long as Naashti had a chance of enriching herself on the black-market with an item that could fetch several millions, then this could carry on.

But she was unpredictable.

Noting an intersection further ahead, Amanda turned calmly. "I would have to unlock the combination of the pouch in my bag. It is very valuable, you know!"

"I know!"

The driver belted out some orders. They were approaching the East Gate.

"If you move when you show your passport at the gate, you will lose this child instantly, do you understand?" said Suti.

"I do!" said Amanda, carefully extracting her passport from her bag and moving forward to show the MP at the Gate.

 He looked at the passport. "You are expect Mrs. MacDonald. You and your children. Please proceed to the East Hangar. I will inform the security authorities...Thank you!"

The driver did speak English. He did not step off the bus accelerator before he gestured to her, over his shoulder.

"You..." He was grinning "You will be found, unfortunately, forced to land because of a malfunction once you have lifted off...The jet is rigged to explode thirty five minutes into check with the comptroller's tower. The pilot will start ignition in approximately five minutes...You have been an easy target Mrs. MacDonald. I am not accustomed to having my victims step so easily into my trap!"

To Amanda's utter disappointment, no one at the gate was responding to the situation. Airport Shuttle buses drove through here every hour. Who would suspect the driver? This had been anticipated, evidently.

He must have read her thoughts. He turned to Suti and spoke before slowing down the bus, checking the rear view windows. "Of course, we will keep the child..."

Amanda's thoughts were a whirl. How long they had been on to her was hard to know. She knew she was in trouble. Amanda felt trapped. These assailants had her exactly cornered where they wanted. The would collect their loot; the child *and* blowing up the plane with her and Adam in it.…
What a rigged job. Totally undetectable!
Amanda looked back, and saw that Suti had helped herself to Amanda's duffle bag, assuming that it held the sacred relic of St. Paul's Scroll.
Amanda knew the minutes were ticking and her options, diminishing. She had to weigh her risks. Decisions had their costs.…
"Mummy!" yelled Sandra, unsure of what to make of the woman Suti, now emerging as angry in manner and gesture.
What could Amanda do to protect them? What did she know… to defend herself and her children. How to explain…?"
Yet a calmness took over. As if an icy bucket of water had been tossed at her. She started to calculate. She knew the motions of a bus!
Naashti Suti stood upright holding onto the chrome rail bar of the mid-entry steps, the firearm dangling from her shoulder.
It was dusk as they approach the jet, its wheel-jams gone, red beacon-lights twinkling. That meant they had less than twenty minutes before it was scheduled to explode.
They were less than half a mile away. She could see the jet's reflection on the wet tarmac even. It was in a taxiing mode, facing the runway in a commercial zone designed for smaller planes, beside a white hangar.

The Shuttle Bus would have to turn towards it, and Amanda picked precisely that moment. Just as he bent forward with the wheel she lurched up and reached for the overhead luggage rack cords. She yanked down and thrust the cord quickly around the driver's throat and laced it back over the rail behind him with a half-hitch pull that sent him backwards, hands up. She still held the cord as she stretched forward to push down on the mechanism that opened the doors while pressing hard on the driver's right knee which accelerated the gas pedal. Already in mid-turn, the sudden jerk teetered the bus to its side, both doors opening. Suti lost her footing, slipped into the well of the midsection steps and her body tumbled out before the doors closed on her hand holding onto the firearm, its leather strap weaved around her wrist.

With the driver choking, Amanda pulling viciously at the half hitch cord and grabbed the steering wheel while leaning hard on the gas pedal knee to drag Suti half mile before the bus stopped close to the airplane.

The driver was immobile. With the luggage straps around his throat wrapped tightly to the pole behind his seat, his back was arched, hands tugging at his throat for air. She yanked hard down on a double hitch behind his seat, and left him there, gaping.

She ran to the back of the bus, screaming at her children to get out of the front door.

Amanda, now at the steps of the mid-section door, grabbed the hand that lay limp in the strap of the gun. She tied the gun strap quickly to the chrome rail so that whatever life was left in the body outside could not break free. The woman was attached to the bus, damaged perhaps, but not dead since wheels were beyond range of her fall.

But when she opened the door, Adam leapt out and Sandra squealed as Amanda bounced over a pair of legs that began to kick out from beneath the body of the bus.

Amanda ran the twenty yards to the waiting Jet, her arms waving.

"Get out!" she screamed. "There's a bomb on that plane!"

He saw her and put his hand up to the glass to acknowledge her.

"*A bomb..*" she mouthed, pointing to the back of the plane.

He understood what she was saying, having been trained in airport security and passenger safety long enough to know that the probability of sabotage on air transportation was exceptionally high. He unbuckled, leaving the Jet ignition on.

The children were standing in the tarmac between the bus and the plane.

"Run!" she screamed to them "Run over there…"

Sandra was wailing out in panic as her mother swept her up and carried her as fast as she could away from the Jet, Adam running beside her.

The Jet's pilot had exited the craft and hesitated, looking back at the bus that was parked too close to the plane.

"No!" yelled Amanda. "No time!"

But he would not be deterred.

He approached the side entrance and saw the woman Suti with her arm trapped in the door jam. He reached down to help her, her body now leaning against the bus, and her shoulder badly lacerated, but alive.

Her face was unspeakable.

He misread it.

He did get her hand free. And he was helping her up when she reached over with her other hand and pulled loose the firearm. She unloaded a round into his belly, point blank, and was searching for the real target of her mind.

She aimed at the figures running, and fired away the semi-automatic pin pulled.

Sandra jerked forward in Amanda's arms, and Adam, who wanted to go back and save the driver, dove to the ground.

"No!"

Amanda could only scream at them with enough despair to get him scrambling up and running with her, Sandra limp in her arms.

Suti was able to free herself, and stood up against the bus which she knew was too close to the plane. She aimed her firearm at them for another solid round of shots.

* *

The Apache flight training contingent were rigged for rescue when the helicopter pilot lowered the craft.

"We have visual contact" said the Chief.

Trevor took off his headset. He unstrapped himself, and clipped on his braces to be air-dropped to the tarmac.

He was a trained Airman, after all.

"No time Sir!" said the pilot. "The craft is hot!"

Two paratrooper trainees attached to hoists dropped out the hatch and dangled from the chopper. The pilot hovered, calculating the risk of remaining too close to an incendiary explosive device.

Amanda understood the danger, running hard from the Jet towards them, Sandra in her arms.

The two trainees swung gently before her. Fifty feet ahead. Thirty. Twenty five.

One explosion peeled out of the rear engine of the Jet. The Jet's port tire collapsed, as did the wing. The craft collapsed sideways, on fire but not entirely damaged.

The conflagration that followed ignited a second explosion.

The chopper surged.

It was at that moment that one of the trainees laced his arm around Adam and embraced him to the chest, just feet off the ground. As the chopper shot forward with Adam secured in the clutch of one paratrooper, The other releasing himself to the ground.

He had fell to push Amanda down to the ground with Sandra, spread eagled over them, sheltering them from fireballs and flying projectiles that flew out and away from the second explosion of the Jet's fuel tanks.

Later, when he was helped up, his fire-retardant gear was singed; his helmet gone and his arm bleeding.

His equipment had saved their lives.

"Sandra is… alive!" said Trevor, his voice penetrating the panic on Amanda's face as he gathered her into his arms.

* *

END